I'LL PRAY
WHEN
I'M DYING

Stephen J. Golds

RED DOG
UK

Published by RED DOG PRESS 2020

Paperback ISBN 978-1-914480-26-3

Ebook ISBN 978-1-914480-27-0

www.reddogpress.co.uk

*Dedicated
to
Those
Who
Count*

"Yesterday, upon the stair,
I met a man who wasn't there!
He wasn't there again today,
Oh how I wish he'd go away!"

Antigonish – William Hughes Mearns

"In the desert
I saw a creature, naked, bestial,
Who, squatting upon the ground,
Held his heart in his hands,
And ate of it.
I said, "Is it good, friend?"
"It is bitter—bitter," he answered;

"But I like it
"Because it is bitter,
"And because it is my heart."

In the Desert – Stephen Crane

Seaport Boston, USA
Monday, February 18th, 1946

EVERYTHING STARTED TO rot with a photograph in a newspaper.

The bar awash in a dim cool. The only light filtering through grimy windows that occasionally flashed black with the passing-by of pedestrians on the street outside. An automobile horn blasted insanely somewhere. A radio playing static softly at the end of the bar top. Dead noise.

Ben Hughes stared at the picture of the young boy on page four of the Boston Herald. Something like a bullet in the back. A blade across the throat. A headache like a hammer blow to his skull and the start of a fever boiling underneath his clothes.

SNORT

A muscle in his cheek twitching.

SNIFF

The boy in the ink spotted photograph. Wide eyed and toothy grinned. Freckles. Cow-licked hair. Nine years old. The son of a well-to-do upper-middle class family.

A heavy, frigid, solid mass spread in Ben's guts. A poisonous kind of sudden emptiness.

He scratched at his face and neck. Itchy. Blinked slow. Closing his eyes briefly and then snapping them open again to escape the memory that burst, scurrying within the darkness behind his eyelids. Pinched the crease in his slacks with trembling fingers and readjusted the newspaper on the bar so it was in line with everything else. Symmetry. Order. He knocked on the oak bar top. Touch wood. Trying to focus on the words printed beneath the photograph. The boy's irises screaming, empty, black holes assaulting his concentration in a heavy, stinging rain. Distorted images passing through his head like the headlights of a speeding hearse down a black street.

He caught his own murky reflection in the mirror at the back of the bar shelves. His eyes cast in shadow. The image contorted into something else. A black figure. Ben looked back down at the newspaper again.

SNORT.

Trying to read the words. Concentrate on the facts. Focus on the real. The now. Slow his heartbeat down. Counting to seven. Slow. One. Two. Three. Four. Five. Six. Seven. Breathe. One. Two. Three. Four. Five. Six. Seven. Breathe.

The child had disappeared two days ago while out playing in the park with the family's maid. She'd gone to buy a baked potato from a street vendor for the kid and when she came back, he was gone. No witnesses. No ransom notes. Nothing. Just gone. Another child. Vanished into the vapor.

SNIFF.

Ben tried to remember how many children had been in the newspapers since the end of the war? How many had been the talk of the precinct? A lot. Too many.

SNIFF.

Knowing what made the headlines was usually only the tip of the iceberg.

SNORT.

Like cockroaches, if you glimpsed just one, there were another hundred of the filthy fucks hiding in the darkness you only witnessed once you'd taken a torch to the grungy corners and squalid crevices. Crawling on their bellies and scurrying around spreading sickness. Missing children were a plague. A disease that wasn't ever talked about. An epidemic. Black Death. A lot of the children reported missing had been poor negroes from the Eastside. Not one of *those* pitiful bastards had even made the newspapers. Fucking Boston. A city of missing children's posters pasted to tenement walls, ripped to shreds by the wind. Backwards and inbred little shithole.

Ben pinched at the crease in his slacks again. His eyes stung. Clenching his jaw so hard his gums ached. Skull pounding.

SNIFF. SNIFF. SNORT.

He shuddered, took off his hat and placed it on a sheet of carefully laid napkins. Picked up the sterling silver flask his mother had gifted him when he graduated from the police academy and shook it at Sammy the bartender. His eyes flickering over the inscription etched into the metal '*Love Always, Mother*', and then the boy's face ripping through his conscience like a gunshot. Ben's guts clamped up. He winced, rubbing at his stomach. Sammy took the flask and refilled it from the bottle on the shelf marked by a piece of white tape that read '*B.H ONLY*'. Brought it back over held aloft with a thick manila envelope which he waved in the space between the two men. Thin lips opening and closing.

"Ben, you listening to me here?"

"What?"

"I said, you get a chance to watch the Red Sox lately? I caught a game last week. The fucking—"

Ben cut the bartender off by holding a hand up.

"Don't attempt to small talk me, Samuel. You know I couldn't care less about the Red Sox or a bunch of yokels hitting a ball with a piece of wood and running around in circles like morons. Get straight to the point would you."

"Well, I guess," Sammy swallowed. Straightened. "I guess I was just wanting to ask about who exactly this envelope is going to this time, Ben? All this bullshit-bad blood between your man Stevie Wallace and the guineas, Phil Buccola… I got you coming in, and then twenty-five fucking minutes later the greasers from the North End are coming around here wanting to get paid as well. I'm at a fucking loss here. They broke Fergus's jaw last week. Poor guy's scared to leave his mother's house. I can't get anyone else to help out behind the bar now."

Sammy wiped his hands up and down his grimy, stained bar apron. Ben peered at the yellow-brown stains smeared there, quickly turned away. Tried to focus on the words typed below the boy's picture in the newspaper again but found himself dragged back to the boy's eyes. Cast in ink shadow. Black gaping holes. Empty graves. Just a scared, lost kid. Painfully familiar.

Counting.

Inhale.

Exhale.

Knock on wood.

"Do I even remotely resemble an Italian to you, Samuel?" Ben said, his eyes not leaving the boy's face in the photograph.

"What? No, course not, but…"

"We are *still* currently located in Seaport, Boston, are we not?"

"Yeah, yeah, of course Seaport but…"

"Stevie's still in possession of Seaport and Southie. I make collections for Stevie. You pay Stevie because your bar is located in Seaport. That's why I'm here in this shabby little pit you dare deem a drinking establishment. To collect. I'm not here because I enjoy being in your company. Now, that's not all too dreadfully complicated to comprehend for your thick skull, is it, Samuel?"

"Well, what am I supposed to tell the dagos when they come sniffing around here asking, shoving me about? I need that kind of trouble like I need another asshole to shit out of."

Ben cringed. Exhaled hard through his nose. Massaged his temple with a fist.

"You communicate with Leary at that time and he'll remedy it. The Italians shouldn't be encroaching onto Stevie's territory anyway, and they're going to get their grubby little hands caught in the cookie jar sooner or later."

"Talk to Leary? Why I gotta talk to that exiled IRA maniac? What's going on with Stevie, anyhow? There's a lot of rumors flying about, Ben. They true? I don't know what to think over here."

"And what are the rumors, Samuel? Enlighten me, why don't you?"

Sammy pulled at the sweat yellowed, crumpled collar of his shirt and smacked his lips together "people are saying he's sick, is all. In the head. That kind of sick."

"Stevie's fit as a fiddle. An Olympian. You'll talk to Leary because I told you to talk to Leary. Stevie doesn't have time for your kind of petty bullshit, Samuel. He's got more entertaining things to do. You speak to Leary. Clean?"

"What?"

"Clear. Are we clear? Clear. Clear."

"It's a lot of fucking hassle is what it is. I'm paying protection ain't I? What is it that I'm paying hand over fist for here if I still got these kinds of problems? I got a family to feed, Ben. I got kids."

"I see. I see. You've got kids," Ben knocked on the picture in the newspaper with his fist. "Children like this little one?"

The bartender gawked at the headline in the newspaper, sucked air through a gap in his front teeth. Cords in his neck standing out like the roots of a grotesque tree for a moment. Ben continued, still not looking Sammy in the face. "Perhaps, this filthy little brat's father didn't pay what he owed either. Perhaps, he was complaining too much, too. Yes? So, stop giving me this kind of fucking grief and just pay the fucking fee that is fucking owed, Samuel."

"Jesus Christ, Ben. We're pals ain't we? Known each other a long time. Since we were kids ourselves. No need to go and get all heavy like that. Go and threaten a man's kids. It's not right. Not right at all."

Ben still didn't look up from the newspaper and the bartender placed the flask in front of him on the bar with the thick manila envelope beside it, shook his head slightly. Brought over the bottle and then went back to wiping down the back shelves with a stained, crusty brown rag that made Ben feel raw underneath the fabric of his linen shirt, as though small insects were crawling over his flesh. He took a long hit of the flask. The whiskey burning its way down his throat. Cleansing. He peeped at the newspaper again, his heart still palpitating, making him breathless. Sick. A sick man. He drank deeper from the flask. Trying to work himself through it.

Counting. One. Two. Three. Four. Five. Six. Seven. Counting to seven made things all right. Normal. Ordered. Lucky seven.

Reset.

Restart.

Breathe.

SNORT. SNORT. SNORT.

After a moment, he picked up the light brown envelope, weighed it in his palm, slipped it into the side pocket of his grey, tailored jacket. Squinting at the newspaper and trying to calm himself on the columns of printed words in the missing child's article again. He couldn't. A hot sweat trickling down his chest and stomach. The child's eyes a midnight sable and gasping. Familiar. Ben drained the remaining contents of his flask and attempted to blink away the thoughts of his own childhood. The thing that had crawled and scurried through the empty hallways and doorways of his childhood home. Darkness. Bile surged into his mouth. He gagged it back down.

SNORT.

SNIFF.

SNORT.

SNIFF.

SNORT.

SNIFF.

SNORT.

He snapped his head towards the slovenly man further down the bar sniffing and snorting incessantly. Like a pig. Something akin to Chinese water torture. Every sniff, every snort, every grunt an icepick chipping away at Ben's exhausted consciousness. He had tried to drown it out. Endure it. Ignore it. He couldn't any longer. Finally having enough, he closed the newspaper with hands that shook and folded it on the bar. Placing it perfectly straight so it was in line with the symmetry of the bar-top, his hat and the flask again. Symmetry. Order. He twisted slightly on the stool to face the man. A construction worker in faded denim dungarees, sweating up the place. Tufts of his greasy, shit-colored hair sticking out wildly from his head like an insect's antennae. Twitching. The man had a thick mustache like Ben's father had had.

A flash of memory, a razor strop ripping into the flesh of his back and legs, drawing blood, making him wince. All those nights he slept on his stomach. His pillow soaked with tears. Just a scared, lost kid.

He twisted further on his stool, scratched at his chest suddenly feeling completely empty inside. Hollow. As though he'd been eaten from the inside out. A shell. That fucking photograph.

"Excuse me. Excuse me. I beg your pardon, friend," Ben said, clearing his throat.

The small, ugly man fixed small, ugly eyes on Ben.

"Yeah? What?" he picked at his nostril and flicked something to the floor. Ben placed a fist to his lips, swallowed slow. Blinked heavily. Breathed.

"Marian White," Ben croaked, running his fingers through slick, blonde hair and then pinching the creases in his slacks. The suddenly rough fabric unbearable against his skin. Irritated. Itchy. Raw. Sick. Filthy.

"What?" the man dug into a nostril with his finger a second time and examined what he found between his fingertips. Smiled to himself.

"Marian White," Ben frowned.

"Wrong guy, pal," the man shrugged and wiped his hands on the bar edge.

"No, no, no. Do you know of *her*?" Ben's eyes felt very wet, slippery inside his skull and he wondered if he was going to cry. The missing boy's face hacked and cut into the very tissue of his brain. He had been working so damn hard to get his problems under control, to manage his behavior, incorporate it into his daily life and now everything had gone to fucking shit because of that one single picture in the fucking newspaper. As damaging as a bullet to the back of the head. Point-blank.

"Who?" the man grunted.

"Marian White. Are you familiar with her?" Ben spoke slowly. Enunciating every word clearly.

"Nope, never met her. Never poked her, neither. Not yet, anyway," the man hahaha'd.

"Yes, very quaint. That charming Boston humor." Ben gritted his teeth. "Marian White was a young negro woman."

"White?" the man gulped at his beer, burped. "What a name for a spook, huh? White? They always got names like that, don't they? White, Chalky, Milky. It's like the hebes with their gold and silver and rubies and what not, ain't it? What the hell is this country coming to? I don't even know no more," the man sneered, and wiped his mouth on the back of his hand. Fingernails black, caked with dirt. Ben's stomach flipped. Flesh screaming.

"That's not currently relevant to what I'm telling you. Marian White was a negro woman who got the electric chair in '39 in Mississippi. Dreadful fucking inbred, hellhole that the state is," Ben said.

"Yeah, that right?" the man gulped at his pint glass again. Beer dribbled down his greasy chin. "Good! Should do the same with the lot of them, I say. Fry the whole lot of them." He placed down the glass on the bar top loud and went back to fingering his nostrils.

"I always felt she got the chair rather unfairly. Twelve jurors and every single one of them a white man. Justice is blind *they* say. More like a dumb bitch, *I* say. Anyhow, *they* gave her the chair. Old Sparky. Just like that," Ben clicked his fingers together. "A poor negro girl. Twenty-two years old. *Twenty-two years old.* Electrified to death. A crying shame, a crying shame," Ben said, shaking his head.

"What are you? Some kind of dark meat lover? That it?"

"That's neither here nor there and none of your fucking business, friend. Anyhow, do you know what her crime was? Of course, you don't. A fellow as brainless and ignorant as you appear to be, wouldn't, would you? I'll elucidate for you, shall I?" Ben waited for him to respond. The man stared with eyes like rotten broken eggs. Ben went on anyway, "she murdered her husband with a knitting needle. Slid it straight through his eyeball and up into the soft mush of his little brain as he slept one night," Ben gestured the actions of the murder on his own face and then squeezed his hands together to stop the trembling there. "She turned herself into the law the next morning and gave a full confession," he said shrugging. He knocked his fist on the bar top again. Touch wood. The shakes eased off.

"Crazy shine bitch, *I say*. Does this little story have a fucking point, pal, because my patience is running kind of short over here and I just finished the night shift?"

"Snoring." Ben tried to grin. Couldn't. Wiped his hands up and down his slacks and thighs.

"What?"

"I said snoring. Snoring, I said. She killed her husband because he snored. All the night through. Every night. For years. She should've pleaded temporary insanity; she'd still be alive today. Locked up tight but alive at least," he said, picking a piece of white flint from his jacket sleeve. Squinting at it and blowing it from his fingertips.

"Like I already said, crazy fucking spade got what she deserved," the man shrugged and picked up his pint glass, examining the foamy contents collected at the bottom of it.

"No, no, not particularly. I can understand her motives fully. Empathy, it's important to have empathy in this life, you know? Every person you meet is fighting a battle you know nothing about," he said, tapping at his temple with a finger shaped like a pistol. "Imagine it, snoring every single night for years on end, it would drive any sane person completely looney, no?"

"Yeah, right. Sure. Now, what's your fucking point?"

The snorting man drained the remaining bubbles of his beer and belched. Ben eyeballed him; his left eye twitched. He massaged it impatiently as he spoke. "My point is actually a question. The question being what exactly the fuck is that revolting snorting noise you keep making? I'm sat over here attempting to enjoy the peace and quiet of this here dim, little bar, shithole that it may be, reading the funny papers, or fucking trying to, and you continue to *snort, snort, snort, snort, honk, honk, honk.* Incessantly. You sound like a fucking disgusting pig. It's quite maddening, I assure you. Knitting needle through the eye kind of maddening. Are you sharp enough to comprehend what I am trying to tell you, fuckhead?"

"What's it to you? I've gotta cold, so go fuck yourself, you little limey prick."

"I see. You're the hardheaded type, are you? A hardcase? That's a shame."

Ben reached into the inner pocket of his jacket and took out his detective's badge, flashed it fleetingly at the man's gawping sweat-stained face. The gold shimmered softly in the shadows and he placed it on the bar in the center of the neatly folded Boston Herald. Unclipped the .38 Smith and Wesson service revolver from the shoulder holster inside his jacket and placed it next to the badge. The symmetry was slightly off, he adjusted it. Readjusted it. Touched the newspaper. Touched the revolver. Counted to seven under his breath. Nodded to himself. Symmetry. Order. The guy at the other end of the bar stared, mouth gaping. When Ben felt better about the placements, the order of things, he slid off of his stool slowly, sighing like a man returning to work after a short lunch break. Went and leaned on the bar next to the man. Took a step back. Not too close. The man stank of congealed sweat. Congealed. Ben gagged. Swallowed. Slapped a fist to his mouth and nose. His skin burning, prickling. Festering. He scratched, scratched, scratched at his stomach and chest. Took another step back and tried to compose himself. Breathed slow. The man glared. Sneering.

"A race traitor and a copper, huh? I should've known it. What? You gonna fucking arrest me for breathing too loud? Who the fuck do you think you are? I served *my* country in Europe. France. Lost a lot of buddies to the Krauts, so cowards like you could scurry around the streets free and clear hiding behind a badge. You can go fuck yourself, if you think I'm letting you slap cuffs on me because you don't like the way I'm breathing over here. Now, lemme drink in peace you limey, powder poof fucking cop."

"Scurry? Scurry? Scurry." Ben scratched at his jaw and moved down to his throat again, drawing blood from an old shaving cut. He winced. Frowning at the man. His face contorted into lines and creases.

"What you say?"

"No, no, no. *You say*. You *said*, 'scurry around'. '*Scurry*'. That's an exceedingly unkind word, isn't it? I want you to tell me why you elected to use the word 'scurry'? Of all of the words in the English language you could have chosen, and you decided on 'scurry'. Why that word in particular? I want you to tell me. Tell me. Tell. Tell me. I want you to tell me." The stuttering repetition, his sickness. When he was upset. Anxious. Disturbed. The compulsion to repeat certain things. To get them out of his mouth correctly. Sounding right. Ordered. A curse since childhood. Ben pinched at the flesh of his hand to break off the garbled words. Counting to seven in his head. Counting the lines in the construction fuckhead's face. Twelve lines. He counted beads of sweat. Four. Four beads of sweat. Four was an unlucky number. He knocked on the wooden bar top. Touch wood. Knocking on wood stopped bad things from happening.

Breathless. Pulse ratcheting. The oxygen seemingly sucked from the bar. His breath came ragged and short. He pulled at the knot in his plain, navy necktie.

"What? What are you talking about? It's just a word. You can't arrest a working man, a veteran, for breathing too loud and the kinds of words he says," the man glanced at Sammy the bartender as he spoke, trying to hook some kind of eye contact, some kind of moral support. The bartender sunk deeper into the back shelves, avoiding eye contact, and rubbing obscenely at a glass with the same rag he'd used to clean the surfaces. Ben dry heaved, glared back down at the man on the stool in front of him. Wiped sweat from his temples and eyes with a jacket sleeve. Inhaled deep.

"No, no, no. You're sadly mistaken. I'm not going to arrest you, friend. It's gone past that point now, unfortunately. You escalated the situation. Escalated. The situation has escalated."

"You ain't gonna arrest me? Then what the hell you crowding me for, you darkie loving, buggy, stuttering freak?"

"I'm not going to arrest you," Ben shook his head, faux sad. "No, not at all. I'm going to have to put you out of your misery because you sicken me. Sicken me. You literally make my skin crawl. You make my flesh scurry. That was the word you used, wasn't it? '*Scurry*'? Like I'm some kind of a fucking insect? An ant? Or a fucking cockroach? Is that what I am? Something that crawls naked in the dark? A cockroach? A bug?"

The construction monkey laughed it up. The laughter a forced, unsure kind. Brittle and fragile in the sudden vacuum of the bar's atmosphere. The bartender mumbled something about needing to take a piss, wiped his hands on the chest of his grimy apron and stumbled into the toilets, slamming the door behind him. The glass rattled sharply in its frame. The man chuckled uneasily again and twisted on his stool to size Ben up; a grin torn rigidly across his face like a flesh wound. Ben gagged again from the stale stink of the pig, winced, pulled his 'drop gun', another .38 with masking tape around the handle and the serial number scraped away, from the base of his spine, stabbed it into the man's soft guts, pulled down on the trigger. The bullet thumped home with a muffled 'POP'. The man pulled a ridiculous, shocked expression. Eyes and mouth stupidly wide. Breath stinking. Ben jumped back and shot him again in the chest as he collapsed from the stool, gasping. Sucking air.

Ben preferred not to shoot people in the head because the impact of the bullet caused the blood to mist minutely into the air. Blowback. A toxic vapor. Diseases could be breathed into the lungs causing all kinds of infections. Diseases. The kind his mother had wasted away from. The chest less messy and safer. Cleaner. More sanitary. Especially in an enclosed area like a bar.

"Scurry?! Scurry around?! Go ahead! Make that filthy fucking pig snorting noise again," Ben panted, out of breath, at the man lying on the dark, chipped tiled flooring spreading a thick puddle of deep red. The man didn't answer because he was dead. Eyes like beads of glass fixed unseeingly on Ben. Wide and white. Very different from the boy's in the photograph.

Ben wiped his sleeve across his mouth, paced in circles, gulped a mouthful of whiskey from the bottle on the bar, gargled it, spat it onto the ground. Exhaled loud. Pushed the lank blonde hair hanging in his face back over his head. Walked quickly around the back of the bar, opened the cash register and scattered dollar bills and loose change around the place like confetti. Counting aloud as he did. One. Two. Three. Four. Five. Six. Seven. Seven that lucky number. Wiped off the .38 with his handkerchief, placing it into the still warm dead man's hand and fired off a couple of shots at the bar doors. The oak paneling shattered and splintered. Someone let out a surprised scream from in between the rumbles of traffic outside. The bartender peered his bald head out from behind the restroom door, Ben wiped the hanging hair from his grey eyes again and tried to smile. To seem all right. Normal. Ordered.

"Sammy, my good friend, this gentleman just tried to rob your drinking establishment while you were indisposed. Can you believe that? It's a damn good thing I was here, wasn't it? You should probably call some of my pals to come and clean up this mess though," Ben said waving a hand towards the dead man. "You'll have to close up shop for a while, too. Inconvenient, I know, I know, but these things can't be helped any, can they?"

"Jesus Christ, Ben! Why'd you have to go and do that again? I'm trying to run a fucking business here," the barkeep stuttered.

"Are you fucking deaf, Sammy? I just told you, he was trying to rob the place blind. Now, is there going to be a problem?" Ben picked up his service revolver from its resting place on the newspaper and span it on the oak bar top. The muzzle went round and round before finally settling on the barman. Ben shrugged and span it again.

"No! No, there ain't no problem of course. He was trying to rob the place. Sure. Whatever you say, Ben. I was just checking, is all. Getting the story straight."

"Well, what do you say?"

"What?"

"What do you say? I just saved your fucking livelihood, did I not?"

"Oh, right. Sure. Thanks a lot, Ben. You saved my bar… Thanks a lot," Samuel sighed. Wiped his forehead with the bar towel. "Who do I gotta call, anyway? Which pals of yours do I have to call this time? The Seven Shamrocks on Dorchester or the BPD?" he muttered staring at the dead man crumpled on the floor.

Ben shrugged. "It doesn't really matter, I suppose. The results will be the same, but probably the latter is best this time around, don't you think, Samuel?" Ben twitched, went around to where he had been sitting, picked up the bottle of whisky from the bar top again and splashed the contents over his hands, rubbing them together. Cleansed. Sanitized. He then sat back down on his stool, replacing the slowly spinning revolver and detective's shield back into the inside of his jacket as the bartender bitched and moaned into a telephone behind the bar. He flicked open the Boston Herald, drawn to the article about the missing boy again. An uncontrolled compulsion to all things unpleasant, repellent, another sign of his dysfunctions. To get stuck inside his mind on ugliness. The unreal. The nightmarish lies that span like a spinning top in his skull. He sighed deep. Feeling a little more relaxed about everything. A kind of peace at last. The voices resurrected from the photograph that flashed screeching through his head like raging house-fires faded to black. Dead like the piece of shit sprawled on the floor. The renewed silence of the place almost spiritual, a church from his childhood...

His fucking childhood.

The frightened little boy.

Fuck!

No, he couldn't relax. Too fucking itchy. The boy's eyes in the newspaper still screaming at him. The ache boiling up in his guts, burning. The dark silhouette from his childhood scurrying through his mind unchained and free. The black shape at the end of a bed. Twitching. Ben's left eyelid blinked uncontrollably. He placed a palm over it. Stood up. Wanted to scream, but didn't. Hands grasping at the stool for support. Vertigo. His nostrils detecting the stench of shit radiating from the corpse at the other side of the bar. He cursed repeatedly under his breath, "Fuck! Fuck! Fuck!"

About to leave, he snatched up his hat then hesitated. Frowning, he ran his fingers through his hair, shoved on the fedora and ripped the photograph of the missing child from the newspaper. Folded it carefully into his pocket with the envelope of cash and staggered twitching into a chilled Boston afternoon. Sammy shouted something as the doors slammed shut. Ben ignored him. Counting. Three sets of seven and reciting the poem his mother had taught him.

A GROUP OF pedestrians stood clustered on the sidewalk outside muttering hushed to each other. He was sure he'd seen the same crowd in a recent nightmare. No animal uglier, stupider or more vicious than a crowd. How he hated most people. His body ached suddenly. Sirens wailed in the distance. He pulled the brim of his fedora low, flashed his badge at the disgusting gawkers, told them everything was all right, to go back to their business. Thought about ripping the .38 from its shoulder holster and shooting blindly into the crowd, saving the last bullet for himself. The image of his own suicide something ingrained into him scar-like since adolescence. The reason why he kept the rounds to the .38 in the glove compartment of his Cadillac when he finished working. He'd sat in his pitch-black apartment, pressing the muzzle of the empty revolver against his temple and pulling the trigger so many times he'd lost count.

Click, click, click. Click, click, click. Click. Seven—a lucky number.

He shook his head at the thoughts and walked down the block to where he had parked his Cadillac.

Sitting in the automobile, listening to the engine. The newspaper page in his fingertips. Trying to catch his breath. Counting to seven.

One.

Two.

Three.

Four.

Five.

Six.

Seven.

London, England
Thursday, February 18ᵗʰ, 1926

BIG BEN CALLED out eleven times.

Metropolitan Police Sergeant William Hughes counted the chimes, watching the couple. The two shadows that swayed and shook together. Darkness draped around their forms like funeral shrouds. A subway train rumbled underneath his heavily shined boots through the rain dampened cobblestones. A stony weight in his guts, a heaviness in his bollocks. A cool sweat freckling his brow. He watched them. The lovers. Writhing together like snakes in heat. A feminine laugh took flight into the night on papery wings and lingered along with the woman's acrid perfume. A breathless, intoxicated conversation whispered hushed along the weathered, pockmarked bricks of the glue factory they were huddled against. He ran fingers over his thick mustache and breathed in the damp February night air. Lost in thought. Locked elsewhere for a transient moment.

Paris, 1918. A woman's smile in candlelight. A sigh. The taste of perfume on the slender nape of a neck. Long golden hair underneath his fingertips.

Memories, a bloody, aching wound in the mouth to be tongued at.

He nodded to himself, a decision made and slid the truncheon from the worn leather belt on his hip. Making his way over to the two slow dancing forms. The sounds of his heavy footfalls echoing off of the tenement walls. The woman's face as pale as the moon gaped and hissed a curse in his direction.

"Now, now, what the bloody hell's going on here then?" the smiling policeman said.

The young man startled, squeaking out a weak moan, fumbling at his trousers and jacket. Readjusting. Correcting himself.

"Nothing at all, Constable. I'm sorry. I'm just escorting my lady friend home, that's all."

"Sergeant."

"I beg ya pardon?"

The policeman tapped at his upper arm, at the golden insignia sewn into the dark, rough fabric of his uniform jacket, with the heavy oak truncheon bringing their eyes to the rank patch but their focus stuck fixed to the cruel glimmer of the cosh in his large fist.

"Ah, I see. Yes. Yes, of course, Sergeant. Sergeant. I am dreadfully sorry, Sergeant," stuttered the boy.

"This your *lady friend* then, is it?" the policeman asked, roughly running the truncheon over the woman's hip and then up to her swollen breasts. Stabbing the nub of the truncheon hard into the place her nipple pushed through the thin fabric of the cheap dress. She pouted and rotated her leg on the heel of a muck covered shoe, turning away from the blunt object and closer into the young man.

"Not much of a friend, nor much a lady neither, I suspect. And dressed pretty loosely for February weather too, I might add," the police sergeant chuckled humorlessly.

"Leave off, would ya, please Constable. We ain't botherin' nobody. Are we?" hissed the woman. Her breath reeking sweetly of poteen and bile. Something intoxicating, maddening about the stink of it that the policeman savored. Relished. He stared at the man, ignoring the woman,

"Shut your trap a minute, woman. Males are talking. What's your name, boy?"

"George. George Gamble, Sir. I mean, I mean Sergeant."

"And where do you presently reside, boy?"

"I… I…"

"Cease the stuttering and answer the God-damned question, boy."

"I'm staying at a lodging house over on Commercial Street. Spitalfields."

"Yes, I know the street very well. A haven for degenerates. How old are you, boy?"

"I'll be twenty-three this coming November, Sergeant."

"Well, George Gamble who is twenty-three in November, your *lady friend* here is a brass. A tart. A Babylonian whore. A succubus. You know that fact, do you, boy? Soliciting a prostitute is a crime. A very serious one at that, I'll add."

"Oh, leave off, for Christ's sake," the woman sighed. She sagged back against the pockmarked brick wall again, lit a cigarette from a dull tin tobacco case and flicked the spent match at the feet of the Sergeant. He felt his face burn up. Sunburnt and windswept raw. The little fucking whore was testing his resolve. His patience. He hadn't even started in on her as of yet. The cunt. Cunt whore. Fucking cunt whore. Harlot. Betrayer. Betrayer. Betrayer.

The policeman stepped forward; his fist snapping out a jab that sent the woman sprawling onto her back. Hard and heavy. Her long white dress spread over the glimmering cobblestones; her milky thighs illuminated in the moonlight. She looked so very beautiful, the policeman thought. Something to be destroyed. Wrecked. So achingly beautiful. Painful. He could smell lavender and red wine. A phonograph bleeding out music sadly. Paris on the night air. He shook his head to try and clear it.

"You should retire and return to your residence now, boy, if you know what's best for you. I'll escort your lady friend home. No need for you to trouble yourself now," he said, rubbing the knuckles of his fist with the hand still gripping the cosh.

The woman, slack-mouthed, remained frozen, sprawled on the wet ground. Weeping softly and holding a trembling hand to her jaw. She moaned a few times. Gazing imploringly at the young man with muddy eyes. Shaking her head violently from side to side. Lips shaped deliciously desperate. The young man avoided eye contact, turned, hesitating a moment and then the sound of his boots quickly echoed his departure down the street towards the Thames riverside, fading away into the darkness.

The policeman chuckled again, sighed, reaching down a blood sticky hand to the woman. She slapped it away, scowling.

"Get off. I'll get myself up. You've given me a bloody fat lip, you 'ave."

"You'll come along with me now then, unless you'll be wanting more of the same."

"Down the nick? But I wasn't doin' nothin', honest to God. We was just talkin' for Christ's sake. No crime in having an innocent conversation, surely? Is there?"

The policeman threw back his head and laughed. A large heartless sound. Hollow. An echo in a churchyard. Laughter with a hard edge, a rusty clawhammer.

"You think I'd waste my time dragging your worthless state down the station? Embarrass myself like that? No, darlin'. You'll accompany me over to Brick Lane. There's an unlit courtyard there I use often where we shan't be bothered none."

"I should 'ave known it. Just another ruddy cozzer lookin' for a giveaway ain't ya? I've heard about you. You're the one that's been beatin' on the girls. Everyone's been warned about you."

"You want another fucking smack for your lip, harlot?" He grabbed the woman by the scalp, shaking her head backwards and forwards violently. She screamed through crooked clenched teeth. Sobbed and screwed her face up. Still nothing more than a very young woman. Her creamy face in the streetlight angelic.

Lavender. Red wine. Milky skin. Paris.

Her hair in his fist like the threads of something very fragile and the Sergeant felt himself become hard. He pushed her roughly up against the brick wall.

"I love you so much and you always hurt me so," he whispered, panting, reaching up her thighs, pulling roughly at her knickers. She pulled herself free from his grasp, hitched up her filthy dress and took off quickly in the direction of the young man's retreat. Running like a ghost story into the night.

"George! George! I'd rather go along with you? I'm frightened! Wait for me, please. George?! Please! Wait. George?!" her voice came breathless and desperate down the empty street.

The policeman growled, grinned bitterly and stalked after her, bringing the worn, smooth brass knuckles casually from his trouser pocket and sliding them over his right fist. Placed a long silver whistle in his lips, gripping it between his teeth. Tonguing, tasting the bitter metal. Something like a fever burning through his body. A biblical combustion. The dull ache of an aged betrayal as hot as a straight razor in his guts.

He spotted them then, standing outside The King's Head pub, squabbling like a couple of infants. The whore had a hold of the boy's arm, pulling him back towards an alleyway. Wide eyed in the twilight and desperate to make the little amount that would enable her to get a place in the bunk house for the night.

They saw the policeman and froze. Two hares caught in a game warden's torchlight.

"Sergeant, please," said the boy in a tired voice. He slid his hands out in a gesture of surrender and the glow from the nearest streetlamp gloved his palms in a taint of sickly yellow.

"It's all right, son. It's all right," The policeman mumbled soothingly through a clenched jaw, biting down hard on the whistle and giving the boy a vicious one-two combination. A flickering jab with the brass knuckles and then a straight over the crown with his truncheon, splitting the boy's head open. Blowing down hard on the whistle as he backhanded the whore and kicked her hard in the stomach to shut her trap from screeching. The boy collapsed unconscious to the wet ground. His skull cracked against stone. Teeth rattled across pavement like rain drops. The policeman continued to blow out on the whistle as he kicked the boy's legs open. Wider, splayed. Satisfied with the length of the space between, he began to stamp down on the boy's crotch. Stamping and kicking. He spat out the whistle. Screamed.

"Fuck *my* woman?! You want to fuck *my* woman, do you?!"

Lost in an all-encompassing boiling, bright black fury until another patrolling police constable came running in answer to his bellows and pulled him off the ruined heap of the boy. The girl long gone into the darkness of the East End. Police Sergeant William Hughes, pushed off the arms that held him, sat down heavily on a curb, panting and lit a cigarette. Picking a flake of tobacco from his tongue. Feeling a little better about the memories that burned inside his mind.

Paris. The taste of red wine and lavender on the whitest, purest skin.

He cursed, wishing he had kept a grasp on the filthy, little whore. Betrayer. There was always the next night. Always another harlot.

"Bloody hell, Sergeant. I think this boy might be dead," the young constable said.

Sergeant Hughes dragged long on his cigarette, flicked it onto the cobblestones and stood up, brushing down his rain-dampened trousers. Exhaled a cloud of smoke into the other younger man's concerned face.

"Well, he was resisting arrest. You shan't be needing an ambulance wagon now in any case, will you? Saved a lot of time and grief, I did," he placed a hand on the young constable's shoulder and squeezed hard. Glaring into his eyes until the other policeman stared down and away.

"You deal with this, constable. If anyone asks, you tell them I've gone to The Ten Bells pub for a nightcap and they're more than welcome to come search me out if they've got any fucking questions that need asking," he said walking into the darkness and smog of Whitechapel.

South Boston, USA
Monday, February 18th, 1946

THE SKY A clotted kind of grey. Dorchester Street an icy kind of dead.

Stevie Wallace washing the windows of The Seven Shamrocks social club, a limp cigarette hanging from his thin, scarred mouth. Grey hair windswept. Hunched-shouldered and wearing the same ratty, faded blue bathrobe he always wore as of late. The bitter reek of whiskey emanating from him tangible as Ben came up from behind swinging the leather doctor's bag. He spoke to Ben, squinting into the soapy reflection of the glass.

"Here he is now. Fucking Sherlock Holmes himself. The Englishman with the rent," he grinned, scratching at the salt and pepper stubble on his chin. Ben grinned too, couldn't help himself, placing his hand on the old man's shoulder. Stevie "Boxer" Wallace, one of only a few people Ben could touch without a jarring feeling of disquiet. Without having to wash the prickling, dry irritant of filth from his hands in the nearest sink. He almost loved the old man. Stevie had been the boss of Southie since '33 when King Solomon, the old boss, caught a few bullets in the back of the head while taking a piss in the swanky restroom of The Cotton Club.

"Everyone's paid up, Stevie."

"Of course they have. There was never any doubt. Did you take your boss's percentage and god forbid, your own?"

"You know I did," Ben grinned again.

"That I do. Never a doubt. Also know you made another fucking mess over in Seaport not an hour before."

"That was unavoidable, unfortunately. Crime in progress. News always travels fast around here, doesn't it?"

"Sure, the news? I made the news in '20. Olympic Featherweight contender for these United States of America. The fucking Olympics. You know that, Benny?"

"Yes, I'd heard, Stevie. More than a few times, actually."

"Went all the way to Antwerp. Never even been out of Southie before that. All the way to Europe. Benny, they didn't even let me fight, you believe that shit? I could have gotten the gold. People, they called me 'The Tommy Gun Kid', the fastest jab in the whole of this white America," said Stevie, dropping the sponge into the bucket of water and shadowboxing his reflection.

"Sure, you could've, Stevie. It's freezing cold today. Come inside. You're going to get sick standing out here in that bathrobe. It's February in case you hadn't noticed."

Stevie stopped the punch combinations and snatched up the sponge from the bucket again with a deep sigh. "Of course I fucking noticed it's February, you English moron. Someone's gotta clean these windows. Not going to clean themselves, are they? March weather be damned."

"February. February weather be damned, Stevie. Anyhow, I was inferring about the bathrobe."

"'*Inferring*? '*Inferring*' were you? Now that's a lace curtain word if I ever heard one. Don't trust words like that, nor the men that utter them, Benny Boyo. Then there's that fucking British accent. And you wonder why the lads don't trust you any?"

"I don't wonder. I couldn't give a fuck about them either way. Come on inside and have a drink with me. Sit down for a while."

"Sit down? I've got shit to do. These windows ain't gonna clean themselves, are they? The club is starting to look like a dump. Where the fuck is that kid Tommy Shea? He always helped me out around here. Good kid that boy."

"You know where he is, Stevie."

"What do you mean? Where is he?"

"Shea's six years into his stint at Charlestown Pen. Armed robbery. Him and that little fuckhead Blondie, both. You held their going away party here. Blondie pulled a knife on the Mulligans. You remember now?"

Stevie frowned confused at Ben a moment, then looked down at the bucket of water, nodding as though he understood.

"Sure, sure, of course I remember. You think I'm some kind of an eegit? Is that it?"

"No, not at all, Stevie. You're the boss of Southie. Now, come on inside."

"I gotta go and do some collections. Jimmy Noonan still owes my brother vig for the last three fucking weeks."

Stevie shambled off into the street, his bath robe catching in the chilled breeze and exposing pale flesh. A rusted Chevy pickup swerved, honked its horn irritably. Ben jogged after, took the old man gently by a skinny arm, guiding him back towards the safe confines of the sidewalk and the club.

"You can't do the collections now, Stevie. You have to clean these windows, remember? Besides, your brother and Jimmy are both departed. Years back now, Stevie."

"What are you yammering on about?"

"Never mind, it's all right. Now, you want this money or not?" Ben placed his hand softly on the old man's back, feeling

28

bones protruding through the matted fabric of the bathrobe. Lifted the leather doctor's bag aloft.

"Sure. Sure. Go inside and give the bag to the Fat Man. Have a piece of cake that's on the bar, my Debbie made it."

Stevie went back to sponging the windows with scummy icy water and then glanced at Ben again as though for the first time. "Here he is, now. The Englishman with the rent."

Ben tried to smile; his face hurt. Shook his head and went through the doors he'd been going through since he'd been a child new to America and the streets of South Boston.

THE BIG KIDS had dark brown freckles on their faces and orange hair. The freckles looked like insects crawling angrily across their cheeks. Ben was running as fast as he could. His legs hurt bad. Heart pounding a hole through his vest. He could hear the boys behind him. The sounds of their dirty shoes slapping down on sunbaked concrete. The bad words they shouted. Why did everything always have to be so ugly? He didn't know. They were gaining on him. Too quick. Running as fast as he could. Biting into his bottom lip painfully to stop the tears from coming. They'd beat him worse today if they witnessed him crying.

"Stop! Stop running, you cowardly little chicken shit!" the tallest boy shouted.

"You little limey piece of shit," the one with the brightest orange hair shrieked.

Ben kept running.

The smallest of the bad boys held a cockroach in his enclosed hand, and they were going to put it in Ben's pants they'd cheered. Knowing from school how much he hated the things. How he screamed at the sight of anything with six legs scurrying. A peculiar little phobia, his teacher had said.

An old man stepped out of the barbershop suddenly and Ben twisted to avoid hitting him, losing his balance. Falling hard to the street. Stones and grit cut into the palms of his hands and knees. He screamed and hated himself for it. The old man chuckled and walked away whistling as Ben struggled back to his feet.

The two larger boys collided with Ben, knocking the breath from his lungs. Wrestled him back down to the asphalt. Shoving their knees painfully into his arms. Ben tried to say the words of the poem his mother had taught him thousands of miles and a year ago, but the words didn't come. Refusing to form into sounds willing to leave his throat. Abandoning him. One of the boys punched his nose and banged his head against the ground. Ben screwed up his eyes and wept. The tears slid burning hot down his face. Not knowing why life always had to be so hateful and ugly.

"Look it, the little limey baby is crying for his momma."

They cackled in unison.

The smallest boy placed his filthy foot on Ben's chest, brown stains smeared over cotton fabric. Ben squealed.

"This roach is going stir crazy in here. Think it's pooped on me. Quick open his mouth before it bites me," the smallest boy said, waving his cupped hands in the air excitedly.

Ben squealed again. His father's face flashing through his mind. His mother's lips. He clamped his mouth shut.

The older boys twisted Ben's ears, one of them hissed, "when he screams again shove that bug in the little sissy's mouth."

They all hooted. An ugly sound bouncing off bricks, tarmac and cobblestone.

Then a different noise. The sound of a door gliding open. A man's boots stomping into view. Ben squinted up at the shape towering over them all, shrouded by the afternoon sun.

"What the Jesus are you little shits doing outside my club?"

The older boys let go of Ben, standing up quickly. Backs straight. "Nothing at all, Mr. Wallace, honest to God," the tallest said.

"Be honest to me, not God. Sure as hell don't look like nothing. Three against one? That's how the wops and the coloreds and those rats in Charlestown fight each other. It's not the way we do it here in Southie."

"He's an Englishman, Stevie," the smallest one murmured under his breath.

"I don't give a shit if he's an Englishman or a man from Mars and it's Mr. Wallace to you, you little gobshites," the man said, cuffing the three boys around the backs of their hung heads in quick succession. The boy with the brightest orange hair started to snivel. The smallest one wailed and dropped the cockroach he'd been carrying since the school yard. It scurried into a drain, dragging a leg behind it and disappeared. Ben sighed audibly.

"Now, get the hell out of here before I tell your fathers," Wallace growled.

The boys ran. The boys ran fast.

The man gazed down at Ben for a long moment grinning and then ruffled his hair roughly. "Your nose is bleeding, and your head is cut, Englishman. Come inside the club and we'll clean you up. My Debbie's got some iodine. It'll sting like a bitch, but it'll clean the dirt out of the gash. You thirsty? We got some tonic. Soda pop, I think."

"Thank you, Sir," Ben said.

"Call me, Stevie. And don't worry about those little hooligans. They're mad dogs like their fathers. It's in the blood."

"What's in the blood, Mister Stevie?"

"Our father's madness... passed down in the blood. You like boxing, kid? You know, I went to the Olympics in '20?"

Ben followed Stevie into the Seven Shamrocks holding his burning ears and almost smiling.

WAY PAST ITS glory days, the place stank of disease. Diseased hopes. Diseased regrets. Old beer, stale tobacco. Piss. The same group of Irish heist men sat around the same table, playing the same game of poker. Talking the same shit. Ben's guts coiled up and dropped. The muscular, flame haired Mulligan brothers, Connor and Christopher, and skeletal, pale Hughie IOU. They hushed, pausing to gaze at Ben coolly, nodded and then went back to their game. Fat Man Leary behind the bar eating a large slice of grey, dry looking sponge. He nodded at Ben as he entered the place. Engulfed the last of the cake into his swollen, pink face and wiped the crumbs from his mouth with the back of a bloated hand that had the last three fingers missing. Smooth stumps of a past mistake. Ben hung back, eyes darting from Leary to a barstool. Cake crumbs clung to the fat man's dark, scraggly beard.

"That punch-drunk fool still out there freezing his balls off, English?"

"He is. And if word gets back to the Italians that Stevie is a few sandwiches short of a picnic, wandering up and down the street in his bathrobe and piss-stained undershorts talking to himself, they'll hit you all hard and fast. Buccola's already testing the waters over in Seaport. I've been telling you to try and keep him inside," Ben said, dropping the bag down on the bar.

"Stevie don't listen none. Don't stop yammering on about fighting in the 1920 Olympics, neither. Sick to the back teeth of hearing about it, truth be told." Leary hefted the bag into air, shook it and then dropped it behind the bar out of sight. "That everything? How'd you say? Consolidated?"

"It's everything that's anything," Ben said sitting down at the end of the bar, the stool furthest from Leary and the table of Irishmen. He didn't remove his hat. Hughie IOU muttered something; the Mulligans laughed it up. Ben eyeballed IOU until he looked down at his cards. The Mulligans stared at the tabletop grinning. They were talking about him. Laughing at him again. Ben knew it. Sure he heard someone whisper the word *'buggy'* under their breath. Ben shook out a handkerchief from his jacket pocket and rubbed at his moist hands. Whispers rattled like dry leaves blown across concrete. *Crazy. Sick. Father. Mother. Weak. Ill. Dishonorable Discharge. Sick. Filthy. Sick. Crazy. Buggy.* Ben pulled the necktie from his throat, rolled it up and placed it in a jacket pocket, wiped sweat from his brow, his eyes and turned to glare at the table again. His heart choking in his chest. Someone whispered *'buggy'* under their breath again.

"What are you talking about over there?" Ben called out. His voice wavering.

"What, Englishman?" grunted Connor through a cigarette pinched at the corner of his lips.

"I want to know what you were saying just now. Say it again," Ben fidgeted and pulled at the creases in his slacks. Heartbeat jacked. A prickly heat running over his scalp and down his spine.

"Huh? We weren't saying nothing," IOU deadpanned. Blank faced blinking.

"Yes, you fucking were. I heard you. Now, say it again."

"No one said nothing, honest to God," Christopher said, shrugging and dealing out the greasy cards.

"Yeah, we're just playing a game of rounders over here. And I'm getting my fucking ass handed to me by these degenerate cocksuckers," IOU said.

"You fucking liars. I fucking heard you. Heard you. I fucking heard you. I fucking. Heard you." Ben scrunched up his face. Slapped a hand to his mouth. Swallowing bitter stutters.

"Ah, shit. He's gone and started his stammering. Look, don't call us fucking liars. We weren't bothering you none, Englishman. Don't come in here making no trouble today. Jesus fucking Christ, every single time with this guy," Christopher said waving his hand dismissively in Ben's direction.

"You Irish fuckheads," Ben spat.

"Go fuck yourself, you stuttering prick, English. People round here getting pretty tired of you throwing your weight around because you got a detective's badge and you're Stevie's little favorite," Connor sneered, snubbing out his cigarette in an overflowing ashtray. Butts tumbled scattering onto the table and floor.

"All right, all right, that's enough you mad dogs. We'll have no fisticuffs today, you hear? You want a piece of cake, Englishman? Stevie's old lady made it," Leary gestured the bloated, disfigured, hairy hand in the direction of the plate at the end of the bar.

Ben dragged his eyes away from the Mulligans and watched a fat, black fly crawl across the dry cake. His guts tumbled. He shifted uncomfortably on the stool. Fingering the cool damp front of his shirt. Trying to control his breathing. He counted. His hands shook and he wiped them again on the handkerchief until the bones in his knuckles cracked. The silence of the bar like ocean waves in his ear drums. The shakes starting to build up in the bones of his fingers. Becoming sicker as the day wore on. Cool mucus slid from his nostril onto his upper lip, and he used the handkerchief to wipe it away quickly. Needing a drink to last him until China Town. Until his cure. His medicine.

"Wakey, wakey!" Leary shouted.

Ben almost fell off his stool.

"Well? You want some cake or not?" Leary held up the plate. Crumbs rolled to the floor. Ben scratched at his chest and tried to compose himself. To be normal.

"No, thank you, Leary. No. Just a whiskey from my bottle... You need to talk to the old man about retiring. Things are getting too much for him around here."

"Who? Stevie?" Leary said filling up a tumbler from a bottle with a small Union Jack cocktail flag taped to the base and sliding it over to Ben. "He won't retire. None of us do in this life. You keep going until a bullet or a pair of cuffs stop you."

"All the same, Stevie should be at home doing crosswords and growing vegetables in the yard. Whatever it is retired bootleggers do," Ben said, examining the glass in front of him and then placing his palm over the top of it.

Fat Man Leary squinted down at the protected glass, placed both fists down on the bar and leaned forward. Ben shuffled back slightly on the stool, pulling the drink closer to him. Leaned back. Cringing. Leary nodded towards the club doors. "He ain't that old yet. Just his mind's going is all. Taken too many shots to the head. Be damned if I know where to put him. Trying my best to keep the fool out of sight. Deborah's trying her damnedest, too. But you of all people know best what he's like. The smallest things set him off. Let me tell you something, things are already on a fucking knife edge with the guineas in the North End. Fucking fragile. Been like that since '31 when they murdered Stevie's brother over at the Hanover Street meeting but now that Stevie don't really know what day of the fucking week it is, things could get real bad for all of us, real quick.

Things ain't been this bad since before me and Stevie snuffed out King Solomon. Hate to fucking admit it, but we're outnumbered and outgunned over here. We all need to keep our heads down and our asses clean for the time being. The last thing we want is a fucking war. And let me tell you, we'll be needing all the support we can get to keep Southie out of their greasy fucking wop hands. Seaport is another question all together. A lost cause. Can we at least be counting on you and your boss?"

"As long as you keep paying more than the Italians are offering."

"Fucking typical English. Working for the all-mighty greenbacks."

"Aren't we all."

"You'll put cash money before the people you grew up with? Southie is your home too, ain't it?"

"You know full well how expensive The Chief already is and with Stevie retiring I'm getting together enough money to get the fuck away from this place and all the people in it. No offense intended."

"Let me tell you something, things get any more heated than they are, there'll be a lot of work coming your way. Cold cash, too. Stevie's had a war fund stowed away for years. You'll not have to do it for free like over in Seaport earlier today, am I right?"

"I take it everyone's well aware of my actions by now then."

"This is Southie. If you fucking stomped on a roach, we'd hear about it before you'd even scraped it off the bottom of your shoe," Leary laughed heartily. The word cockroach brought a dark, murmuring, shuffling mass to the forefront of Ben's mind. He cringed, blinking the thoughts away. The boy. The photograph. His upbringing.

"What was that then? Earlier in Seaport? Business or pleasure?" Leary pulled himself a beer. Slurped at it.

"It was neither," Ben pinched at his creases.

"Whatever it was, you're playing kind of fast and loose with that badge of yours. You're no good to us without it, you know? Stevie pulled a lot of strings to get you where you are. Detective. Don't forget it. Just a friendly heads up, English."

"I'll worry about my side of the street. You worry about yours, Leary," Ben said.

"Talking of your side of the street, that son of a bitch was sniffing around here again. Not thirty minutes before. Looking for you. Forever building his case. That's why you need to be smarter."

"Jones?"

"Yep. Son of a bitch Welshman. They fuck sheep, I'll have you know."

"What did you tell him?"

"What do you think? I told him to get back into his shamrock green fucking Ford Coupe and get the fuck outta here. Stealing our colors. Livestock fucking Welshman."

"Good, that's good, Leary." Ben held up the glass, scrutinized his drink again.

"Covering your ass always, Englishman, but at least we weren't called to clean up your bloody mess this time around," Connor shouted over.

"You were paid well enough the last time, Irishman. It isn't like you're making anything substantial on your own, is it now?" Ben called back over his shoulder.

"Still, nothing worse than cleaning up a mad dog's shite," Christopher chimed in.

"Well, like I said, it isn't like you paddy fucks have anything better to do than sit around playing poker, is it? You'd be best suited working out of the sixth floor of The Charlesgate selling your asses to the degenerates," Ben said pushing his stool out and standing.

"I said that's enough now, lads," Leary clapped the large, deformed hand down on the bar top, motioning Ben to relax and take a seat. "We've more important things going on."

Ben sat back down. The Irishmen went back to playing cards, muttering underneath their breath.

"Let me tell you, English, thank Jesus it wasn't a wop you snuffed out in Seaport. Last thing we need right now is a war."

"Yes, yes, yes, as you've already made me well aware, Leary. Don't you start repeating yourself too," Ben finished his drink and shook the empty tumbler in the air. The whiskey hitting his empty stomach like splinters of ice.

Leary refilled it, pushed the cork back into the bottle and returned it to the shelf apart from the others. Shoved another piece of cake into his mouth and smirked, speaking with his mouth full, "perhaps I'm going a little squirrelly, like the boss man. Maybe it's this fucking bar that does it to all of us. I'm sure the place is fucking cursed. Came in here early one morning and was sure Solomon was slouching at the bar sipping at a cold one, the whole of his face gone where me and Stevie put the slugs in him. Fucking creepy. Yep, this place makes a man buggy," he shrugged. Crumbs tumbled down his beard and shirtfront to the floor.

Ben swallowed a gag, mouth dry, eyeballing Leary's face for signs of an insult. "Just talk to Stevie about taking it easy from now on. I'd stay, but I've other matters to attend to and this place stinks like an Irish bog today." He raised his glass to the table of poker players. "Slainte fellas." Tipped it down his mouth. Smooth. Clean. The Irishmen shrugged their shoulders. Their faces empty.

He stood up, throwing a crumpled dollar bill on the bar, thought he heard the word *buggy* hissed in his direction again. Why couldn't people just leave him the hell alone? Suddenly dizzy. He started counting the shapes of light cut golden yellow across the picture frame clustered walls. Knife blades causing his eyes to ache. Staggered, pushing hard through the front doors, the brass handles slammed against brick, out of the bar. His fist clamped in his mouth.

Stevie pissing against a streetlamp that had the remains of a black child's missing poster stuck to it and growling words towards a repair garage across the street. Ben started to go to him but stopped, turned and walked hurriedly in the opposite direction, pulling his jacket tightly together against the icy breeze. Tremors ripping through his body. Migraine tearing his brain into two. Nose starting to run again. He wiped the cold sweat from his face with the handkerchief, blew his nose and tossed it at a fire hydrant. Junk sick or the photograph. Cramps tearing through his guts. Losing himself. Needing China Town. Needing Li Yu.

SINCE A CHILD fresh off the ship from Southampton, England, Ben had always loved Boston's China Town. His mother had forbidden him to enter its boundaries. Had said it was filthy and rife with sickness, he had disobeyed her and played truant from school just to explore its streets. He supposed he loved it still. There was something supernatural about the place. An atmosphere that seeped out of the very brickwork and ran slick over the streets, like a hot summer rain. He enjoyed the vibrancy of it all. The oriental people with their mysterious language and mysterious, ageless faces. The signs that glowed alongside lanterns that burnt a luminous red. Scents of the food—a curious enticement he never partook in but could appreciate all the same. Strictly the odors. Eating the filth they served in the restaurants was a good way to become ill. Hospital sick. His mother had been correct about that. The people ate chickens' feet. Sucked the flesh right off the repulsive clutched claws. Imagining it fleetingly brought a hot, bitter flow of vomit to the back of Ben's throat. He spun into an alley and cleansed himself against an overturned trash barrel. The stench of rotting garbage. He heaved again. Eyes burning. Trembling hands on his knees. Mucus running from his nostrils. He waited for the convulsions to end and wiped at his face with a fresh handkerchief. Cursed. He needed to purify himself.

To purify himself. The only reasons he had started frequenting Chinatown again since his mother passed away from the illness that had eaten her from the inside out. Opium. Opium and Li Yu. The only things that could ease his mind. Take the jagged, bitter edge away from things. Stop the screams, the whispers, the chatter, the counting, the festering within the prison cell of his skull. Li Yu and Opium. They had come into his life together and he needed them both. Became ill, weakened without them. Junk sick.

Glimpsing another missing child's poster pasted to a dented lamp post, ripped and weathered, he spat the nasty taste from his mouth and stumbled quickly on.

IN THE GARMENT district a couple of Chinese kids ran giggling from the early evening darkness of an abandoned storefront with boxes of matches and toothpicks to hawk but recognizing his face sank back into a shadowed storefront with disappointed, black eyes. One said something to the other in Mandarin and they both giggled. Ben knew enough of the Chinese language to identify the words '*crazy*' and '*Englishman*'. Insolent little shits. He turned into Ping On Alley where Li and her mother ran a small teahouse and nodded bluntly at the old, toothless, bald-headed Chinaman who stood out front every evening underneath an intricate banner of green double dragons. Rain or shine, staring and rigid. A cigar store Indian.

Antiquated women with faces like crumpled, brown paper bags playing mahjong and sipping at tea slowly from delicate white porcelain cups glanced at him suspiciously as he entered into the warm glow of the tea house interior. In the basement was the opium den. Poor blacks, poor whites and poor Chinese all slumped over wooden pallets together, sucking on the ends of pipes, gawping into their pasts or their futures through a haze of cheap opium that stung the eyes like a brittle gun smoke. One of the handful of opium dens scattered, hidden around Chinatown.

"Good evening, ladies. You must love the tea here. Every time we meet like this. Every single night," he said it faux casual as usual, and they said nothing in response as usual. Li's mother one among them, he assumed. Didn't know which. He slid past their tables, through the spiderweb vapors of their drinks and jogged up the stairs, passed what looked like a waiter in a white coat, smoking a cigarette on the middle step. Ben knew he had a pistol concealed on his person and would use it on anyone the old ladies pointed their ancient fingers at.

He made his way towards Li's room. Anxious to feel the smoke wash through his lungs, over his flesh, soothing and smoothing out the aches and pains. The shakes. Anxious to feel Li's gentle fingers on his body, massaging away the putrid decay that settled there from the streets of Southie, from his job on the Vice Squad and the things that nested in the crooks and crevices of his mind, spawning shadows that flickered in moonlight, deformed, putrid things. The corridor lit a dull yellow by small paper lamps on the walls. At the end of the hall, a small shrine with a jade statue of Buddha smoldering incense that burnt twisted spirals of fragrant smoke to the narrow wooden ceiling. He tapped lightly on the rich brown door at the end of the hall. One knock. Wait. Two knocks. Wait. One knock. Three knocks. Lucky seven. Their agreed signal.

Li swung the door open smiling something akin to sunshine through a thick fog. Ben breathless. Like a feline in myth, her coffee black almond eyes sucked the very air from his lungs. She was something else. The very embodiment of smoke. Ethereal. His woman. His medicine. Li Yu. The warmth of her body. The embrace of her opium.

The daughter to a dead negro and a Chinese mother. A girl of two worlds, wanted in neither. Too black for the Chinese. Too Chinese for the blacks. He'd led a raid on the house of prostitution she'd been enslaved in a year and six months previous. Had fallen in love with her as soon as he discovered her laying naked on stained silk sheets in that small, smokey room. Just a child. There had been a pale, bloated cockroach crawling over her body. He'd tried to kill the fucking thing. She said he'd saved her.

Li standing in the doorway, draped in a deep maroon, silken kimono, gazing at him with those limpid eyes of hers. She let the robe fall open displaying her caramel-colored breasts, dark nipples and the thick patch of hair between her legs. Ben licked his dry lips, stuttered something and she laughed out loud, pulling him into the sweet aroma of her. Chanel Number Five and poppy. The room a deep maroon-red matching her kimono, fragrant, aglow with soft lighting, cushioned and draped with silks and velvet. Reminded Ben of a womb and he ruminated sometimes about the psychological implications of the girl and the room, China Town and his dead mother. *Mother.* He knew he thought too much. Another symptom of his sickness. His mind would catch on something. Become fixated. Twisting and writhing like a diseased fish on a rusty hook until he had spent hours counting in circles. Touching things and counting things to take the thoughts away only for them to resurrect stronger. Counting himself dizzy. Counting himself out. It was something that had to be managed, dulled and drowned out by whiskey, opium and her.

He passed Li the envelope of bills and she took it with a small, shy bow. Peeked inside and placed it in the drawer of a cream-colored vanity desk with other similar envelopes.

"You should be careful someone doesn't rob you." Ben raised his eyebrows towards the drawer of cash stuffed envelopes. A sharp pain in his stomach. Trying to recall if all of them were from him. Suddenly cold and clammy underneath his shirt. The audience of malicious critics in his head started chattering. Images flashed up on a large cinema screen behind his eyes. Ben pinched the bridge of his nose. Hard.

"It's my rainy-day fund. Besides no one will get in here with Mister Chun on the stairs. He was the Hong Kong police pistol champion three years running, don't you know?" She smiled, letting herself fall onto the large bed. Propping herself up on an elbow watching him undressing carefully. She'd prepared three coat hangers as usual. For his jacket. His pants. His shirt. He hung them intricately on the curtain rail away from other things and walked over to her in his jockey shorts and white vest. Placed his hands on her head, standing over her, feeling her kinky, thick, jet black hair in between his fingers. She lifted the vest, kissing his stomach, gazing up at him with eyes that shimmered in the glow and then ran her fingertips tenderly over the inflamed pink patches of flesh that crisscrossed his lean torso.

"You've been scratching at yourself again, haven't you, Detective?" she said examining his body.

"It's this February climate, perhaps. An allergy. I'm not quite sure. Everything seems to make me itch as of recent," he scratched at the back of his neck impatiently as he said it and she kissed the deep claw marks that were yellowish and healing over, gazing into his grey eyes again. He ran a hand over her face and her lips were a rose underneath his thumb. Closed his eyes. Her warm tongue flickered over his skin.

After a while, she paused and spoke "do you want me first or the smoke first? You look as though you need the smoke first."

"You know fully well I always want you first, my flower. But I need to ask? Did you?"

"I did it, Ben."

"You did it?"

"Yes, I did it. You know I always use *that thing* before I see you, my Detective. I use it after, too. Clean before and clean after," she pulled him down onto the bed next to her, "I don't want any babies. Not yet, anyway," she said speaking the words to the door.

"I know. I'm sorry, it's just... I think too much, I know. I know."

"My body is healthy, Ben. Clean. I'm not doing those bad things anymore. That's my past. I've only been with you since then. I don't even talk to other men nowadays. I'm so very glad of it." She chewed at her bottom lip as though considering something. Whispered. "Do you remember my friend, Wei Ping?"

"I think so. The young girl who was with you when we first met?" he peered at fresh, raw grazes on the flesh of her knees. They looked like friction burns. Felt his guts twist and knot up. His mind sharpening itself to a knife edge over her words. Examining every sentence and intonation for truth or deceit. Dishonesty. Betrayal.

"Yes, when you came to rescue us, you and the other policemen. When you saved us, Ben. She always liked you so much. But she went back there a couple of weeks later. Started again. It's not her fault. She knows no other life. She needed the money. For her family."

"What is it? What happened to her?" Ben yawned.

"She went with a man last week and he slashed her face with a straight razor. She's all stitched up now. He forced himself on her, too. Raped her. She's very… What's the word? Melancholic. It makes me feel so melancholic, too. I have been having the worst nightmares. Simply the worst. I can't sleep at all."

"Why would someone do a thing like that to a woman? Cut them like that?"

"He couldn't get it up? Drunk? I don't know. He's crazy, maybe…"

"Do you know his name?"

"Yes, I do. I mean, I think so. He's an Italian man. One of the Italians from the North End. His name is Fantino. I think. All of the girls call him Frankie."

"Call?"

"I'm sorry?"

"You said they *call* him Frankie."

"So?"

"So, you used the present tense?"

She giggled, slapped at his shoulder playfully. "Don't tease me because my English isn't good. It's my mother's fault. A lifetime here in this country and she still refuses to speak the language."

He felt as though he were freefalling through the pine floorboards into hungry shadows. Vertigo again as though his life was the constant walking of a tight rope. Head swimming. He dropped his face into his hands a moment trying to focus on solid objects around the room through the gaps in his fingers. The vanity desk, the stool in the corner, the cupboard, the sink, the large gold framed mirror on the wall. Solid things to anchor him back into normalcy. Order. Symmetry. He shoved the echoed tormenting words from his mind, but they came back stronger until he was compelled to speak them as a release valve before spontaneously combusting.

"Have you fucked him, Li Yu? This Fantino man?" he placed his palm to her face, turning her head gently to look her in the irises. His reflection shimmering back at him.

"No, never," she said, frowning. Turning her gaze away abruptly.

"Are you sure? You can tell me," he whispered, watching her very carefully. The way her fingers stroked at her throat. Soothing herself. The way her eyes bounced over everything in the room but him.

"I said *no*, Ben! Why are you always fucking questioning me like I'm some kind of a criminal you've arrested? You think I'm just a piece of filth? Some kind of a trashy woman?"

"No! No, of course not. I just want us to be honest with each other. Don't be upset. It's good. Fine. Fine."

"You still don't trust me? Is that it?"

"No, I believe you. I trust you, of course." It was his turn to swing eye contact towards something else. To change the subject quickly. "Do you want me to do something about him? This Fantino man?"

"Could you? Would you? For me?" She kissed him hard on the mouth as she spoke.

He answered into her hot, wet lips. "For you, my flower? Anything. She's your friend and I don't like to see you upset like this. I'll find him tomorrow and arrest him. Give him a good working over down the station, if that's what you want."

"*Arrest him*? Is that all you think he deserves?"

"Well, I'm not quite sure what else can be done. I'll trump up some charges, make it so the little piece of shit goes away for a long while. Cools his heels."

"You said you loved me?" She said, moving away from him.

"What? I do! I do, Li Yu. I do. You know I do."

"Tell me you love me, Ben. Say the words to me."

The words were like a slap in the face, and he was a child again.

"I love you, Li Yu." A single tear slid from his eye, trickled down into the stubble on his cheek. He brushed it away with his knuckles.

"And I love you. Even though I know all the terrible things you've done; I *still* love you. I want you to make it, so he never hurts anyone *ever* again. He's a bad man. I hate him. Do you understand me, Ben? I want you to hurt him, hurt him real bad, so the nightmares will stop. He'll kill someone next time. I know it. Do you understand what I'm asking you to do for me? I thought you promised to always protect me? You promised." She kissed him again, pulled the vest from over his head. Running her hands over him, caressing. Began licking his chest and nipples. Working her tongue over his pale skin.

"Yes, I understand. I'll do it for you. I'll do anything for you," he said, closing his eyes.

"Good. Good. Thank you, my kind detective."

He sighed, "I warned you whoring was no good. You could have caught the syphilis or gotten all sliced up like your friend. You're my woman now. I'll look after you, Li. Always protect you."

"Yes, I know. I'm sorry, too. I'm your woman. I'm sorry."

"Why are you sorry?" he pushed her away a moment and held her firm. "You're not deceiving me are you, Li? You're finished with that life? You promise me?" He snatched looks at her knees again as he asked. Those red wounds on her knees that looked like carpet burns. A mental image of her naked on all fours, splattered with blood, being fucked by the dead man from Seaport tearing through his mind and he blinked and twisted his head away from the thoughts.

"Yes, I promise to you. No men ever *really* wanted me. They just wanted to use me. Only you've ever wanted me. *Really* wanted me. I was just a dirty half-breed to them then and I'm just a dirty half-breed now."

He lifted her chin gently, so her eyes were on his again. "Don't say things like that, it hurts me. I want you. I need you. You're beautiful to me. Anyhow, something mixed is something stronger." He kissed the chocolate-colored freckles that star-crossed her cheeks, tasting rouge on his lips. She let out a breath and turned her face away again.

"Like what?"

"I'm not quite sure. Metals… Cocktails…" he smiled.

"I'm none of those," she crossed her arms.

"Perhaps, you're a Singapore Sling." He took her hands in his, pulled her to him again.

"Don't tease me, Ben. I feel like I am nothing good, sometimes. Nothing."

"You're something better than everything. To me," he said, pushing her down on the bed. Her hair twisting its way in dark waves across the pillows. Kissing her mouth long and hard. Her tongue moving against his. After a while he pulled away from her to inspect the bedsheets and mattress, running his fingertips over the fabrics and cushions, squinting. She sighed heavily but he was too engrossed in his task to notice her resigned impatience.

"Are you going to fuck me already or are you going to just examine the bedsheets for God knows what, Ben?"

He nodded the affirmative a few times and then dragged his eyes away from the bedcovers. She had undressed quickly, seated on the edge of the bed, dark brown naked like something fragile and innocent from a renaissance painting. Waiting for him. He went to her. Her skin clean enough, pure enough to drink from. Tasting her everywhere and then like smoke she engulfed him completely. He fell into her like a baptism of smoke and opium. Moving inside her, their mouths and bodies coming together again and again, he could forget everything. The voices and images in his head faded to a pure white. Pure. And then the boy's screaming face like a blow to the head with a sledgehammer. Eyes became mouths, agape, shrieking. He kissed Li's lips harder. Concentrated on her breasts and skin and eyes. Screaming eyes.

He groaned, cursed and pulled himself free from her embrace.

"What's wrong? Did I do something wrong?"

"No, it's not you. I'm sorry. I just have too much on my mind recently, I can't seem to…"

"I'm sorry." She pulled the blankets up over her breasts and pouted.

"Please, don't apologize, Li Yu. It's not you. There's a case I'm working on at the moment and it's disturbed me, is all. A missing kid. Causing me a great deal of stress. It's not you, I swear."

"A missing child. But you work Vice, I thought?"

"I do. Never mind. It's complicated."

"Will you talk to me about it?"

"I can't. I don't think you'd be able to understand it, anyhow. I can't seem to make sense of it all myself."

"Let me try and help you forget then." She pulled him back underneath the covers and they kissed each other slowly, working themselves up together in a strong momentum. Ben could forget.

Only momentarily.

AFTER, HE THOROUGHLY scrubbed at himself with the bar of soap he'd brought with him, splashing at his body in the sink in the far corner of the room while she smoked a cigarette, the blanket pulled up to her stomach, sleepily observing the rituals she knew almost as well as he. No longer offended by the routine and more accepting of the man's madness. He finished with the soap and dropped it out of the window into the alley behind the building with the others from past meetings. A cat screamed and knocked a pile of garbage clattering to the rain-soaked ground. Ben stared out at the night for a moment. A ghost of himself in the evening tinted glass.

Li had slipped out from the blankets and was setting up his pipe as he dried himself off, folded the towel neatly, and set it carefully on the rim of the porcelain. He lay down on the bed again, rolling on his side and taking the stem of the pipe in his mouth as she burnt the opium for him, watching his body unclamp, the muscle definition release and disappear as he inhaled deeply. Her hand pressed to his face.

"You should grow a mustache. It would suit you, I think," she smiled, running a fingernail playfully underneath his nose.

"No. No, my father had a mustache. I remember he used to wax it up at the ends. He looked like some kind of a sideshow magician." He held the smoke in his chest and released it slowly through his lips. "I'm not sure if I hated him more than he hated me. He wasn't a good person. My mother and me had to leave England because of everything he did. My mother changed after that. Or maybe she'd always been that way and I'd never known because I was too frightened of my father. Sometimes, I fear I'm becoming like him... It's the anniversary of his death this week. Twenty years gone, but I still see him out of the corner of my eye sometimes. Hear him shouting my name. A giant to me then. A giant to me still. Haunting me like a fucking ghost."

"Breathe. Hush. Sleep, Detective." She stroked his forehead, running her hands over the dark blond hair that hung damp from his clammy brow.

"Sleep well. Sleep deep. Joyous dreams, Ben."

His eyes half-closed, gazing at her as a child to a mother, and then he was gone. Lost in the smoke.

Memories of a fractured past.

His past.

The boy's past.

THE WATER VERY cool on the boy's skin and his mother's eyes held little ghosts of gold from the lamps in the deepest blue of them.

The creeping light of the early hours of morning flowing through the small window and the water making sounds like rain trickling from the roof in a summer storm.

The moist flannel his mother held in her fist passed softly over his flesh, cleansing him. The young child crouched in the tub, gazing at his mother's face, the way her hair hung down in long twisting blond lines. The way the fabric of the silk nightgown moved over her flesh akin to the water moving over the boy's.

Turning his eyes to his father's shaving set stood carefully in its place on the sink, reaching out his hand and running his small fingers over the black and brown hairs of the shaving brush. Badger hair; his mother said. Rough to the touch. He withdrew his hand because the texture of it made him feel strange inside his stomach. Looked away. His view snagging on the razor strop hanging noose-like from a rusty hook. The boy flinched and scrunched his eyes closed. His small hands to his mother's face, and she closed her eyes and smiled underneath his featherlight fingers. Radiating absolute warmth and absolute beauty, as all mothers to their sons.

"You're all dirty, Benny. We have to get you all clean now. All clean. All clean and all better. Filth makes sickness, you know? Wash away all the bad now. Wash away all the sickness and all the bad," she whispered softly.

"Yes, mother," the small boy said, used to his mother's repeated worries. Her mantras.

"Did you have another bad dream, Benny? A nightmare? Is that it?"

"Yes, mother."

"About whom or what was it this time? The Beetle Man nonsense again?"

"Yes, mother. But it isn't nonsense. He's all black and shiny. He stands at the end of my bed at night. He makes strange clicking and slapping noises and he wants to hurt me. He has large black eyes that watch me while I'm sleeping, too. I hate him, mother. Hate him."

"We searched your room together, Benny. There was nothing there, remember?"

"Yes, mother. But…"

"Do you remember the poem I taught you? 'Antigonish' by Mr. Mearns?"

"Some of it, mother. It's a little difficult."

"'Yesterday, upon the stair, I met a man who wasn't there. He wasn't there again today, oh how I wish he'd go away'. Say it with me, Benny. Repeat it with me. Repeat it until everything is all better. Repetition makes everything better. Drives away the cobwebs and the blues."

The boy chanted the words after his mother. Eyes closed tightly as though reciting a Hail Mary.

"You see Benny, my darling, there's no Beetle Man. It's just your imagination playing tricks on you is all. That's what that poem's all about. Your imagination playing tricks on you. Everyone's a little afraid of the dark, of course. They just don't speak of such things. Even me! Your mother! Can you believe such nonsense? But it's perfectly normal to worry about things that aren't real. It's all right to be lonely at night sometimes. However, you mustn't let your mind run away from you or you'll never get it back. You'll get sick like your uncle George. You don't want to end up in Bedlam Hospital like him, do you? Now, there is *no* Beetle Man, is that understood, Benny?"

"Do you promise, mother?"

"Of course, my little darling. I promise you, there's no Beetle Man and I promise I'll always protect you," his mother said smiling, "cross my heart and hope to die, stick a needle in my eye," her palm pressed to his chest. His heart.

"Now, the next time you feel scared or worried, you repeat that poem over and over until everything is all right with yourself again. Yes?"

"Yes mother."

"Do you love me, Benny?"

"Yes, mother."

"Say it, Benny, say the words. Tell me you love me."

"I love you, mother."

"There. Now isn't everything so much better? Do you feel good now, Benny?"

"Yes, mother. But what's the matter with Uncle George?"

His mother's face fell into crooked lines. Her eyes began to shine more. The boy watched her bottom lip shake a little. She poured more warm water over his small, pale body. The droplets creating sounds like the piano downstairs that his mother often played after supper.

"He thinks too much, worries too much about things that aren't real, and it makes him very sick, so he stays in the hospital where the doctors can look after him. Where he can be properly cared for. That's why you mustn't worry too much about that silly Beetle Man and other such nonsense. There are more important things to be worried about in the world."

"Such as what, mother?"

"Well, for instance, sickness and disease. The Spanish Flu. The consumption. Yellow Fever. Typhoid. Lice. That's why you must stay clean, Benny. The world is a very dirty place. Filthy. A filthy, filthy place."

"Is that why I'm not allowed to play outside with the other children, mother?"

"Yes, Benny. Lord knows what those scruffy little mites that run around the streets at all hours have. Absolutely filthy. They're probably crawling with lice for one thing."

"What are lice, mother?"

"Lice are truly disgusting little insects that live in the hair of dirty people. They suck your blood, like Dracula. Yucky!" she cringed, laughed and tickled her son under his armpits. He giggled and felt his shoulders relax; his stomach untwisting itself.

Then his eyes moved over his mother's face to the darkness in the hall.

A black figure clambered into the doorway. The boy's face collapsed. Whimpering. Not the Beetle Man, but the boy's father, infinitely large and hard, leaning into the bathroom doorframe. His cheeks scratch marked and his face a cloudy red in the lamplight. His thick mustache and the ash hair on his head askew and askance and not right. His sudden appearance frightened the boy, and he tried to make himself smaller in the bath. The father was wearing dark grey one-piece underwear and the boy didn't like the stains on it. Their existence made him feel irritable and uncomfortable. As though his tummy were drying out. Glancing at the shapes of them, it felt as though he was standing on the ledge of a tall building looking down. Vertigo, that feeling was called, his mother had said. He wanted to cry out. Making himself as compact as he possibly could within the confines of the white porcelain and willing his father to leave. Just leave. Just go. Father's presence never ended well for the boy. Or for his mother.

"What the bloody hell is going on here then? Who's singing and what the hell are you doing with the boy again?" the father shouted, unreasonably loud into the silence of the house. An unreasonable man in unreasonable times and the boy felt a cold, sharp certainty he would become his father as all boys become their fathers in the end. Rage, violence and sickness passed down generation to generation as though it were the color of the eyes or the tint of the hair.

"I'm so sorry, Husband. Benjamin just had a little accident, that's all. No one is singing. There's no cause for concern, Dearest. Please go back to bed and I shall join you soon," his mother murmured, her eyes on the faucets. She was Welsh and her voice sounded like fragments of song sung in snatches on the coast somewhere by the sea the boy sometimes imagined. Though he had never seen a beach or even the ocean except in his picture books.

"You don't tell me what to bloody do, woman. You were singing! I heard you!" the boy's father shouted louder, a croaking roar.

"I'm sorry, Dear. I didn't mean to be disrespectful, I'm sorry. I'm sorry. I'm sorry," the mother repeated the words quietly, a whisper. Twisting the flannel violently in her bloodless hands.

"Yeah, right. Anyway, what do you mean, the boy's had an accident? What kind of an accident? You don't mean he's fucking shit himself again? That's not your meaning is it, woman?" the father demanded.

"No, Dear. It's fine. You must be tired after your work today. I'm so sorry we disturbed your rest, I'm sorry. I'm sorry." Tears came to her eyes, and she hurriedly wiped them away.

"No? No? It stinks like fucking shit in here, it does. I told you to stop mothering the boy this way. You're gonna make him bloody soft as a little sissy boy. Little mummy's boy hanging from his mother's apron strings. Don't think for a single minute that I'm a dunce and I don't know what's going on in this house… He's going to continue shitting himself if he doesn't learn," the father said. "We shall have to train him the same way you would train a stray mutt that kept shitting and pissing on the living room rug. Teach him."

"Yesterday, upon the stair, I met a man who wasn't there!" the boy whispered.

"Hush now, Benny, Darling," the mother said.

"What did he just say to me?" the father said.

"Nothing, Dearest. It's just a little poem we were practicing together."

The boy closed his eyes and repeated the words. "Yesterday, upon the stair, I met a man who wasn't there!"

The father moved like a thunderstorm across the bathroom. Grabbed at the child. His thick fingers pinching and pulling at the scruff of the boy's hair at the nape of the neck, ripping him from the bathtub as though ripped from the womb and birthed into the world a second time. Shit out into the suburbs of Chelsea, London again.

The mother squeezing her hands to her face, a mask of fingers. The fingernails made many eyes like a spider and the boy couldn't breathe. Wailing from the immense pain of his hair being yanked and torn from his scalp. The high-pitched shrieks of his child enraged the father further. He backhanded the small boy around the face. Once. Twice. Wrenched the child's head up. The boy's feet slipping and flailing, the condemned dropped through gallows, standing tiptoed on the bathroom's slick tiled flooring, but the father pulled him up further, higher. The pain at the back of his scalp something suffocatingly awful, immeasurable. The mother tried to wrestle the boy from her husband's grip. The boy's vision going blood red. The suffocating stench of whiskey and something hot pouring from the father in electric waves. The child screamed, wrenched himself free, collapsing naked to the soaked floor. The mother fell into the bathtub. Water splashing over the father causing him to slip to his knees. He roared, a prehistoric noise that would haunt the boy all his life. Dragging the child then by arm and neck, naked, and wet, out of the bathroom, down the hallway, tumbling down the stairs of the affluent home.

Wrenching him out of the front door and into the violently cold early morning air of the street outside.

The sky the color of bruised flesh. The cobblestones slippery like the tiles in the bathroom had been. The father forced the boy down into the road. A couple of street sweepers stood smoking, chatting across the street, glanced at each other and quickly walked away in the opposite direction.

"I am sergeant constable William Hughes of the Metropolitan Police, and I would like to announce to the inhabitants of this street that my nine-year-old son has repeatedly, *repeatedly,* shit his fucking bed at night!" the father bellowed.

Lights in windows flashed on, illuminating black silhouettes behind net curtains. The father kicked a trash can clattering violently into the street. Tins and glass jars rolled clattering and old newspapers tumbled in the frigid breeze.

The boy shivering, naked, hugged himself into a small ball.

Many tiny fingers trickled over his skin. He brushed them away. The fingers continued moving intricately over his naked body. Incessant. Over his back, legs, arms, and stomach. Tickling. Scratching. Stroking. Caressing. Benjamin pinched one between his fingers, something that scurried behind his ear, screaming out when he glimpsed what it was. A little black thing with small ebony eyes and sticky delicate legs writhing inanely between his trembling fingertips. An ant. Ants! Ants scurrying all over his body. His father had forced him to kneel in an ants' nest built at the side of the road. Burrowed down between the gritty gaps in the cobblestones, waiting for the beginning of summer to take a choking grasp of the street.

The boy attempted to stand up but each time he tried, his father forced him back down, scattering the ant's mound, angering them further. They scurried over the boy's little body nipping and biting like a disease carried on sticky little legs over his face and eyes, into his nostrils. His mouth. Down into his throat. His heart. Infesting him. Infecting him.

The boy from the newspaper photograph screamed. Ants crawled from his dead eyes and gaping mouth.

A black shape standing at the top of a grand flight of stairs gesturing to Ben. The Beetle Man.

Gun shots exploding.

A child's screams.

Ben.

The boy in the photograph.

BEN SAT UP choking for air, biting into a bedsheet clenched to his mouth. Li's light coffee colored face the first thing he recognized when he snapped open his eyes. Opium hazed and baptizing. Plump lips pursed in a horrified curiosity. Dark almond eyes shimmering in the lamplight. She anchored him back into reality. Sanity. Sanitization. Safety.

"Are you alright, Ben? You were yelling out in your sleep again," she said, rubbing his chest.

"Was I? I'm sorry," he said, wiping at his eyes and taking the glass of water she offered him.

"Don't be sorry and the glass is clean so don't worry yourself about that." She reached out a hand to his face and ran her fingers over the stubble there again. "Where did you travel to in your dreams tonight?"

He gulped at the water. Spluttered. Coughed. He shrugged at her. "The past."

"Not a good past then?"

"No, not good. Not good at all. I don't have anything good in my past. Nothing. You know that."

She nodded at him like she understood and began cleaning away the pipe and the smoking set. Started humming softly, the lamplight catching on her skin like flakes of gold.

"Do you feel better for it? The smoke?" she asked.

"I don't know. It's wearing thin. Losing its effectiveness. If I go a few days without seeing you I become sick. Feverish. Almost as though I have influenza. Runny nose. The shakes. You always make me feel better though. In this room with you." He got up and kissed her mouth. She tasted sweetly of incense. She pulled away. Stood up and pulled the kimono around herself.

"By the way, I saw a picture of your Chief in the newspaper today. What's he like?"

"Disgusting, really. I avoid him as much as I can. As if the filth in the streets wasn't enough, I have to take orders from it in my place of work," Ben said, sitting up and resting his head against the wall.

"You don't work directly underneath him? I thought you did." She continued cleaning away the opium and the smoking set. Speaking as she tidied.

"No, not really. There's a whole hierarchy of empty shirts just like him." Ben sipped at the water.

"Some people think he's pretty crooked."

"Who?" Ben asked, peering at her closely.

"How's that?" she shrugged.

"Who do *you* know that thinks the Boston Police Chief is corrupt?"

"I don't know. I just heard it, is all." She shrugged again.

"Just heard? Around here? In China Town?" He chuckled humorlessly.

"Yes, I've heard a few things about you, too, actually."

"Really? That's interesting. I'm curious. Enlighten me, would you?" Ben said, kicking down the blanket and swinging his legs out of the bed.

"Well, people say you're working for the Irish in Southie. The mob. That you're a bagman for The Chief."

He tried to chuckle again but couldn't. "That's ridiculous. Utter fabrication. You shouldn't believe everything you hear so easily. Besides, do you even know what a bagman is, Li?"

"No, not exactly. But…"

"Well, there you are then. Now let's talk about something else," he said cutting her off.

"You don't trust me enough me to tell me honestly."

"I trust you with my life. But there are things about me that you shouldn't know. Things you don't want to know."

"If you trusted me as much as you say, you'd open up to me completely. Sometimes I feel like you treat me like I'm your personal whore. You come here, fuck me, smoke my poppy and leave. You don't tell me anything about your life or your work." She waved the opium pipe in front of his eyes before cleaning it away into the box.

"Li, I do have something very important to tell you."

She paused a moment, stood frozen in the center of the room. The walnut smoking box still in her hands.

"What is it, you wish to tell me?" She held her breath.

"I have put in for a transfer, Li."

"What's your meaning?"

"I've asked to be moved to another police department. I'm not happy in Boston anymore. It's making me unhappy. Sick. I want to go somewhere else."

"I see. Where will you go?" she breathed out the words.

"I've asked to be moved to Los Angeles. The L.A.P.D need good men and the sunshine and dry air may do me some good.

Los Angeles is a boom town now. Lot of great things happening out there. A lot of possibilities and opportunities since after the war."

"I understand. So, you will leave here?" She placed the smoking set into a drawer, swallowed a lump in her throat and stood holding her hands tightly against her chest.

"Yes, I hope to, but I want you to come with me, Li. We can both start again, fresh. Be new people. Better people. If we don't leave Boston, it'll kill us both eventually. It sounds ridiculous, but I can feel it, somehow. Will you? Come with me? Start new? Start clean. Fresh."

"Yes, Ben. That sounds just wonderful. Wonderful," she said, not looking into his face.

"That's the best news I've had in a long time, Li. You've made me the happiest man in Boston. I'll sleep well tonight." He genuinely smiled. The sensation felt strange across his face. Unnatural. He kissed her, walked over to the window, shaky, and hungover. Still feeling the effects of the opium. Pulled his slacks down from their hanger and turned them inside out and started examining the fabric, running his thumb and fingers along the seams. Satisfied finding nothing he shook them violently and pulled them on. Repeating the ritual with his shirt and jacket. Wiping beads of sweat from his brow with his forearm as he did so. Took out the scrap of newspaper from his pocket, unfolded it and examined it a moment, cringing, before refolding it and pushing it back into his breast pocket. He didn't know why.

"Why are you always checking the insides of your clothing like that, Ben? I always wonder so." Her eyes narrowed on him.

"Insects. They get into everything. Everything. They hide inside the seams of your clothing, you know?"

"There aren't any bugs here, Ben. I hate them too, so I would know."

"Insects are *everywhere,* Li. Everywhere. They're here. They're just hiding. Waiting until darkness. Crawling around in between the walls and underneath the floorboards. Ants. Cockroaches. Fucking disgusting things. Ants. Disgusting. Disgusting fucking things. Fucking. Underneath the floorboards. Underneath the floorboards. The floorboards." He bit into his fingers and chewed at a hangnail.

"I've never met a man like you, Ben. Why do you hate bugs so much?" she giggled.

He glared at her. "I just fucking do. They're filthy. They spread disease; you know? Don't fucking laugh. It isn't a laughing matter."

"Diseases? What do you mean? What diseases?"

"Fucking disease! Sickness! Fucking disease, that's what I mean. Now change the fucking subject, will you, Li? Change the subject, will you? Change the subject. Subject change, please."

He started to hyperventilate, gasping. She went to him and held him in her arms like a child. Soothing him. Reminding him again momentarily of his mother.

"I'm sorry, Li. I'm sorry. I love you, Li. Please, leave with me for California." He spat the words out like a scream from a drowning man.

SHE FELT EACH wet syllable against the nape of her neck. Her flesh prickled and got goosebumps. She stared at the vanity, her reflection in the mirror. This man hanging from her. Pulling her down. Holding her too tightly. Suffocating her. Drowning her too.

He held her face tightly in his hands, looking fixed into her eyes, "I have to go now, I'm afraid. There's something I need to do. Something that will help me, I think. I want to be better. I want to be better for you, Li. We'll be happy in Los Angeles, I promise you. Just have to do this one thing and it'll wipe everything clean. Wipe it all away. All clean and all better…"

"You promise to protect me from that Italian man?"

"Yes. Yes, I said I would do it for you."

She kissed his rough, clammy cheek, his cool forehead and held him until his breathing leveled out because she didn't know what else to do. Pleased he was finally leaving. A frown creasing the space between her fine eyebrows, wondering if she was right or wrong about this man. She *had* needed him before. But the last few months she had come to realize she was riding on the back of a wounded tiger up a mountain, and now she didn't know how to get off. Stuck between a rock and a hard place. Didn't know of any other way to escape someone so dangerous, so volatile. Her plan was the only one. She told herself she really had no choice. No choice at all. She had to protect her mother. Had to protect herself.

She grasped at the vivid memory of the raid when they first met, how she'd stood helplessly by and witnessed him beating the handcuffed man he'd found her with near to death for simply spitting at his feet. She remembered the way the man's blood had splashed over the flesh of her naked legs. Hot. Scalding almost. She held the detective tighter. Too fearful to risk letting go. Knowing what she had done was the only way. The only way to be free of him. Riding on the back of a tiger. She could only escape once the tiger was preoccupied with other tigers and other wolves. She had to save herself. This man, she knew, was beyond saving. The detective wasn't drowning. He was already at the bottom the ocean. Dragging her down into the darkness with him.

The moment he left, the door clicking shut, his footsteps fading out down the stairs, she dropped her head in her palsied hands, exhaled a deep sigh of relief and erupted into tears.

London, England
Friday, February 19th, 1926

WILLIAM HUGHES' BASTARD uniform itched. Mouth dirt dry. Damned thirsty. He wanted a drink. Needed it. Hands shaking, he grabbed at his knees and squeezed. The morning grey flooding into the room through the open window like smoke. His skull throbbed like an open wound. The Superintendent of the Metropolitan Police, Harewood, sat primly behind his oak desk all high and mighty. Little fucking toff sodomite. The Superintendent flushed in the face and goggle-eyed at Hughes as though reading his mind. The grandfather clock in the stuffy office chimed eight times. Hughes leaned back in his chair and lit a cigarette with a hand that tremored visibly.

"William, I…" Harewood cringed.

"We aren't mates nor associates, Superintendent. Address me by my rank," Hughes said, brushing flakes of ash from his navy-blue uniform trousers. Pinching at the creases.

"You act as though we weren't at the Somme together."

William chuckled between clenched teeth. "We weren't. I was down in the blood, the muck and the filth and you were behind a shiny desk. Same as now. Same as it'll always be."

Harewood cleared his throat. "Very well, have it your own way, *sergeant* Hughes. You're not making this any easier on yourself, are you?" He flushed crimson and pulled at the collar of his shirt.

"I don't need to," Hughes grinned. All teeth.

"You don't *need to*?! Don't be so ridiculous, man! You beat a boy to death! In the street! And there's a witness for God's sake. Get your bloody head out of the clouds."

"There's a witness is there? A witness. A whore, I'm assuming?"

"I just said there's a witness. A Katherine Jones. A married woman from South Wales or some such. Lives in that dreadful pit of a lodging house over on Flower and Dean Street. Known to a few of your fellow officers already. States she was a friend of the deceased. Says you attacked them both and molested her, Sergeant. Molested. Not her words of course."

"The words of a drunk whore are the words of a drunken whore," Hughes shrugged and snubbed his cigarette out in a brass ashtray holding loose foreign coins on the desk. Harewood frowned, fingering his neatly trimmed moustache.

"Yes, a drunkard and a prostitute but an eyewitness all the same. She's down in the drunkard's cells presently. One of the constables brought her in early this morning for Public Indecency." He opened a desk drawer and brought out a pipe, thumbed tobacco inside, got it started and puffed on it. His face lined in disturbed thought. "There'll have to be an investigation, of course. An inquiry, Hughes. It'll be the bloody Royal Commission on The Met all over again. We'll have mobs and crowds gathered outside the station and the newspapers will be all over this like ants to sugar. They'll have a bloody field day. I can see it now, Metropolitan police sergeant murders bank clerk. A bank clerk, Hughes. Good Lord! A right ruddy mess you've brought down on us all. And I will refrain from even bloody mentioning the rumors circulating of the money you're receiving from clubs and all the other establishments in Soho for your little so-called *licensing* fees. Oh yes, old boy, we've heard about those. The brothel on Greek Street, we know about that as well.

Known for quite some time, I might add. A right little nest egg you must have hidden away, William."

"So what, Harewood?" Hughes sniffed at his fingertips. Breathed in deeply. Lit another cigarette.

"I am sorry, Hughes, but you'll have to swing for this one. I'm sympathetic because of our history together. Really I am, but someone has to take the fall and the horse manure rolls downhill, doesn't it? As from this morning you're suspended without compensation." The Superintendent patted down his hair, massaging his pink Adam's apple and throat.

William stood up and went to the window, watched a horse and cart carrying a group of small children to school, dropped his cigarette out onto the street and closed the window, "Suspended? Without pay? For how fucking long?"

"Two weeks. Thirteen days to be precise," Harewood said, leaning away from William as he passed by him back to his chair at the front of the desk.

"I see. Well, perhaps I have a better newspaper headline. Read all about it! Read all about it! Police Superintendent's nightly visits to young rent boys in infamous Berkeley Square house of ill-repute popular with very high-ranking politicians. Now, how's that for a headline, Superintendent? Reckon it'll sell more than a few copies; don't you agree? Tabloids'll be all over that like, what was it? Ants to sugar? Flies to shit?" William lit another cigarette, coughed and grinned, clasping the butt between his ivory teeth. Glaring down at Harewood.

"You've always relished hanging that over my fucking head haven't you, Hughes?"

"Yes, I have, Superintendent, and I shall continue to do so for as long as I need to. When needs must, as they say. Now, onto the more pressing matters at hand, who's on duty down at the drunk cells?"

"Albertson, I believe. Why do you ask?"

"Have him called him away."

"Jesus Christ, Hughes. Look, we'll just attempt to charge the woman for something and have her sectioned in a mental asylum for a few months until it all blows over." The Superintendent ran his hands over his face and sighed. "There's no need for any of your heavy-handed tactics this time. Things are really quite bad enough as it is."

"She'll not cease her squawking. Women like her never learn and no one wants headlines, do they Superintendent? After all, I've my nest egg to worry about and you have your illustrious career and little queers to ravish," Hughes tapped ash onto a pile of files stacked on the desk and smirked.

Harewood spoke softly to the floor, his pipe burned out and held stiffly in his hand. "No, Hughes. I can't. I won't be a party to something like that. Not again."

"You're already in the filth and muck with me, my friend. If I go over the top this time, I'm dragging you and your friends with me into the line of fire. I've quite the little dossier on you all tucked away with that nest egg of mine. Read all about it! Read all about it!" "A Dossier? What the Hell are you on about man?"

"Let's just say I have quite the little scrapbook collection on you and your pals. If I swing, you're all swinging with me."

Harewood moaned high pitched, stuttered slightly, "bloody hell, Hughes. How long will you need?!"

"I'll make it quick enough. Quicker than you and your Eton friends were with that unfortunate little nancy I had to dump in the river two winters ago. You really went to town on him, didn't you all. The body didn't even look like a human when you sent for me, begging me to clean up your drunken, perverted mess,"

William said, standing up and flicking ash from his cigarette onto the floor.

"Get the hell out of my office, Hughes! You lunatic fucking degenerate!"

"Let he who is without sin, Superintendent. Read all about it! Read all about it!" he called over his shoulder as he left The Superintendent's office, closing the door quietly.

Superintendent Harewood picked up the internal telephone on his desk and told the person on the other end to call Albertson off his post. He sighed, rubbing at his throat and staring at the door. After a while he took a pen and scribbled a note. Addressing it *Dearest Kate*, he slid it into an envelope marked *urgent* and called out to his secretary in an adjoining office to have it included in the day's outgoing post right away.

WILLIAM WATCHED ALBERTSON and another officer light up their pipes and then stroll up the stairs to the main hall from a crack in the locker room's door. Could hear the whore singing snatches of song. The words clumsily tumbling down the sparsely lit corridor and chipped marbled flooring. Some kind of nursery rhyme. Made him feel uneasy. Thirsty. Squeezing his hands into fists, trying to ease the tremors that were running jagged throughout his body. Breath struggled up from his chest and crawled from his lips. As though his first time. So long ago. The only person he might have ever loved. The only person who had hurt him. Lavender perfume. Words of love whispered breathlessly in French. Red wine lips. Music twisting sickeningly from a phonograph. Fucking thirsty. He wiped a fist across his mouth and went to her. Following the tune and lyrics into the drunk cells with the smells of rotten sick, damp and mold. His eyes adjusting to the dim. The woman. His woman. The whore laid on the metal frame of a bunk, braiding her disheveled hair.

On hearing his footfall she turned her face to him and snarled from the dim.

"You?! And what do you bloody well want?"

"I've come to apologize to you, Miss," he bowed his head in a parody of shame and regret.

"*Apologize?* You can shove your apology where the sun don't shine, cozzer. I ain't buying what you're selling. I'm telling everyone what you did to me and that poor boy. Everyone that has ears to listen and mind to know."

"Yes, yes, I know, Miss. I acted atrociously. Lost my temper, is all. I've come to let you out of these cells and take you to meet some of my superior officers. They wish to hear your account of what really happened. It looks as though I'm in for an awful lot of strife. Now, I'm coming in, Miss. Sit down on the bunk and calm yourself woman." He unlocked the cell, swung the door creaking open. The cell awash with the whore's scent.

Betrayer.

Harlot.

Maddening.

He held out a trembling hand to the woman and she glared at it hanging before her with suspicious eyes.

"Yes, you are. You're gonna be in so much trouble. In this life and the next one," she spoke, frowning at the palsied palm. Avoiding eye contact.

"The next one? Whatever do you mean, Miss?" William tried to smile.

"The Hereafter. Kingdom Come. You need to pray and repent. Pray. You need to pray for forgiveness." She placed her small, pale hand in his. Yes, she looked like so pure now, bathed in a beam of ghostly light stabbing its way through a small rectangular barred window at the end of the cell block. An innocence corrupted. Stolen. Ruined. He crushed her palm in his fist. Bones cracked. She screamed out shocked, trying to pull her hand free. He wrapped his other hand around her throat, cutting off her shrieks and squeezed.

"That's pretty hypocritical advice from a fucking whore, ain't it?" he spat.

She gasped deep, bucking her hips against him as he pushed a knee hard into her chest. Holding her down to the bunk with his weight. Her eyes so wide. So white. He blinked and, for a moment, was in the small bedroom of an apartment in Paris. A bottle of red wine seeping into disheveled white sheets and his lover in his arms. Her long blonde hair twisting through his fingertips like spun gold. A mahogany crucifix hanging from a nail above the headboard bringing vomit to the back of his throat. Margaux.

The whore gasped, clawing at his face.

"I need to pray? I'll pray when I'm dying and not a fucking minute sooner," he winked, grinning into her choked, purpling face. Watching the life in her eyes fade like the flame of a candle burning out while she scratched weakly at his cheek. He closed his eyes.

Back in the room in Paris again. Candlelight flickering over the milky white flesh of his woman. Both of their faces slick with tears. The bottle of red wine spilt and soaking into the white fabric. The crucifix above the bed. Jesus staring into a black abyss. The flesh in his grip so soft and slippery with sweat.

William moaned. Snapping his eyes open wider. Back in the cells. The black of the woman's irises glazed, and her body long ceased its bucking. He took her small wrist in his fist, checking her pulse. Dropped it back to the bunk. Stroked the long blonde strands of hair from her forehead. Ran his fingers over her freckled cheeks remembering again the woman who had damaged him so detrimentally, "I loved you so much, Margaux. So much. You did this to yourself. You have only yourself to blame. Did it all to yourself."

He ripped the spoiled sheet from the bunk, twisted it into a rope and knotted it about the dead woman's neck. Dragged her body from the cot and then heaved her body up, leaving it hanging limply from the bars in the cell still smelling fragrantly of her perfume. Just another pathetic suicide while in police custody. No eyebrows would be raised. He tried to whistle as he locked the cell behind him with shaking fingers. Couldn't breathe. Gulping back something heavy that had settled in his throat. So fucking thirsty. Margaux in candlelight fixed in his mind. He hurried back up the stairs as though the spirit of the woman was crawling the floors after him. Stalking him like so many other hungry ghosts. He ran, bursting out into the disorientating buzz of the street outside the station, ignoring concerned shouts and cutting down the nearest alley to have a drink before he died of thirst.

Boston, USA
Tuesday, February 19th, 1946

THE NEXT MORNING, an unenthusiastic, stilted applause greeted Ben as he entered the second-floor duty room of the Boston Police Department precinct building.

Patrolmen stood around in creased, stale blue uniforms, trying to appear tough, and detectives glanced up from their desks smirking. Lewis Jones, a detective from the Homicide Unit, a degenerate gambler and moonlighter for the Italians, waddled over, eating a fried egg sandwich and clapped Ben spitefully on the back. Ben jumped, startled and blanched.

"Long time, no see, Hughes old-boy. You finally decided to show up for once, huh? Wonder why? I swung by that shitty little dive you paddy fucks call a social club yesterday looking for you. You were someplace else, I guess. Ah, that's gone and reminded me, well done. Looks as though you foiled *another* attempted robbery yesterday." Jones held his sandwich clamped in his mouth to clap a few times, then took it back out, waved it at Ben. A piece of egg tumbled to the floor and broke into tiny yellow pieces. Ben stared and readjusted his necktie, straightening it. Loosening it and then tightening it again. A drop of sweat ran down his spine and settled into his waistband.

"How many is that now? Four? Or was it five? Been so many I'm starting to lose fucking count. Another notch on the belt anyhow, right, Huey? Who would've thought an average schmo with a wife and four kids would try and rip-off a bar connected to the Southie mob? It's a fucking mystery if you ask me," he said, his mouth full. Flakes of yellowed egg and bread caked the corners of his lips in greasy little clumps. Voices in the background whispered incessantly. The words like needles pricking the nape of Ben's neck. *Crazy. Sick. Father. Mother. Weak. Ill. Dishonorable discharge. Sick. Filthy. Sick. Crazy. Buggy.*

He shook Jones' hand from his back as though it were plagued and squinted, twitching, at a swarm of large gravy stains spotted down the fat piece of shit's crooked necktie, unable to tear his eyes away from them. Jones noticed and grinned. Took the tie in his oily fingertips and wafted it like a bad stink towards Ben's face. Ben stumbled backwards, his calves hitting the edge of a desk painfully. Files fell and papers flew. Someone cursed. An ice-cold fever breaking out all over his body. He could feel eyes scurrying over him cruelly. Merciless pests sucking his blood. Lice. Cockroaches. Ants. The ringing of telephones, eye-watering. The harsh murmurs in the room relentless. *Crazy. Sick. Father. Mother. Weak. Ill. Dishonorable discharge. Sick. Filthy. Sick. Crazy. Buggy.*

Jones licked yellowed teeth and kept coming. He'd been harassing Ben for over seven months. Always sniffing around. Always there. Bullying. Trying to destroy Ben. He reached into his jacket and placed his hand on the cool wooden smoothness of the .38's handle hanging in the shoulder holster. He didn't know why. Was he going to finally shoot Jones or shoot himself? The handle was wood. Touch wood. Touching wood stopped bad things from happening. Images like bullets ricocheting around his skull. The boy. Eyes. Lips. Buzzing telephones. Stains. Crumbs. Congealed. Corners. Filth. Ants. Cockroaches. *Crazy. Sick. Father. Mother. Weak. Ill. Dishonorable discharge. Sick. Filthy. Sick. Crazy. Buggy.* Why couldn't people just leave him the fuck alone? Why did everything have to be so fucking ugly all the time?

"Yesterday upon the stair…" he whispered.

"What you say, Hughes old-boy?" Jones's grin split deep and wide. Egg and bread stuck between teeth.

"Yesterday upon the stair…" Ben panted the words out, cringing.

"You're looking a little peaked there, pal. What're you mumbling? Spit it out," Jones laughed.

"I saw a man who wasn't there," Ben blurted.

"Is that poetry, Hughes? You really *are* a sensitive boy, aren't you?" Jones said in a booming, lispy lilt that made laughter break out from all corners of the room. "Hey everybody, get a load of this! Hughes is reciting poetry to me! I told you all he was kind of fruity."

Cackling laughter roared and cut like shattered glass.

Ben unclipped the holster and held his breath. Reciting the poem in his mind over and over like a mantra. The only thing that could calm him. Save him. His mother had promised.

Crazy. Sick. Father. Mother. Weak. Ill. Dishonorable discharge. Sick. Filthy. Sick. Crazy. Buggy.

Jones clapped him hard on the shoulder again and laughed longer and harder. Ben stepped further away his hand still in his jacket.

"The Chief wants to see you in his office, Hero Hughes. In his office. Everybody around here knows you're the bagman for Sully but maybe the crooked, old drunk's finally seen sense and you're gonna get dishonorably discharged from the department the same way you did from the army, pal. Sure, we all take a little taster here and there. Hell, everyone pretty much knows I work for the dagos on occasion, but you Hughes, you ain't one of us and you'll never be one of us. You're a dirty, murdering freak and your time is running out around Boston. I'm gonna get ya. I'm gonna be the one that gets ya, Hughes. It's gonna be me to put the cuffs on. I want you to know that. I'm not going anywhere. Your fucking two-bit, Irish hoodlum pals over in Southie too, you'll be sharing a cell in C-Town Pen together." He spoke it loud, to an audience. Everyone in the room.

The department broke out in an applause again, but this time they meant it. Someone whistled. Someone shouted, "You tell him, Lewie!" Oily faces murmuring to each other. *Crazy. Sick. Father. Mother. Weak. Ill. Dishonorable discharge. Sick. Filthy. Sick. Crazy. Mother. Buggy.*

Ben's face blazing, he swallowed something that caught scratching at the back of his throat, shoved his way past Jones towards the stairs leading to the third floor and The Chief's office. The greasy windowpanes hacked shards of retarded sunlight across wood paneling and nicotine-stained walls. The room began to tilt. Floorboards warped. Heads elongated freakish. Limbs stretched abnormal. A hive. A nest. Insects. He had stumbled into a nightmare. He tripped over, staggered back up to his feet. The cackling laughter pursuing him unforgiving.

"I'm looking forward to reading your report on what exactly happened over there in Seaport, Hero Hughes, Old Boy!" Jones called after him.

Ben slipped again in the hall; his hands pressed to the filthy, cold marble. A face reflected in the marble—a ghost. An office girl with make-up smothered acne, clutching files to her flat chest, wide-eyed him pitifully. Bile crawling at the back of his teeth. He lurch-ran to the restrooms, kicked open the door and vomited into a sink. His empty stomach burned. He snatched out the soap from his jacket pocket, ripped the paper packaging from it. Scrubbing his palms and fingers raw. Splashed icy water from the faucet over his face and slouching over the sink stared at his trembling reflection in the cracked mirror, promising himself he'd find the child, get out of Boston. Beat the shit out of that fucking animal Jones sooner or later. He pulled out his flask, took a long hit. Eyes stinging. His fingertips running over the grooves of the inscription. His guts rolled. Dry heaving, he slipped it shakily back inside his jacket. Holding his hands under the ice-cold water and counted to seven seven times. Eye fucking his reflection and breathing deep. Reciting the fucking poem because he didn't know what else he was supposed to do. It was all he had.

THE OFFICE WAS brightly lit, but smelled decrepit, rotten and musty. A morgue stench without the chemical aftertaste.

Police Chief Sullivan was seated behind his large oak desk with his feet up, lighting up a thick cigar and chuckling horse with a tall, well dressed, slim man. Ben recognized the piece of shit as soon as he turned around and fixed those mocking icy blue eyes behind round-framed spectacles on him. Ben had seen him in the Dailies more than enough. A man from a family very well known in Boston. American royalty. A dynasty of wealthy barons and investors. Joseph P. Kennedy. America's blessed. He'd been a big wheel on Wall Street. A big wheel everywhere that mattered. People said he was one of the richest men in the country. Gotten the majority of his wealth through dishonest investments, insider trading on the stock market and bootlegging with gangster partners. Incredibly well-heeled. Incredibly well connected. A golfing buddy of ex-president Roosevelt. It seemed to Ben, the elites were the only criminals that ever got away scot-free. He'd heard whispers on the streets of Southie of big-time rip-offs. Heroin imported from Europe. Invite only parties with armed guards—sex orgies for the rich and famous. Investments in skin flicks starring drugged up casting couch Hollywood starlet wannabes. Yes, Joe K was corrupt as they came. Allegedly. A cunt with a sickly smug face. For Certain. Ben clenched his teeth to veil his disgust.

The Chief jabbed his cigar at them both, rubbing at his protruding gut, "speak of the devil and he shall appear, eh Joe? Our hero of the moment, Detective Benjamin Hughes."

Joe Kennedy stepped forward, raised his eyebrows appraising Ben coolly. "Damn pleasure to meet you finally, Detective Hughes. I've heard a heck of a lot about you. Quite the dashing British hero, by all accounts."

"Sure, nice to meet you too," Ben lied. Tried to smile. His jaw locked and clicked.

"As you're probably already acutely aware, I was the ambassador to your fair homeland a few years back. Didn't end too well. Differences of political views and some such nonsense. Damned shame. Hitler wasn't hurting anybody but the sheenies in my humble opinion. Damned shame. Lovely place, however. Britain. Just lovely."

Joe stuck out his hand to shake and Ben slid his hands into the pockets of his slacks. Took a step back. Nodded several times.

"I've not called England home for over twenty years," Ben took off his hat, held it for a moment and then pushed in back onto his head.

The climate in the room became a few degrees hotter.

The Chief cleared his throat as though making a point and waved his cigar again. "Like I mentioned earlier, he doesn't like to shake hands, Joe. Doesn't like to touch anybody. Don't take it personally. He's our precinct neurotic, aren't you, Hughes?" The Chief said, grinning with stained chipped teeth, eyeing Ben as coolly as Kennedy.

Ben stared at a black stain on the sole of Sullivan's shoe. It looked as though he had stamped on a cockroach. Could have been chewing gum. Ben didn't know but couldn't drag his eyes from it. He broke out into an electric sweat. Guts, solid and aching, groaned audibly. Felt similar to crashing, opium withdrawal again but wasn't. The Chief shrugged, gazing at the tip of the cigar thoughtfully and continued to talk.

"Another robbery in progress foiled due to your eagle-eyed diligence, Hughes. The Boston Police Department owe your heroics a debt of gratitude. Hell, the whole of Boston does. Isn't that right, Joe? A real Boy Scout we got here."

"It certainly is and we certainly do. I was just saying to your boss here, Ben, that I could very well use someone with your type of moxy. Your drive. How would you like to come and work for me this weekend? With the big man's blessing of course."

"What are you talking about?" Ben avoided the man's eye contact. Focusing on a gold and mother of pearl stick pin lanced through a blood red necktie.

"A little work, is all, Sport."

"What exactly would this *little* work entail?"

Joe Kennedy glanced at The Chief and the Chief shrugged, nodded at him to go ahead.

"Well, it would be a kind of security detail."

"I would've imagined someone of your reputation would have their own security already. Armed guards and what have you."

"I have a couple of good fellows, yes, that's true. But they'll be engaged in other matters this weekend. Short notice. I'll need yourself and a few suitable men, of your choosing of course," Kennedy slipped a small candy tin from his pocket, shook some breath mints into his large mouth. Lips puckered. Ben looked back to the stain on the bottom of Sullivan's shoe. The Chief interjected and picked up the ball.

"We aren't talking about men from the department either, Hughes. We're talking about your other friends. The lads over on Dorchester Street," Sullivan winked.

"What do you need *that* kind of security for?" Ben asked, even though he had a good idea. Southie rumors always had a hard edge of truth about them.

"Well, that's not something I'm willing to go into with you just yet, Sport," Kennedy said.

"I don't walk into a dark room without switching on a light or two, Joe. That's a good way to cause injury to yourself."

"*Joe?* It's as though we're becoming fast friends already. All right then, *Ben*. I wouldn't want to you feel in danger of stubbing your toe. Let's just say some little upstart Italian gentlemen are somewhat dissatisfied with a business relationship that came to an end last month. I'm having an important gathering of people in Salt Lake City this weekend. A lot of important people. Movers and shakers from the most prestigious fields. People creating a new kind of America. A better kind of America. And I don't want any disgruntled, hot-headed fucking guineas spoiling all the fun and disrupting the flow of things, if you follow me."

"I follow you. Thus far. Who'll be attending the party?"

"Well, it's a private affair, as is the guest list, Sport. However, I will say that the head of a major movie studio, one or two governors, some other upper echelon politicians and some well-known Hollywood types will be in attendance. A cardinal, if you're impressed by that sort of person. Those are just some of the minor players of course. But real movers and shakers, like I said. The old blood, if you will. King makers. Good people to know and better people to have on your side," Kennedy winked.

Ben glanced at The Chief. The Chief tapped cigar ash into an ashtray, stony faced.

"I'm working a couple of cases here. Besides, Salt Lake City is pretty far away. Why would I want to involve myself and my associates in babysitting a bunch of spoilt elites? We've better things to be doing with our time. No offence intended, of course, Joe."

Kennedy chuckled, cleared his throat and looked over the lenses of his glasses towards The Chief. Sullivan examined the tip of his dress shoes as he spoke, "Hughes, my boy, this is a stupendous opportunity for you. As Joe said, a lot of important folks'll be there. The kind of people who really know how to return a favor. What we're saying here is, we need men with a little bit of discretion. Guys who know when it's best to look the other way. Like you Ben."

"Like me?" Ben caught his reflection in glass of the office door. He straightened his shoulders and shook his head.

The Chief threw his head back, crowing out a loud 'HA!' then looked Ben up and down slowly. "Just like you, Ben. Look lad, see this little job through and tell you what, I'll finally push through that transfer request you've been hounding me for. I didn't want you to go out to Los Angeles, but I'll sign the damned paperwork and push the damn thing through. All right? I won't be able to find a man as good as you, but fuck it, I'll send you to California. If that is what you want? That *is* what you want, isn't it?"

Ben nodded slow, unsure of how to respond.

"You could even take that young girl you've been frolicking with as of late. Li Yu, isn't it?" The Chief stood up, brushed ash from his slacks and came round the desk. Leaning his soft, sagging body against it. Peppery hair out of place and his face a flushed, red. The vile stink of something corrupt drifting out from his stained, creased shirt. Ben stepped back again, wishing there were an open window in the room. He felt too hot. Placing a hand on the door frame to steady himself and automatically regretting it. It was sticky. He rubbed his fingers together grimacing. Yanked out a handkerchief from his jacket, pretended to sneeze into it and then thoroughly wiped at his hand. Joe and The Chief made slow eye contact with each other.

"Los Angeles… Too many spics and hebes for my liking. But what the hell, the heart wants what it wants. How long's it been, anyway?" Sullivan went on.

"Been since what?" Ben asked, folding the handkerchief back into his breast pocket.

"Since you saw your kids? That's why you want to go out there, isn't it?"

"You know about my children? And you know about Li?" Ben asked frowning.

"Of course I do. I'm the Chief and I like to know what my favorite little underlings are getting up to in their free time, Hughes."

Ben's face burned up. The Chief slapped his knee and guffawed. "Well I'll be damned! I got the boy blushing! Lad, I don't care if your wife ran away taking the kiddies with her. I don't even care who you fuck, Ben. A lot of people around here they wouldn't understand any of that, but I understand you. The restraining order your ex-wife has out on you can be our little secret. And as for the whore? Hell, I've been known to dip into China Town myself on occasion. Get myself some of that exotic erotic. We all have our little peccadillos, I'm more than sure." He laughed too heavily and broke out into a hacking cough.

Ben felt another headache stretching out in his skull with clawed legs. Sullivan cleared his throat, spat phlegm into the wastepaper basket and puffed at his cigar thoughtfully. "No, it wouldn't be good for you if it got out at all, like so many other things. Say for example, did you know, Ben, the revolver that was used in the attempted robbery you foiled yesterday was last recorded missing from our evidence locker two fucking years ago?" The Chief shook his head faux concerned, sucking on the cigar. "That's pretty damn peculiar, isn't it? Some people around here would have a hell of a lot of questions about that, like Detective Lewis Jones. He'd have you in cuffs in front of a tribunal faster than a twelve-year-old shoots his load at the sight of a pair of big titties. But not me, Ben. Not me."

Ben swallowed bile and closed his eyes. Needed to piss. Needed to sit down. Vision topsy-turvy.

The Chief grinned at Kennedy, continuing. "No, not me. You're my good pal and one of the very best men I've got around here. I could add that the bullets we took from the stiff also matched the other bullets at the scene. The bar door. I could also add that you're a fucking moron, Ben. Killing the perp with the same gun you framed him with."

The Chief and Kennedy erupted into a cackling laughter then cut it off abrupt. Glaring at him. Ben gulped. Scratched at his chest and stomach. His legs trembled and he tried to shift his weight to stop it. Staring back. Sullivan slapped his knee. It sounded like a gunshot in the suddenly silent office. "I *could* say all those things, but I won't. I won't say a damned thing. You're as safe as houses with me and Joe here, lad. Anyway, all's I'm trying to say here is, you're looking a little under the weather. Having to put a perp down, especially a violent perp is always a very stressful business. Very stressful. Maybe a little personal time away in Salt Lake City is exactly what you need. A holiday. A vacation. All those mountains and fresh air will do you the world of good."

"I'll also pay you and your pals handsomely, Ben. Very handsomely. One thousand dollars per man, per day," Kennedy chimed in.

"Two thousand dollars for a weekend of security? For a party in Salt Lake City?" Ben's interest peaked. He would be able to add the cash to his savings for a new life with Li Yu in California. He rolled his shoulders back.

"That's exactly right, Ben. Two thousand dollars for two days. I'm renting the entire Peery Hotel. It'll be empty of clientele and staff, with the exception of a few maids, cooks, and what have you. Easy work for you and your buddies."

"I'll also be one of the lesser important people attending the party, Ben," The Chief cut in, "so you'll be in good company." He smirked.

Kennedy eyeballed Sullivan and went on. "Yes, The Chief here will be the man with the guest list. Making sure those who come up to the top floor are invited to the party and not unwanted interlopers. You just have your men positioned around the hotel lobby looking rough and tumble. There will be rooms for you to use on the lower floor. I imagine you'll work in shifts. But I'll leave all those kinds of arrangements in your very capable hands. However, I want to add, no one, and I mean no one, is to come up to the top floor or enter the banquet room for any reasons whatsoever. That's the sine qua non. I don't care if the devil himself rolls through the front doors of the hotel and commences claiming the souls of the wicked. No one is to bother the party. Now, tell me, Sport, is that easy money, or isn't it? Think of all the great things you could do with four thousand dollars."

"Four thousand dollars?"

"Well yes, obviously I'll be paying you double for your trouble and that certain moxy, I spoke of earlier, of course."

"How can I reach you to let you know my decision?" Ben stepped back towards the door. The two men's faces seemed to be distorting. Something slithering underneath the flesh. His hand itching where he had touched the doorframe. The smell of shit and breath mints. Something awful in the atmosphere of the office, drifting from Kennedy and Sullivan both. Ben held his breath. Pulled the handkerchief from his pocket again. Wanting to get the hell out of the office and away from them both. Fast. Needing to scrub his hands desperately.

"He still needs to think about it? Jesus H. Christ," Sullivan slapped his knee again, blowing thick pungent smoke towards Ben's face.

"No, I don't reckon so. I worked in Hollywood for a little while. He's already sold. Like a slutty little starlet desperate for a part in the movie, he's just playing hard to get, aren't you, Ben?" Kennedy grinned.

Ben shrugged. Balled the handkerchief in his fist tight. It looked as though the two men were wearing masks. Rubber Halloween masks of human faces pulled too tight over something grotesque and ancient. Insectile.

Kennedy rubbed at his jawline as though hearing Ben's thoughts and guffawed. "Let the boss here know and I'll know. You and I won't be seeing or hearing from each other again after today, Sport. Our little discourse here is done and dusted." He stuck out his hand to shake again. Ben ignored it again.

"I'll give your proposal some thought and send word within twenty-four hours," he spat out, going to leave, gasping for oxygen. The Chief threw a hand in the air, telling him to stop, went back around the desk, took a thin, white envelope from a top drawer and handed it to Ben.

"I've been trying to get in touch with Wallace, but no one over there is answering the fucking telephone. Line is deader than Abe Lincoln."

"Stevie had the telephones taken out of the club a couple of months back."

"Why the fuck would he do a thing like that? I knew the street gossip must've been true. It always is, isn't it?"

Ben looked down at the envelope in his hand and then glanced out of The Chief's office window at the golden dome of the New State House shining in the distance. The building was meant to stand for everything righteous in Boston, but Ben could never help but think it just underlined everything that was wrong with the place. It started to rain again. Droplets trickled down the glass like a child's tears. Ben thought he heard a child crying. The kid in the photograph. The cries metamorphosed into screams. The Chief snapped his fingers four times, snatching Ben's attention and pointed at the paper envelope in his fingers.

"Take that to Wallace."

"Sure, I'll do it after the morning's briefing."

"When have you ever given a rat's ass about the morning briefing, Hughes? No, do it now, *right away*, it's important. Very fucking important. Can't stress that enough, lad."

"What about the briefing?"

"I said don't fucking worry about the briefing. It's the usual bullshit. A dead whore with her tits hacked off in the North End and another missing brat. You're on holiday leave as from this moment. I want that envelope in Wallace's hand within the hour, you hear, Englishman?"

Kennedy and the Chief chuckled and slapped each other on the back as though sharing a private joke. Ben's flesh itched and prickled all over. His heart lodged in his throat. Tears running down the windowpane. Needing to wash his hands desperately. One. Two. Three. Four. Five. Six. Seven.

He swung open the door to leave. The sweat scalding, trickling down his back.

"Uh-uh, aren't you forgetting something, Hughes? Gimme, gimme, gimme," Sullivan said, holding out his palm and wriggling his fingers back and forth. A pale cockroach on its back.

"Yes, right. Of course," Ben said, pulling the thick Manila envelope from the inside of his jacket pocket and letting The Chief snatch it out of his hand, licking his thick blue lips.

"Good boy, Ben. I hope you didn't take more than your percentage. Be a mistake to start getting greedy. Now, go and get some rest and recuperation. Take that little Chink girl out somewhere nice. I'll see you in Salt Lake City. And, don't get into any more fucking trouble, for Christ's sake." He winked again the same way Kennedy had.

"I'll need to write the reports about what happened in Seaport yesterday morning before I go."

"That's not going to be a problem, they've already been typed up and filed."

"What?"

"Just say 'thank you', Hughes."

Ben croaked out a thanks, nodded. Turned around and left quickly. The sounds of their laughter crawling after him down the musty hall. The clatter of typewriters machine gun fire in the typing pool. Feeling filthy. Dirty. Contaminated. Needing to decontaminate his hands and rinse his mouth out.

Kennedy frowned at the closed office door, "Sully, I do believe that boy is a certifiable bed bug."

The chief fell back into his chair, coughed up more phlegm, spat it into a wastepaper basket again. Spittle dribbled down into the crevice of his double chin. "Hughes? Shit, what did I tell you? Crazy as a shithouse rat, but those are the best kind of guys. Trust me, ain't no one better to pull security for your get-together. The amount of shit I got on him would make your head spin around. He's definitely the guy for the job."

"It's on your head, Sully," Kennedy took off his spectacles and cleaned the lenses on a silk handkerchief.

The chief chuckled and shrugged, puffed on his cigar and leaned back in his chair to gaze out of the window at the dome of The State House.

"Shit, that's a risk I'm willing to take."

They both laughed, but at different things and Kennedy glanced at his wristwatch trying to think of a good remark to leave the fat slob behind the desk on.

DETECTIVE MELLON WAS smoking one of his French cigarettes and drinking an old coffee from a paper cup, his brown hair pomaded back on his head catching the morning light from a grimy window when Ben approached his desk.

"What the hell you want, Hughes? Don't just loom over me, scratching at yourself," he said in his thick New Yorker's accent without looking up.

Ben took out the photograph from inside his pocket, unfolded it and dropped it onto Mellon's cluttered desk. Mellon took a long drag on his cigarette and examined the photograph ripped from the newspaper. Shrugged, took off his spectacles, glanced up and blew smoke into Ben's face.

"Yeah, another missing, kid. So what? What the hell you asking for? Got any tips or what?"

"I wanted to know if you have any leads yet?" Ben shot back, waving the smoke away.

"No, not yet. We got jack shit, as per usual. No one talks to cops in this town, you know that. All we got is a couple of crank calls. The maid the kid was with when he did the Houdini is clean. No suspects. Nothing. Like all these other missing kids. It's like the Pied Piper of Hamlin came to Boston. Only difference is Boston is still full of fucking rats."

"What do you reckon?"

"We're leaning towards a kidnap for ransom, waiting on some kind of communication right now. Nothing else to be done. My private, personal opinion, the kid ran away, probably got a den stashed away somewhere. You know the kind we had as kids. He'll come home when he gets hungry or lonely enough."

"Still, a white child from a middle upper-class family goes missing, I would've thought your squad would be all over that."

"We're fucking swamped at the moment. This kid is the fourth to disappear into thin air in the last three months and that ain't even including all the spade kids that have turned up gone. It's a shit show around here and I've got enough on my plate. Besides, word came from up on high, The Chief and even the fucking commissioner himself told us to concentrate on the cases we can actually fucking solve. None of these kids are the Lindbergh babe, that's for sure."

"I see," Ben said stepping away from a dust ball skittering across the floor like a cockroach.

"You don't really see shit, Hughes. Why do you give a damn anyway? I ain't seen you around here for weeks and this kid ain't even on your beat."

"I was just curious is all. Do you think I could I take a look at the file?"

"Just curious, huh?" Mellon snubbed out his cigarette in an overflowing ashtray and lit another. Coughed. Ben stepped back. Mellon raised an eyebrow. "I think you're full of shit, Hughes. Why don't you go loiter around your own department or Dorchester Street or wherever it is you spend all your time nowadays."

Ben turned around to go. That dull ache in his guts again. A cold blade tearing through him.

"Hey, Hughes. Take this with you, I don't fucking want it," Mellon held up the scrap of newspaper and waved it distastefully through the air.

Ben hesitated a moment, took it slowly and folded it carefully. Placed it back inside his pocket and turned to go again.

"And Hughes?" Mellon said, holding Ben's eyes, evaluating.

"Yes, Mellon?"

"You know I can't let you take a look at the file. But I don't really give a shit anymore. My transfer to L.A went through and I'm counting down the days. I'll be L.A.P.D real soon. Leaving this shithole behind me. Look, I'm going out for coffee and a bagel now before this morning's briefing." He rummaged through the piles of manila folders scattered on his desk, pulled one out and dropped it on top of the column. "Maybe it'll be here on my desk when I'm gone. Just saying. Knock yourself out."

"Thank you very much, Harold. We worked well together once. I'm sure we will again someday."

"You're a very strange man, Hughes. I don't think I'll ever understand you, but you were one hell of a detective once. Where the hell did that guy go to anyway?" Mellon said, getting up, readjusting his shoulder holster and pulling the brown suit jacket from the back of his chair. He ran a comb through his slick hair and nodded.

Ben watched him leave not bothering to answer the obviously rhetorical question. Yes, he *had been* a good detective once. Before the sickness got too much. Negativity ruled. He was in the wrong line of work. He didn't know a lot, but he knew that much at least. He glanced around, snatched up the manila file from the clutter on the desktop, shoved it underneath his jacket and followed Mellon out of the precinct into a cruel, unforgiving Boston February rain. He glanced at his wristwatch. Still early. He had someone to talk to and time to kill.

"MY FATHER WHIPPED me with a razor strop throughout my childhood. Any minor infraction and that razor strop would be taken down from its rusty hook on the bathroom wall. I used to fear the damn thing so much. That fucking strop. But the human being is an amazing animal, isn't it? We can become acclimatized to any form of pain or humiliation. It changes us. We mutate to suit our environments. Father stopped whipping me the day I didn't flinch or whimper. Just stared straight through him. I had acclimatized. Adapted. Mutated. Become better. Stronger. Father. The day he didn't come home to mother and me was a huge relief. Almost as though we had rid ourselves of a terminal illness. Cured. Reached some kind of an immunity. The atmosphere in our house changed, lightened instantaneously. Yes, my father's death was a huge relief, but then my mother changed. A last crippling blow from my father. She became… needy. Taking from me more than I could ever give. I was the man of the house. I didn't want that. I didn't want it. But what a child wants and what a child gets are rarely the same. I often wonder where my problems stem from? My mother or my father? Both? It doesn't even matter now, does it? The damage has been done and what's done is done and can never be undone," Ben said, crossing his legs and picking flint from his slacks. He opened up his arms and shrugged at the man seated opposite him as though inviting critique.

"Why are you telling me all this?" the man asked, straining against the handcuffs that were holding him confined to the chair. A bloody gash in the center of his forehead trickling a thin stream of blood down his face. Ben watched the stream of red's progress. It looked like a leech twisting its way down the Italian man's gaunt, pale features.

"Because I want you to know that I've suffered too. I've suffered more than most. My mother was too weak. My father was a very brutal man and now his son is a very brutal man. We all become our fathers in the end, don't we?"

"I don't know what you're talking about. I don't give a shit about none of that."

"Yes, well, I feel better for the telling of the story, anyhow. I feel, I don't know, cleansed. Unburdened. Purified somewhat. A burden shared is a burden halved after all, isn't it? Thank you, Frankie. It is Frankie, isn't it?"

"Please, just let me go."

Ben fake laughed. "You know I can't do that. Why do you people always ask foolish things like that? It's redundant and completely pointless. You wouldn't say it to the grocer or the butcher or the lawyer, would you? No, you wouldn't. They're just doing their job. So am I. How do you people say it? 'Capiche'?"

"Please. Look it, there's an envelope of cash over there on the table," the man whined, nodding his head frantically in the direction of a cluttered tabletop. "It's yours. There's at least five c-notes in there. Take it. I'll go away. I'll go away and I won't come back to Boston, I swear it. I'm gone. Gone."

"Five hundred dollars?" Ben tee-heed. Whistled. "Is that how much you're willing to spend to get yourself out of this predicament? Cheap. Real cheap. Sometimes I wonder about *that*. How much the human soul is worth? How much is my soul worth? We are all equal under Heaven but are some souls worth more than others? Would the devil pay more than God? Surely, I would get more bang for my buck from the devil. Perplexing, isn't it? Could go mad just thinking about all those things, couldn't you?"

"You want more dough? I can get more! A lot more. How much you want? You just give me a figure." The handcuffs rattled. Iron dragged over pine wood.

"You people think all of life's problems can be solved with paper money, don't you? It's pathetic. Besides, if I had any intention of letting you go, I wouldn't have told you such a deeply personal, frankly embarrassing story from my childhood, would I?" Ben said, examining the fingernail on his pinkie.

"I can't go back to prison. I can't. Please."

Ben tittered. "You think I'm here to arrest you, Frankie?"

"What do you mean? You're a cop, ain't you? You don't just work for Stevie. You're a Boston Police Detective, I heard it. You're a cop."

"Yes, that's true. You heard right. I'm a detective, most of the time anyway. I'm not here to arrest you, however. We already discussed all this, Frankie. You can't do what you did and walk away clean. Someone very important to me wants me to make an example of you. In life, you have to pay for all your mistakes, you know? It's not personal for me. I don't give a shit about the little tart you sliced up; truth be told. Like I said, I'm just doing a favor for a very good friend of mine."

The man groaned, exasperated, "I told you a hundred fucking times already, I don't know what the fuck you're talking about. I've never cut up any whores. You've got me confused with someone else, I'm telling you! I just run a shy, got a spread of dough on the street. I lend out cash to people who need it. Like a bank but more honest. More friendly. That's it. That's all. Please, I've got kids. I got two boys."

"Are you a good father? Play catch ball with your kids in the park? Buy them shaved ice? Lift them up on your shoulders? That sort of thing, do you?"

"Yes! Yes! All of that! I'm a good father! Good! Fucking great!"

"Looking at you now, I highly doubt that's true, Frankie."

"It's true. I love my kids. I'm a good father."

"Does a good father beat on whores? Carve their faces up like Halloween pumpkins so they can't work any longer? Can't support *their* families? I imagine you probably beat your children too. What kind of a person would hurt a child? A grown adult hurting a tiny, defenseless child. Small, innocent children. Small boys. What kind of a person does that? A child that loves and trusts you. Depends on you to protect them. To comfort them when they're frightened in the night? To betray a child like that? I've never been able to understand that at all. I never will."

"I said I didn't do any of that shit. I'm sorry about the girl, but you've got the wrong fella here. Besides she's just a fucking whore. It's not like she was someone important, for crying out loud."

"Everyone's important to someone though, aren't they?"

"Yeah, me. Me. I'm important to my kids. They need me. I'm all they've got."

"I have a question I've been wanting to ask," Ben said, shifting uncomfortably in his chair. Noticing more flint on his grey slacks and brushing at it irritably. Itchy again.

"Sure, anything. I'll tell you anything you wanna know."

"Have you ever had relations with a woman named Li Yu?"

"How's that?"

"Carnal relations?"

"Relations? What do you mean? Like she's my cousin or something?"

"Jesus Christ, you Boston degenerates need to read a fucking dictionary once in a while. Have you ever *fucked* a woman named Li Yu?"

"The black Chinese whore?"

"She isn't a fucking whore," Ben yelled, getting to his feet.

"All right, all right," Frankie cowered. "Whatever you say. She ain't a whore. Sure, sure. Why you asking me anyways?"

Ben pinched the creases of his slacks and sat back down, "I'm curious, is all. And you're the one handcuffed to the chair, so I'll ask all the fucking questions from here on out, Frankie."

"Wait a fucking minute. She was the one who put you up to this, wasn't she? That fucking sneaky little bitch-whore. She told me she had cops in her pocket," Frankie said, shaking his head and spitting a bitter laugh with a pink bubble of blood.

"You cut up her friend real good, I heard."

"Buddy, you heard wrong. Dead wrong. She's playing us both. She's taking us both for fools, I'm telling you."

"What do you mean?" Ben licked his lips. Frowned.

"She's taking you for a ride. That sneaky little cunt is into me big time. BIG. She borrowed heavy a couple of months ago and now she's sent you."

"What the fuck are you talking about?"

"She's fucking us over. She's lied to you; can't you fucking see that? The whoring two-bit bitch."

"You use the present tense."

"How's that?"

"You're inferring she's still whoring?"

"I don't know about that for sure. Maybe, here and there, I heard it. I *do* know how she's been paying *my* vig every week."

"What did you say?"

"She's been paying my vig, in, how do you say, services rendered? That it?"

Ben started to hyperventilate. His hand to his eyes as if shielding his vision from a burning bright light. A sharp stabbing pain suddenly shooting down his prick and he wondered if it was syphilis. This wop was probably crawling with infections. Sickness. Writhe with venereal disease. A boiling sweat seeping from his pores. A dull ache behind his eyes. His leg started to shake. He uncrossed his legs and then quickly crossed them again. Fingered the wooden arm of the dining chair and counted to seven in a slurred whisper.

"Why would she lie to me? Lie to me? She would lie to me? Lie? She wouldn't lie to me?" Ben bit into his fist. His teeth cutting into his knuckles.

The Italian shrugged. "These fucking broads. Can't trust any of them. They'll kill you quicker than a bullet through the fucking eye. She's really fucked us both. How do you say, literally and figuratively?"

Ben gagged. His eyeballs suddenly heavy in their sockets. Wondered if he was going to start weeping. He pinched at the bridge of his nose and tried to breathe. The air in the room was musty and dry. Filthy. He gagged again. Spat onto the floorboards.

"I have to leave now. I'm going to leave now. The filth and stench in this room is making me quite itchy and uncomfortable." He stood up shakily. Head down and breathing slow. Hand rubbing at the reassuring cool wooden surface of the back of the chair. One. Two. Three. Four. Five. Six. Seven.

"You'll let me go?" Handcuffs rattled. Metal against wood again.

Ben sighed. "No, of course not. Don't delude yourself, man. We passed that moment a while back."

"She's fucking lying to you! This is exactly what she wants, don't you see that?"

"If she wants you dead, there has to be a good reason for it."

"Yeah, cash money. All debts fucking void. That's the best reason there is, ain't it the truth?"

"I don't understand her motives, but I'll still take her word over a slimy piece of shit like you any day of the week."

"You're making a big mistake, pal. You can't hurt me. I'm made. A man of honor. You know who the fuck my uncle is? You can't fucking touch me. You'll cause a war. You must be out of your mind! Fucking buggy!"

That word again like a fist to the face. "What did you just say?"

"I said you must be buggy. Taking the word of some half-spade, half-chink whore? You're fucking crazy! You'll cause a fucking war if you kill me. All you paddy fucks in Southie will be wiped out like the rats you are. You understand what I'm telling you here? Wiped the fuck out, like cockroaches."

Ben stood up, stretched, faux yawned to hide the sadness and hurt he felt clouding his face. Looked around the room properly for the first time since he'd kicked the door in. Sparsely furnished. Peeling paintwork. Dry. Dusty. A lingering ammonia reek. A naked bulb hanging from the cracked ceiling casting everything in a hospital light yellow. Magazines and newspapers littered the cracked floorboards. A disgusting little dump. Takeaway food boxes from a well-known restaurant in China Town tossed in the kitchenette's sink made his stomach twist painfully like a dirty wash rag. The place wasn't far from Li's Tea House. A block away if that.

He spotted what he wanted on the dining table next to the thin envelope of cash. A singular heavy brass candlestick. The long kind. He walked over to the table slow. Weighed the envelope in his hand, as he always did with such things, before slipping it into his pocket. Picked up the candlestick. It was heavy. Good. He went back to his seat and sat down opposite the man cuffed to the chair. Candlestick cradled in his lap.

"Why is there no candle in this candlestick, Frankie?"

"What? There just ain't. Why?"

"It bothered me is all. It seems out of order. Misaligned. Jarring," he said, pulling the handkerchief from his pocket and holding it to his mouth and nose. Frankie screwed his face up. Confused.

"What's that for?"

"Protection," Ben mumbled through the fabric, standing up and stepping towards the Italian.

"Protection from what? I'm fucking tied up here."

"Protection from inhaling any of your filthy blood," Ben swung the candlestick down hard into the man's face. The Italian shrieked high pitched. Teeth smashed and trickled in pieces from his bloody, wrecked mouth into his urine-stained lap. Ben grimaced, cringed, stepping further away from the piss puddling on the floorboards and held the candlestick aloft for another swing.

Frankie flinched, twisting. The chair legs danced. He gurgle-screamed words.

"Wait! Wait! Wait! Okay, I've got information! Important information for the cops. Useful fucking information," he screeched through blood.

"You've already told me everything that needed to be known. Told me too much actually. More than I wanted to know, Frankie, my friend."

"Wait! I'll talk. I'll talk. I know something about that missing kid, the one in the newspaper. The fucking little rich kid that went missing. I know all about it. I'm a witness, I'm telling you. Take me down the precinct and I'll talk. I'll sing like Perry fucking Como," he gurgled, gagged. Spat blood.

Ben dropped the bloody candlestick clattering to the worn floorboards, kicked it towards the grimy window. Went over to the sink, washed his hands. Dried himself on his handkerchief and then took the folded piece of newspaper out from his breast pocket. Unfolding and holding it in front of the wrecked crimson of the man's screwed up face. "This child? You're talking about this child?"

"Yeah, yeah, yeah, that's the one. I got information about that," Frankie slurred. Spitting a tooth rattling across the floor.

Ben dragged the chair he'd been sitting on a couple of feet further away and sat back down. "All right, you've bought yourself a little time, Frankie. Spiel what you know. Everything."

Frankie spieled.

"There's this guy, a fucking degenerate, hangs around with our crew on the North side. He's good pals with the boss."

"With Buccola?"

"Nah, the pope. Of course, Buccola. Anyhow, this guy, he snatches up kids for order, like a fucking catalogue or something," he slurred.

"What do you mean? For order?" Ben leaned forward slightly, focusing on each dribbled word. Scratching at the stubble on his jaw.

"I don't know. I met him through another guy in the crew, told me he's making it rich, snatching kids for some rich broad. She tells him what kids she wants; he snatches them up, leaves them tied up in some empty building on the outside of town and then she pays him off later at some swanky meeting place."

"He abducts children on the orders of a rich woman?"

"Yeah, that's what I'm trying to tell you right now. Some highfalutin' bitch, the guy says. I think you broke my jaw."

"And the woman? Who is she?"

"I don't know nothing about the broad. All he said was she's some rich bitch." Frankie sniffed. Snorted. Ben cringed.

"I want names, concrete intelligence, not idle rumors you heard in some squalid fucking dive-bar, Frankie. I want the name of the man you spoke to."

"I don't know. Fuck! He ain't one of us. He's just an associate. Someone who comes into the café every so often. Buddies with Buccola, like I said. I can't remember his fucking name. But I'll know him when I see him. You can't miss him, if you see him."

"Explain. What's your meaning?"

"I mean he looks like a freak."

"Elaborate." Ben crossed his legs, uncrossed them. Crossed them.

"What?"

"Fucking go on. Explain, fuckhead."

"I mean, the guy, he ain't got no hair. No eyebrows neither. He's as bald as a duck's ass. Bald as an Eightball. He's got some kind of a sickness makes all his hair fall out. Looks as though he's been cut by one of those plastic surgeons too."

"And this hairless man took the child?"

"I don't know if he took that kid. I said he snatches kids up."

"But you think it likely?"

"What?"

"You think that man has the child?"

"Sure. Sure. Probably. Yeah."

"And the man is an associate of Buccola's?"

"Yeah, right. That's right."

"Where does this hairless man frequent?"

"What?"

"Jesus Christ. Where does he fucking hang out, drink?"

"I said I don't know. He's fucking strange. Gives me the heebie jeebies. I think he's a finocchio, maybe. A queer. I try and stay away from the guy. He just comes into the café sometimes to meet with the boss. Fucking disgusting looking guy, smells sick, too. You know that stink sick people get."

"For what reason?"

"Does he smell sick? How should I know?"

"No, fuckhead. Why does he meet with Buccola *that* often?" Ben massaged his temples. Easing back the migraine rushing in like a midnight tide.

"Like I said, I don't know. They're buddies from way back. They always go in the back room to talk. Real hush-hush."

"Tell me about the place outside of town he drops the children at."

"What's to tell?"

"Where is it? What kind of building is it?"

"I don't know. I spoke to the guy once. All I heard was it's an old gas stand or something."

"North outside of town? South outside of town? I'm going to need more information if you want to leave this shithole in one piece, Frankie."

"Fuck! I don't fucking know. It's one of Buccola's old buildings, maybe. He owns property all over Massachusetts, I know that much. You'll need to go to the city hall, research the permits and shit. Listen to me, I could've been a detective, easy."

"That's all your information, is it? It's not much to go on. I guess, I'll have to go and have a little chat with Buccola myself."

"Ha! You won't get close enough to Buccola to ask nothing."

"And why's that?"

"Cos' you're a cop and he ain't no dunsky, that's why. Everybody knows you push buttons for Stevie Wallace. You'd be dead before you even walked into the place." Frankie sneered. Blood dripped from his chin onto his shirt.

"They'd be very foolish to kill a Boston Police Detective, it'd be suicide for every Italian on the North Side." Ben dusted off his hands. "Well anywho, if that's all your information, then I'll be on my way."

"I can get more. I'll find out where the guy is. The gas stand. Give me a day. Please. Please!"

"Your information was frankie rather disappointing. Get it? Frankie? Frankly? Never mind, you've earned a quick death at least."

"No, no, no! You said you'd let me leave here. Let me go."

"I said, I'd let you leave here in *one piece* and you will. I never said you'd be alive, Frankie."

"For the love of God, please! You're making a big fucking mistake! DON'T!"

The Italian rocked back and forth in the chair screaming. Ben's ears hurt and he wished he'd thought to gag him.

He stood quickly, backed up towards the door. Switching on Frankie's Victrola, twisting the volume way up. Coincidently, Perry Como's *Prisoner of Love*. He snorted. Laughed into the handkerchief held to his mouth.

"Hey, Frankie, you can go ahead and sing like Perry Como now," Ben pulled the .38 from its holster. Frankie wailed, rocking backwards and forwards in the chair. Begging, eyes squeezed tightly shut. Screamed "MOMMY!" The word like a boot kick to Ben's guts. He stumbled back a step. The revolver trembling in his hand.

When the Italian took a breath and slumped back down in his seat, Ben shot him in the chest twice before he could start to scream another word. Blood seeped and then drip-dropped onto the floorboards mixing with the puddle of piss. Ben popped the chamber and shook out the spent bullet casings. Retrieved the handcuffs from the dead man using a curtain he ripped from the window as makeshift gloves. Wrapping them in newspaper like Christmas presents he'd given to his daughters in better days. More normal days. He'd throw the cuffs into the river on the way back. Scrubbed his hands in the sink again and left the flop house room with the handkerchief still gripped to his mouth and nose.

The hallway strewn with refuse. People in rooms shouting at each other. Radios blaring out. The type of place that heard screaming and the sounds of violence regularly. An old lady with wavy white hair wearing a stained ivory nightgown opened her apartment door, peeked out, Ben smiled. She muttered something in Italian and slammed the door closed again.

The Chinese takeaway boxes rotting away in the sink, the scratches and scrapes on Li Yu's knees flashed achingly through his mind like developing photographs, mixed with the face of the screaming boy, as he made his way out of the decaying building. He tried to push the thoughts away. Li Yu loved him. She was going to California with him. The dark thoughts came stronger, more vivid and he flinched at each image as it exploded through his mind. Frankie with two slugs in the chest, bloody holes, fucking Li Yu on the bed he'd first found her in. He counted to seven. Lucky seven. Knocking on the wooden banister rail as he made his way down the stairs into the vestibule and out of the building. Tried to think of something good, pure, positive. Clean. Nothing came but sin, filth, the dead and the dying. The thoughts never stopped. The more he tried to block them out, the more vivid the scenes blossomed in his skull like Poison Ivy. He could make it better. He could fix himself. Repeating the words over and over until his mouth was dust dry.

"Find the boy. Find the boy. Find the boy. Find the boy. Find the boy. Find the boy. Find the boy." Seven. Lucky seven.

THE RAIN HAD stopped, and a dull winter sun lit up the slick streets in a tarnished gold. The house, tall and red-bricked, located in the affluent Back Bay, Beacon Hill, several blocks from the State House, hadn't been difficult to find. He pulled his Cadillac Fleetwood up across the street and sat looking the place over. Nipping at his flask to dull his speeding mind. Sweat soaking his shirt through. Watching shapes of light ripple over the windows. A typical four storied town house that reminded him of his childhood home in Chelsea, London. He rubbed at his eyes. Cringing, blinking in the driver's seat, suddenly assaulted by memories of his father that came screaming back on sharp taloned legs pricking at his mind.

He pushed the ghosts away by taking out the manila file and flicking through the case notes for the seventh time. Finished the flask and placed it in the glovebox. Concentrating on Mellon's scribbled notes and a few hastily drawn diagrams of the park. The bandstand where the vendor had been selling hot potatoes. Photographs of the kid's parents. His guts whined. Couldn't remember the last time he'd eaten. Mother and Father. Mr. and Mrs. Goodman. The kid had a beautiful mother and a lawyer father. Ben wondered if there was a connection between the father's occupation and the kidnapping. A lawyer. Upper class society. Perhaps the father had got into trouble with the wrong kind of people. Fumbled the wrong case with the wrong client. That could be how the Italians figured in. He shook his head no. Southie was Southie. Leary, the town gossip, would've heard something. Ben would've heard something. They'd heard zero in regards to the case, or the kid. Frankie said he'd heard.

Frankie said that a highfalutin' woman was involved. Frankie said a man with no hair and surgeon cut face snatched the kids on orders from said rich woman. Frankie said he had been fucking Li Yu. Services fucking rendered. Frankie said Li Yu was lying to him, setting him up.

Li Yu on her knees.

His consciousness a silent movie of sickness and pain.

Fuck!

Frankie had screamed loud and died hard.

Fuck that lying piece of shit Frankie.

Ben counted to seven out loud into the chilled interior of the car. Spitting out each number slow between breaths. When he'd counted to seven seven times he started reciting the poem, repeating it over and over again like a mantra. "Yesterday, upon the stair, I met a man who wasn't there! He wasn't there again today, oh how I wish he'd go away!" The images of Li Yu lost color, faded to grey then black. He exhaled deep. Snatched up the file again and started reading the notes fully focused. Save the boy, save himself. A cure. An antidote. Save the boy.

The sound of a front door rattling shut startled him from the case details and he glanced over towards the house again. A plump, middle aged woman with pale skin and disheveled auburn hair, draped in a heavy black woolen shawl over a light blue apron had come out of the front door and was sweeping damp, dead leaves from the sidewalk outside the house. Ben flicked through Mellon's notes, found what he was looking for and reread the maid's statement over. Fiona O'Reilly. Thirty-nine years old. An immigrant from Cork, Ireland. Unmarried. No children. Had been working for the family for over ten years. Said she'd raised the missing boy as her own. No prior arrests. No untoward associates. Clean. Pure. Ben went back to Mellon's scribbles. Patrolmen had canvassed a ten-block radius from the park. Knocked on doors. Braced known sex offender scum and child molester fucks around the surrounding neighborhoods. Telephone Directory and beavertail sap interrogations. Sniffer dogs. The whole damn caboodle. They came up short. No one saw a thing. Nothing. Not that Boston residents were known for talking to cops, even in the better neighborhoods. A bullshit mistrust that went all the back to The Old Country and their hatred for the British. They'd dragged and dredged the bodies of water in the common and the adjoining public gardens. No corpse. A big fat nothing again.

Ben closed the file, placed it carefully on the seat beside him and drummed his fingers on the steering wheel. Thinking. Hoping Frankie was lying about kids being snatched. Hoping the kid had just ran away from home like Mellon speculated and Li Yu wasn't any of the things Frankie had said about her. Hoping Frankie was a fucking liar.

Liar.

Fucking liar.

Liar fuck!

The maid noticed him watching her and waved apprehensively. He popped a breath mint in his mouth, nodded, tried to smile and got out of the suddenly claustrophobic automobile. Heart beating erratically. He scratched at his sweaty, itchy chest as he crossed the street. Squinting into the filmy, diseased eye of the yellow afternoon sun as he approached.

"Excuse me, Madam? Ms. O'Reilly?"

She propped the broom against the side of the house and wrung her hands into her apron. Her scent carried faintly by the breeze. Rose water and soap. A comforting smell that made Ben feel at ease. Then his mother's smiling face in darkness. He flinched. Blinked. Taking off his hat, running his fingers through his hair and then dropping it back on his head, pulling it down low over his eyes. Could hear children playing somewhere but when he glanced around the street was empty. He thought of ghosts. The dead. The people he'd killed. Their faces pulsing behind his eyelids. An icy chill ran like a bead of sweat down his spine.

"You're a policeman," she still spoke with a heavy Irish accent. Ben still had his British accent, but it had mixed with the Boston intonation into a bad cocktail.

"Yes, I am. How did you know?"

"You've the look to you. And we've been waiting for news. The lady of the house telephoned the police station this morning. She's naturally distraught. Out of her mind with worry. She'll be happy to see you. She's laying down presently, migraine, shall I go and call on her?"

Ben flashed his badge, "I'm Detective Benjamin Hughes. I'd like to talk with you beforehand, if that's all right with you, Mam?"

"You're an Englishman, I see. Far away from home, as am I."

"Yes, I can't seem to lose the cursed accent. I guess you can rip us away from our homes, but you can't rip the homes from out of us, Ms. O'Reilly.

"Please, call me Fiona. And of course, you may ask me any questions you wish, though I don't know what good it'll do. I've already told the other officers everything that I know. More than a few times actually."

Ben noticed her front teeth were rotten black and took a step back grimacing. She noticed his unease and took a step backwards too. A car door slammed shut and echoed down the street, highlighting the sudden awkwardness. Ben swallowed and tried to smile. Stepped forward again.

Save the boy. Save the boy. Save the boy. Save the boy. Save the boy. Save the boy. Save the boy. Fix yourself.

"We have some fresh leads we're currently looking into," he said, the words rolling from his mouth like jagged rocks.

"Oh, really? That's the grandest news." She smiled. Black teeth. Ben stared at the space of flesh between her thin eyebrows. A trick he'd learned in the academy to help him appear to be holding eye contact. Something he'd hated since childhood.

"On the morning the boy disappeared, the reports say you went to the bandstand to buy a baked potato from the vendor there at approximately ten thirty-five, is that correct?"

"Yes, I still have my Finn's pocket watch and I checked it not ten minutes before."

"Finn?"

"Yes, he was my greatest friend. He didn't come back from the war, over there in Europe."

Ben nodded quickly, took out a small notepad and pencil from his pocket, "I see, sorry for your loss. Were you well acquainted with the vendor? See him often? He was a regular in the park?"

"Were you there, Detective?"

"I'm sorry, Madam? Was I where?"

"Europe? The war?"

Ben frowned at her, finally making eye contact. Her eyes were green with flecks of brown in them. He felt strange and looked away, down towards a storm drain. The darkness.

"Why do you ask?"

"You have the same look in your eyes that a lot of the men have, that came back."

"What's the look?" he tried to chuckle, but the sound came out mechanical and shattered on the air.

"Haunted. It's a haunted look, I think. I apologize if I'm speaking out of turn."

"It's quite all right." The image of him bringing the butt of the rifle down on the back of the drill sergeant's neck illuminated his conscience, then the filth and the damp of the brig. A cold shock crawled over his scalp. He shook his head. "No, no, I wasn't in Europe, I wasn't anywhere that mattered. Now, Miss O'Reilly did you happen to see anyone suspicious around the park? The public gardens? Anyone distinctive?"

"I told the other policemen everything I know. The park was empty that morning. It was only me and little James there. He wanted to see if there were any frogs in the pond, so we went after breakfast. Went to the park at least twice a week. Often. Of course, there's no frogs around now. It's too cold. But I don't tell him that. The fresh air was always nice. It was nice before, I mean."

James. It was the first time Ben had heard the missing child's name spoken aloud and the sound of it caught his breath. Gut punched. He swallowed. Scratched. Blinked. *James*.

"Please think hard, Miss O'Reilly. Fiona. Not just about the park. Did you see anyone distinctive that *whole* morning? Anyone at all? Say for example, someone with strange facial features or anyone that seemed out of place on the street or around the house? Or a woman, perhaps? Someone or something that stuck out to you? Anything?"

The maid's features brightened. "Now that you mention it, *I did*. There was. I mean, maybe I did see a rather strange looking man that morning."

Ben raised his eyebrows. His breath snagged between clenched teeth.

"Go on, Fiona. Strange how? Try and describe him as best you can. As best you can. Please, try and describe, describe him as best you can. Please. Describe him."

Ben coughed into his hand. Wiped his hand on his sleeve. Cleared his throat. Halting the flow of haggard words.

Fiona frowned. "Well, it was a gentleman with a face like a newborn baby's."

Ben froze. "Like a baby's? What do you mean?"

"Well, I mean he was hairless. As bald as a coot, my Finn would have said. No eyebrows even. His face was very smooth. Tight looking."

What Frankie had said was checking out. Ben didn't know if he was happy or disappointed. Li Yu danced into his mind. Her long, dark, wavy hair spread over silk sheets. Eyebrows knitted together in ecstasy. Services rendered. Frankie handcuffed to a chair, cockroaches pushing themselves out of the bloody bullet holes. Grotesque births. Frankie hadn't been lying. Ben shook his head violently side to side, trying to dislodge the thoughts. The maid tightened her eyes on him and placed a hand on the crook of his arm. "Are you all right, Detective?"

Ben startled, rubbing at his eye socket. "What was he doing when you saw him, Ms. O'Reilly, I mean, Fiona? The man?"

"Well, I couldn't rightly say. He was sat in an automobile across from the park, and we walked past him. He seemed to be waiting for someone. It didn't look very suspicious, but he just caught my eye because, like I said, he didn't have any hair or eyebrows and I remember thinking what a poor, poor man he must be to have the appearance he did."

"You didn't mention this to any of the other detectives?"

"Well, it just didn't seem relevant at the time. Do you suppose it is, Detective?"

"It could be pertinent. Very pertinent. What was the vehicle, Ms. O'Reilly? Do you remember?"

"Well, I can't rightly recollect. It was black, that I know for sure. Looked a tad similar to yours."

"A Cadillac?"

"I couldn't say. Don't know much about motor vehicles and such. I walk everywhere I go. Always have."

Ben stepped closer, "Ms. O'Reilly is there anything else that seemed unusual. Anything else that stuck out to you? Anything at all. Even the slightest, smallest of things can be of the utmost importance."

"No, I'm sorry, Detective. There's nothing more I can think of."

"Please, think carefully, Ms. O'Reilly."

She thought for a moment, staring off down the street, shook her head sadly, "I'm sorry Detective."

Ben clenched his jaw, speaking through his teeth "you can't tell me anything about the automobile. Nothing more about the man?"

She gaped into his face, sad. "I'm sorry, Detective."

Ben took another step toward her. Her breath stank rusty. "Fucking think, woman."

The maid backed off towards the front door, her hand to her mouth, "Detective! That kind of foul language is wholly unacceptable."

Ben held out his hands to calm her. They were shaking like he was in the final stages of terminal illness. His mother in the hospital. Starched sheets stained with hospital food. Her lips like rose petals underneath his thumb.

"I'm sorry, Fiona. I apologize. I apologize. I'm under a lot of stress. Too much stress. I apologize for my language."

"I see, Detective. I see." She placed her hand on the front door's brass handle. "It's quite all right. Would you like to speak to the lady of the house now?"

Ben's heart stopped.

"No, not right now. I'll be back later. I need to follow up on another couple of leads that have come to our attention. You've been very helpful, Ms. O'Reilly. Thank you." Ben started back to the automobile.

"Excuse me!" A different voice. Softer, higher.

Ben made like he didn't hear. Hunched up his shoulders to the February chill. Didn't want to turn around. Didn't want to see the face there. The mouth. The eyes.

One.

Two.

"Excuse me, Detective!"

Three.

Four.

He kept walking.

Five.

Six.

"Detective! Wait, please?"

Fuck!

Seven.

He stopped mid-step. Glanced over his shoulder.

Fuck!

The mother standing on the stoop. She'd aged a lot since the photograph in the file, or since the kid had been snatched. Ben would've put his cash on the latter. Her blonde hair restlessly swept across her head and old mascara running black from her eyes. A hand pressed to her cheek as though she had a toothache, and the other hanging limp at her side. The fist opening and closing like a heartbeat on the cream nightgown. Her nipples visible through the silken fabric in the chill of the day.

Ben waved quickly and looked away quicker. Fumbling in his pocket for the keys to the Cadillac.

"Good evening, Mrs. Goodman. I'll be in touch soon." He tried to smile, cursing underneath his breath.

As he swung open the door to the automobile, she ran out into the street barefoot. The desperation in her voice brittle and hard. Hysterics thinly concealed. A growling whine rumbling from Ben's throat like a stray dog dying alone at the side of a freeway.

"Please, Detective. Please just a moment of your time. I'm simply going crazy in this godforsaken house without my son. Please won't you give me a little of your time. I need to know what's going on. No one is telling me anything. Nothing. Please, Detective."

She placed a hand the same color as the nightgown on his shoulder to stop him from getting into the automobile. He froze, letting the hand remain there. He didn't know why. He turned around, glanced into her eyes. Holding little ghosts of gold from the dying sun in the deepest blue of them. His mother's eyes. He looked down the street, stuttering "Mrs. Goodman, I just needed clarification about certain aspects of Miss O'Reilly's statement. Another detective will be in contact with you in a couple of hours."

Her hand gripping his shoulder. Eyes narrowing. "Are you one of those vultures?"

"I'm sorry? I don't follow."

Her hand still there on his shoulder as though it had always been there. Since London. He could feel it burning through the woolen fabric of his jacket. The door of the Cadillac wide open, begging him to slide inside.

"Another one of those no-good reporters from the press?"

Her fingers still on the fabric covering his skin. Limp. Exhausted. Elegant.

Ben pulled out his badge, flashing it quickly and then hiding it back inside his jacket.

"I'm so sorry, Detective. I just hadn't seen you before. You're not one of the detectives we're dealing with. Mr. Mellon and another detective. Can't remember his name. It's an Irish surname, I think."

Ben didn't know what to say. He nodded, slid into the front seat of his Cadillac, the leather squeaked. He fumbled with the ignition and started the engine up. His first time drifting back to him like blood-red smoke, pure white steam in his brain.

Mrs. Goodman stood, holding the door open. Ben pulled at his jacket lapels, feeling naked.

Eyes the deepest kind of blue. He remembered the way his mother's eyes had felt when they had fallen on him. As though it were only the two of them in the whole world. Alone together.

"Please come inside for a moment, won't you, Detective? Please."

Ben stared out of the windshield, down the street, gripping the steering wheel so hard it hurt his knuckles. Switched off the engine, got out and followed Mrs. Goodman into the house that seemed to tower over him, making his heart hammer, and his guts twist up.

The maid stopped sweeping. Smiled, showing her black front teeth, and waved at Ben as he entered the house. A shadow. The early evening suddenly haunted by vicious ghosts that gnawed pieces of you while you tried to find your way out from a thick fog.

Ben closed his eyes as he crossed the threshold. Into the upper-middle class home. Holding his breath as though expecting a blow to the face. As though being held under the water of a bath long ice-cold.

THE BOY'S EYES snapped open. Wide. His bedroom cold. Freezing. Goosebumps speckling his pale skin. Toys on a shelf with eyes that glistened in the moonlight. Model airplanes twisted on string like dead men hanging from the ceiling. His blanket had fallen from his bed. Or had it been dragged from him? He lay naked, staring at the purple darkness spread thinly over the ceiling too afraid to bring his gaze down to the foot of the bed. Knowing by the atmosphere of the room that the Beetle Man was there again. Had come for him. In the doorway.

Floorboards creaked. The priest at Sunday School told him the noises he heard were the house's foundations relaxing after a day of constant activity. Ben knew different. Staring at the blank ceiling of the small room, breath leaving his mouth and nostrils in tendrils of icy smoke. Listening to the sounds that edged their way through the silence. Closer. There, moving twisted through the dim. Close. The sound of fabric against fabric. Skin against skin. Another creaking of floorboards. The dragging of feet sliding softly, delicately over the carpet of his bedroom floor. He felt it then. The heavy, magnetic atmosphere of being watched. Observed. He couldn't move. Frozen in place. The dragging of feet moving closer to his bedside. Closer. The wet sound of something breathing. Staring at the ceiling. Too frightened. Too cowardly to look at the thing looming there, leering down at him with eyes that glistened like black glass. Something brushed against his leg. Trickled. His bowels unclamped. The stench of shit and sickness filling the room

His eyes screamed. His mouth screamed. He screamed into an abyss. He screamed the word 'mother'.

"DETECTIVE, ARE YOU all right?"

Ben snapped his head towards the woman. Gripping at the oak stair banister. Woozy. Told himself it was the whiskey. Mouth full of a metallic saliva. He swallowed. Coughed, clearing his throat.

"Yes, yes, I'm quite fine. Just a dizzy spell. Haven't had time to eat something today. Running myself somewhat ragged. Please don't worry yourself, Mrs. Goodman."

"Please let me fix you something. A sandwich? A glass of water, perhaps?"

"No, no, Mrs. Goodman. I'm fine, fine. Thank you. I've not much time."

"Are you sure? You're looking rather peaked."

"All right, a glass of water then, thank you," he said, to shut her up.

She nodded, went down the hall towards a large kitchen and Ben stood staring at the front door before following after her. Wiping at his hand with a handkerchief he couldn't even remember yanking from his pocket. A grandfather clock chimed, Ben startled, chewed at his bottom lip. A snippet from a dead author's novel repeating in his head, '*You can never go home again.*' But he was home. The atmosphere. The light. The smell. He was home. Feeling like a young child, he shuffled further into the home as though it were the mandibles of a slumbering creature.

The kitchen was large, traditional and joined to a lavishly furnished dining room. A chandelier captured light and scattered reflections.

Mrs. Goodman smiled, her eyes dull and unchanged, motioning him to the large mahogany dining table.

"Please rest yourself, Detective," she said, running the faucet over her fingers. She followed Ben's gaze to a large painted family portrait hung on the far wall. "Had that painted last year. Can't for the life of me remember the name of the artist, but he's incredibly skilled. James was a little monkey and wouldn't sit still for a singular minute. As though he had ants in his pants."

Ben blanched, pulled at his collar and undid another button. Suddenly choked. She placed the glass of water on a leather coaster in front of him. Leaning her breasts close to his face. Ben breathed in the scent of her. The natural scent of a woman. Blanched again. Thought of his mother. Pushed the thought away. Li Yu then. Her hands to his face. She'd deceived him. He squeezed his eyes shut. Counted. Counted. Counted. Reaching for the glass, he noticed a fingerprint smudged at the top near the rim and withdrew his hand again, pushing the coaster a few inches away from him.

"My apologies, Mrs. Goodman, I really appreciate your hospitality, but I'm very pushed for time."

"I'd like to show you James' room, if I may."

"Come again?"

"I'd like to show you his bedroom, please. James' room. I'd like for you to see it," she massaged her throat as she said it. Her lips quivered. Maroon red. Desperate. Beautiful. Heartbroken. Needy.

HIS BEDROOM COLD. Freezing. Goosebumps speckling his pale skin. Toys on a shelf with eyes that glistened in the moonlight. He stared at the model airplanes twisting on string like dead men hanging from the ceiling.

Fabric on fabric.

Skin on skin.

"I'M SORRY, Mrs. Goodman, I really don't see how that would be helpful in finding your son," Ben began to scratch at his face. Tried to stop himself but couldn't. Mrs. Goodman's eyes sucked him in. Drowning him. Icy blue. Desperate. He looked down at the table. The way the light crept from the window across its surface. A milky white figure reaching out to him. Chest tight. Breath struggling out of his nostrils in trickles. He gripped at his thighs, squeezing until the muscles ached, unable to gaze into those drowning eyes again.

"Anything to have my son back again. Anything that'll help. Possibly help. Please!"

Her scent again drifting across the table. Intoxicating. Dizzying. He made a show of glancing at his wristwatch. It had stopped days ago. He hadn't wound it. Their eyes locked and he felt like a small boy again.

"I'm very sorry. I'm sorry. Mrs. Goodman, I am very sorry, I am. But I have another appointment that just, it just won't wait," he stuttered.

"Please don't go." She wailed it out. Pathetic. Heartbroken. Beautiful.

Ben got up quickly and walked towards the front of the house. She pursued him. Her hand on his shoulder again as though it had always been there. A childhood memory he'd carried with him always.

"Please, Detective. Please. Please. Please," she begged, clinging to him. A woman suffocating in sorrow. Alone in a house much too large and haunted. "Please, just look at his room. If you see what a good boy he was... *He is*! If you see what a good boy he *is*. You won't give up. You'll find him. Please find him."

Ben spun around, grabbed her by the shoulders, shaking her. "I'm going to find him. I promise you."

"You swear it? You swear it to God?" Those eyes on him again. sickening. Intoxicating.

"Yes, I swear it," he murmured.

"On your soul?" she asked.

He let her go. Stepped back. "What?"

"Do you swear on your eternal soul, Detective?"

The boy's face pulsing like a heartbeat in his mind, Ben put his hands on her shoulders again. Heat radiated off of the mother like sickness. His arms tremored for him to release her, but she pushed her body against his. Her breasts heavy against his chest. The air seemed to shimmer. A mother to a missing child. Mother. The boy. It was wrong. He wanted to move his body away from hers but, as if by magnetism, was compelled closer. Could feel her heart beating. Her eyes bathing him. She needed him.

"Yes," he breathed.

"Say it! Swear on your soul!" Her mouth so close to his. Her breasts. The inside of her thigh sliding around his.

"I swear on my soul, I'll bring your son back to you."

She exhaled hard. Ben tasted her breath. The natural scent of a woman. Mother. Her eyes sucked him in. Drowning him. Icy blue. Desperate. Beautiful. Needy. Intoxicating.

Ben pulled her closer. Kissed her mouth. She fell hard against him. Pushing and pulling at each other's bodies and clothes. Then at the bottom of the stairs he was inside her. His hands to her face, seeing Li Yu there. Hurting Li Yu. Needing Li Yu. Loving mother. Li Yu. Mother. Her whispering the words "Please, please, please, please, please, please, please," over and over again as he thrust into her with each exhalation. And then finishing inside her. As though plummeting from a great height. In the emptiness after, horrified by what he had done, the guilt in him like a disease again, he yanked up his slacks.

"What did you make me do?! What did you make me do?! We shouldn't have done that. It was a mistake. A mistake. It wasn't right. It's not right." The voice not his own. Higher pitched. Unbroken and broken all at once. The mother stared at him dreamily. Eyes half shut to the light. Ben whining under his breath. Drenched in contaminated sweat. Filthy flesh burning. Needing to wash. Scrub. Soap. Purify.

Ben stumbled out of the hallway entrance and slammed the front door on her satisfied eyes. A jolt of pain ripping through his guts. His fingers to his face hysterically trying to scratch away images from his childhood and the desperate promise he had just made to a God he wasn't even sure he believed in anymore. Gambling his soul, unsure of how much it was worth in the first place. The maid was still outside, sweeping, and caught him in her arms as he staggered out onto the sidewalk.

"Are you all right, Detective? What on earth is the matter?"

He screamed into her face and shoved the filthy bitch into the gutter. She let out a startled cry as her skull cracked against the curb silencing her. Ben felt her pulse. Dragged her onto the sidewalk. The blood made a trail like a child's drawing. Tripping over his own feet to the Cadillac. He beat his fists down on the bonnet. Hyperventilating. Counting to seven. Lucky seven. Fucking lucky fucking seven. Squeezing his eyes shut. It seemed as though he was losing everything about himself in this case. Everything. If he didn't find the boy, he didn't know how much of himself would remain. Barely a stain on tarmac.

London, England
Saturday, February 20ᵗʰ, 1926

HER FACE IN the crowd. Paris. The City of Light. Place de la Concorde. He, in his dress uniform. Stomach filled with bread and wine. Lungs full of crisp fresh air and good tobacco. Their eyes met. Blue on grey. The crowd surged and she was gone for a moment in the waving of flags and hands. Faces contorted with joy. He pushed his way through the bodies. Her again. She held his eyes longer. Smiled. Swaying. Electricity on the air before thunder. Lightning. Flowers in her hair. Daisies tied into a crown. Like drops of snow against the gold of her hair. Full-lipped. She mouthed words to him, but they were meaningless in the elated roar of the crowds, gathered to celebrate the end of The Great War. Her lips so completely red against her cream-colored skin, creating intricate shapes. Giggling. Two words or a single two-syllabled one. He shrugged theatrically. She beckoned to him. Drawing him in.

Only weeks ago, he was in the Hell of the trenches. The Somme. The dead. The rats. The constant bombardments, infinite shelling. The stench. The fear. Going over the top. The whistles. The crack of rifles. The unforgiving roar of machine gun fire. The overwhelming mud. Damp. Rot. Decay.

Now Paris. The sunshine warm on his face. A beautiful girl smiling at him with lips painted a rich blood red. Golden hair like English Summertime. He shoved a grinning old fool out of the way, elbowed through the mass of bodies huddled around the fountain to get to her. As though he had been wading through the shit, the madness and the dying from the front line all the way to Paris just to find this girl. An absurd notion in his chest where the dog tags clattered against his skin, he was going to marry this woman. And then he was next to her. His hand on the small of her back. The fabric of her blouse as smooth as skin underneath his fingertips. The scent of her perfume bringing tears to his eyes. She threw her head back and laughed into the space above the crowd. Eyes sparkling like the water catching a golden sun in the fountain pond, dancing like flares ablaze over No Man's Land.

"What's your name?" he shouted.

She cupped a small, slender fingered hand around an ear adorned with a single pearl.

Someone fell into his back and he elbowed them away. Repeated himself, closer, his lips touching the side of her face as he spoke. Almost tasting her. She didn't pull away. On the contrary, leaning closer into him, engulfing him, she shouted her name and the sound of it akin church bells he'd heard a long time ago, somewhere beautiful, "Margaux." The girl he was going to marry. Margaux.

FINGERS DRAGGED SPITEFULLY across his face, startled him awake.

A song sung whispered, strangled. Gurgled from somewhere beneath darkness. Sewer water in the night.

A flash of white rippling through the air like smoke.

A creak of staircase. A dog barked repetitively and crazed from somewhere in the neighborhood. William's throat an old leather dry.

A whisper of words. Hushed. Confessional. Conspiratorial.

He reached out, placing his trembling hand on the sleeping form of his wife beside him. Kicked back the covers cursing. The boy was out of his bed again. He heard the footsteps making their way down the stairs, dragged softly over the oriental rugs and shined hardwood flooring.

He would give the simple child a clip around the ear, drag the little bugger back to bed. He'd regretted his actions the previous night. Dragging the boy from the bathtub to the cold street outside. It wasn't right. He'd been under too much pressure. Drinking too much. How he needed a drink. The constant feeling of thirst, maddening. He'd put the boy back into bed, make himself a drink. Just something to help him sleep again. Warm him up. The moon burning as bright as the sun through the bedroom windows, piercing his eyelids. Yes, he needed a drink to sleep. Thirsty all the fucking time.

He made his way through the chilly darkness and down the stairs. Not caring if his footsteps awoke his wife. Light coming dimly from the lamp in the kitchen. He'd told the bloody boy not to touch the fucking lamps. Disobeying little... A giggle floated down the hallway then. William froze, gripping at the banister. Swaying. His head cocked to the side, listening. He heard the ticking of clocks, the demented dog barks, the pipes in the walls humming softly. Nothing more. No, no, nothing more. Just a touch of gin, that would set him right. Stepping down from the stairs into the hallway still using the banister railing for support. Edging his way towards the kitchen. The light from the lamp a flickering ghostly yellow like the gas the krauts had pumped over the ruptured, torn asunder fields of France. So bright and yet so damned cold. Seeping across the floors and walls. An icy finger ran its nail up his spine and into the back of his scalp. He shuddered. Needing a drink like lover's kiss. He pushed at the door, and it creaked open wide slowly. Ear piercingly loud. Grinding his teeth together.

She was at the sink. Her back to him. Head tilted to the side in thought. A sweet smell like lavender and almonds in the icy air.

He growled, let go of the breath he'd been holding down in his throat, "Jesus Christ, woman! What the bloody Hell are you doing up at this hour? Thought you were in bed."

His wife ignored him, and he cursed in her direction, taking a bottle of gin down from a shelf, unscrewing the lid and taking a long, deep drink.

He sat down on a kitchen chair, sighed. "Ah, that certainly hit the spot. Just a wee nightcap to soften the pillows and sheets. What are you doing, wife?"

No movement of acknowledgment. Her back to him. Long blonde hair tangled in clumps from sleep. The lamp flickered, dancing erratically as though threatening to extinguish itself. The stink of almonds growing stronger. Sickly sweet. His eyes watered.

"Oi, woman! Are you sleeping on your feet or what now?"

He took another long hit of the bottle, squinting his eyes at the back of his wife's white nightgown. Brown stains puddled and smeared around the arse as though she'd shit herself. Not a white nightgown at all, but a dirty white dress. Neither a smell of almonds, but the stench of rot. His breath snagging on his teeth. The kitchen freezing. The thing in front of him giggled, bones in its neck grinding together as it turned slowly to face him. The skin of its face stretched tight. A grin cut hysterically into its purpled features. Eyes a rotten milk white.

You're gonna be in so much trouble…

The flame flickered. Died.

Dead.

William hurled the bottle at the thing, cursing as the darkness wrapped its pitch-black coils around his throat.

Muttering a Hail Mary with gin tainted breath.

A whisper so close to his face he could feel the humid, decomposing breath on his cheeks. *When I'm dying...*

William bucked in the chair.

The chair legs danced and screeched.

Scalding piss splashed down his legs, puddling on the floor.

A clock struck twelve times like a condemnation and William screamed until he choked. Strangled. Gasping. Choked.

The North End, Boston, USA
Tuesday, February 19th, 1946

HANOVER STREET. The Italian North End.

Ben leaned against the hood of his Cadillac, massaging his temples, across the street from Buccola's main hangout, the Italian café. The death throes of the sun cast the place in a coppery, blood-tinged light and his reflection in the large storefront windows rippled like murky water. His guts all knotted up. Pressure behind his eyes. Body aching. Cold, he buttoned his jacket. Blew into his cupped hands. The smell of her there. Sick. He was sick.

Buccola inside sat at a table yapping with his underboss Giuseppe Lombardo, the human personification of a razor blade. The man rumored to have murdered Stevie's brother years before.

Ben squinted into the café.

Checked his wristwatch.

Checked it again.

Trying to wipe the lingering scent of Mrs. Goodman from his hands on the front of his slacks. He'd washed them until the old, dried sores split open again and oozed puss. The smell remained. Unrelenting.

Li Yu in his mind like a moving picture show repeating a reel.

He needed to see her face.

One look into her eyes and he would know.

He scratched at his neck.

Talk with Buccola, get the whereabouts of the bald fuck, drive over to China Town.

Talk to Li Yu. Find out what the fuck was going on. Get the boy from wherever he was being held. Kill the bald fuck. Bring the boy back to Mrs. Goodman. All sins absolved. All wounds healed. Start a new life in Los Angeles. A good plan. The only plan. His jaw locked, clicked as Ben murmured the repetitive words. Slipping a hand into the pocket of his slacks and fingering the ring there. Diamond. Gold. Mother's. She'd pulled it loosely from her skeletal finger as she lay dying in a private room of Mass General hospital. Told him to give it to the woman he loved. He had. That woman had left it with a fucking 'Dear John' letter on the kitchen table and fled back to Los Angeles where she came from. Had taken his daughters with her. Now he would give it to Li Yu. Start again. He didn't give a fuck if she'd lied. Things could be fixed. Bones grow back stronger at the broken parts. A fractured arm grows back stronger. He needed her. Had been a mess before her. She gave him order. Symmetry.

Yes, he'd find the kid and things would get better for him. For both of them. California. The City of Angels. He'd see his daughters again. Start a new life with a new wife. A clean life. He'd kick the junk. Wouldn't need it any longer. He'd be clean. Pure. Baptized.

Save the kid, save himself. Save the boy. Save himself. Save the kid, save himself. Save himself. Couldn't explain it, but there it was. A truth, like a bullet ripping through the center of everything and bringing his life meaning.

He scratched at his stomach. Pinched the bridge of his nose, working the fingers up between his tired eyes. Could feel another headache rolling in like storm clouds. Tumorous mind. He cleared his throat and spat the contents far away from him.

Buccola glanced over, raised his bushy eyebrows in surprise. Pulled at the knot in his necktie. Lifted an expresso cup to his lips, frowning into it as he drank. Spoke animated, gesturing his hand to someone out of view. A couple of seconds later, a skinny Italian with wavy, greasy hair pomaded to the side, a large, loud pinstriped suit hanging from his body, swung open the door and waved Ben over impatiently. A hand shoved inside his jacket. Ben walked over slow; his badge clasped in his outstretched clammy hand. Reflecting terminal rays of sun. The wind cut through him like a blade. Holding his body taut. Trying not to shiver. The Italian had the face of a starved rat. Acne scars. An overbite and eyes like dirty one cent coins. Moving jerkily like an insect tangled in a spider's web. Revolting. Ben's stomach plummeted. Flip flopped. He swallowed saliva that tasted of exhaustion and the whiskey he'd been nipping at since he'd done what he had done. Since he'd been in that house. With the child's mother. Mother. A guilt like acid pooled at the bottom of his guts eating away at his insides. Mother.

"Hey! He wants to know what the fuck you want?" The Rat said in a thick New York accent.

Ben snapped his head up, startled, lost in his own thoughts. "Tell him I'm here as a Boston police Detective, nothing more."

"That badge don't mean so much to you or us. We know who you are. Know all about you."

"Just fucking tell him I wish to speak for five minutes. It's about a missing child."

The Italian pulled an ugly grin, eyeballed him up and down, slow. Disappeared back into the café, the door swung shut and Ben looked at his face in the smokey reflection of the window. A shadowed creature stared back. He heard mumbled Italian chatter. After a moment, the Rat came and pushed the door open again. "You can come in, but you leave the piece in the automobile."

Ben almost laughed out loud, "No, no, no, that's not going to happen."

"Your fucking piece stays in the fucking car or you don't fucking come inside," Rat Fuck said.

Ben hesitated.

The boy's face burst like a supernova in the jagged mess behind his eyes again, as though begging him to hurry. To be quick. Screaming. A cockroach scurried across his cheek and forced itself into a nostril and disappeared. Ben dry gagged. The Italian stood there repeating himself like he was practicing his English intonation. "Piece stays in the fucking car or you don't come in here. Simple as that."

"Fuck!" Ben twisted around, went back to the Caddie, swung the door open, pulled the .38 from his shoulder holster and pushed it under the driver's seat. Slammed the door closed. Locked it. Strolled back to the café. Stopped. Spun around. Returned to the vehicle and pulled on the door handle. Counted to seven. Touched it. Counted to seven. Breathless. Touched the handle. Unlocked it. Opened the door and slammed it shut again. Counted. One. Two. Three. Four. Five. Six. Seven. Cursing under his breath. The kid in his mind whispering silently with lips a dark, cold blue. Black, shiny cockroaches for eyes. Pulsing. Shitting out eggs from their fat abdomens. Hurry! Hurry! Hurry! Hurry! Four times. That cursed fucking number. Fuck! He stumbled back to the café. Stopped. Hesitated. The Rat stood there, tapping a wingtip impatient. "What the fuck you doing over there? We ain't got all fucking day."

"Mind your own fucking business. Your own fucking business. Mind your own fucking business," Ben spat. Panting. Saliva dribbled down his stubbled chin.

STEPHEN J. GOLDS

The Rat stood eye fucking him, sneering for a moment, and then cut his hand through the air, motioning Ben forward.

"All right, I gotta check you over, see, make sure you ain't carrying nothing else," he said, running his greasy hands over Ben's body in the doorway. The man stank of stale sweat and cheap cologne. Ben swallowed bile and grimaced, glaring over at Buccola and Lombardo talking machine gun heatedly at the table nearest the large floor to ceiling window.

"Okay, he's all right." Rat Fuck nodded over to his boss and Ben pushed past him into the café.

The interior a dusty kind of hot, smelling sickly of three-day old coffee, licorice and burnt pastries. Ben peeped at the door to the office. Non-descript. Closed.

Buccola, dressed to the nines in a dark grey, tailored three-piece suit, blood red cravat, nodded at Ben, wiping at his fingers and mouth with a paper napkin.

"What a pleasant and unexpected surprise this is. You coming to us like this. What is it you are wanting, Detective Hughes?" The first time Ben had ever heard Buccola's voice. Surprised at how refined the gangster and murderer spoke.

"I came here to ask you a couple of questions pertaining to an active investigation."

Buccola raised his fat caterpillar eyebrows and turned in his chair to Lombardo, muttered something in Italian. They laughed heartily. Lombardo glaring at Ben with eyes pitch black, lit a cigarillo and shrugged, clearing his throat.

"An active investigation and you came here to ask some questions, huh? Am I needing my lawyer with me now, Detective? You have me worried; I must say." Buccola leaned back in his seat and tilted his head to the side, jutting his chin in the air. Arrogant piece of shit.

"No, it hasn't reached that point, yet. I want a few answers and you're the man that's going to provide me with them."

"Am I really, Detective Hughes? Are you alone? I don't want to answer any questions in front of a crowd of bulls in blue, you know? I'm a very discreet man, have a reputation to uphold."

Buccola grinned, waving his finger at Ben like a disapproving father. Ben thought of his own father. The twentieth anniversary of his death was the day after tomorrow. Surprised he still remembered the man at all. A man with a head full of sickness and a heart full of hate. Haunted by the ghosts of all the evil things he had done. One thing Ben and the old man didn't have in common. Ben wasn't haunted by anything he'd done. All the killing and all the stealing he'd done were more than justified. No, Ben wasn't haunted by what he had done to others. He was haunted by the ghosts of the things that had been done to him. Betrayed his whole fucking life.

"Hey!" Buccola slapped a hand down on the tabletop. Ben flinched. "You don't come in here and waste my time. Are there other bulls around my business now, or no?"

"No," Ben swallowed. The hiss of the expresso machine behind him pain inducing.

"No? No, what?" Lombardo sneered.

"No, I'm alone as your eyes can very well see. However, my partner is waiting down the block with a few other officers, real head breakers just in case there's any trouble."

Buccola's lips pulled tight across his lower face. He said something softly in their language to the Rat and then grinned back at Ben. Eyes a narrowed pitch-black like a snake coiled to strike. Nudged Lombardo. "This man, he speak so, how do you say, *raffinato*, not like these Boston dogs in the South. *Britannico*."

Lombardo pulled his mouth down, inspected his fingernails.

"Alright, okay, I'll hold my patience and listen to your questions. We talk business now." He gestured airily to the chair opposite him. "Please sit, Detective. You want an expresso? I have the beans imported especially from Palermo. They're a robusta arabica blend. The very best. The beans here in this country, they taste like shit, don't you think? How about something to eat, perhaps?"

"No, thank you and I'm fine to stand."

"You treat me with such rudeness and *vilipendio* in my own place of business, yet you expect me to answer your questions? I thought you were a man to reason with. A gentleman. Perhaps, I was wrong about this, huh?" he said over Ben's shoulder to the Rat.

The Rat bit down on a toothpick and giggled. Lombardo sipped expresso. The sounds made Ben shudder and cringe. He wiped sweat from his face with the forearm of his jacket. Pulled out the chair from the table, sat down opposite the two Italians, and placed his badge on the crisp white tablecloth. Rubbing his hot, clammy palms on his slacks and pinching at the creases. Twisted his head to glance over at the Rat, standing behind the coffee bar making an expresso from the steaming, silver machine that seemed to be hissing louder as the minutes rotted away. A telephone attached to the wall, the receiver cradled at his ear by his shoulder and cheek. Grunting Italian down the line.

"Now, that's better, isn't it? Like we're all old friends, yes? Talking of friends, how is my old *amici* Stefano? You see him lately?"

"I saw him today. He's good. Tip fucking top. An Olympian," Ben pulled his lips into something resembling a smile. A muscle at the top of his left cheek twitching uncontrollably.

Lombardo grinned, hissing out Italian to Buccola. They talked low animatedly for a moment and Ben waited for them to finish. Touching his badge and counting to seven in his head.

"He's good, he says," Buccola said in English to Lombardo jerking a thumb at Ben. They turned their focus on Ben tight lipped. He glanced out of the window at the Cadillac. His .38 underneath the seat. Suddenly miles away. In his stomach, it felt as though he were on the surface of the moon. Cold. Isolated. A child in a bathtub. A child naked in bed, shivering. Fingertips like ants scurrying over his body. Fuck! The boy's face there again behind his eyes. The child's jaw dropped open in a silent scream. Insects poured crawling from the gaping orifice.

Buccola knocked on the table with a fist. Ben snapped back into the café.

"Wakey-wakey! Well, go ahead and ask your questions, Detective. I'm very curious as to why you had the balls to come here into my world today," Buccola said, sipping his expresso.

"I want to know where I can find a man with no hair. No hair. I want to know where I can find a man with no hair. No hair. None." Ben bit into his bottom lip hard. Swallowed. Fuck, he couldn't afford to show weakness now. He pinched hard into the flesh of his thigh. Took a napkin from the chrome dispenser and wiped at his hands.

The mobsters glanced at each other frowning. Buccola shrugged. "You work in Vice, do you not? You should know where to look. If *that's* your thing, Detective. Bald *men*," he winked, clucked his tongue at the end of the sentence. The Italians hahaha'd.

Ben ignored the insult and licked his sandpaper lips. Left eye twitching. Pulsing. The chime of the telephone receiver being replaced back on its cradle causing him to snap around, checking behind him. Rat Fuck slurping at his expresso, playing with what looked like rosary beads in his fist. Ben hid his trembling hands underneath the tabletop.

"This man is an associate of yours. Comes around here. You talk business with him in *that* back room, I'm told," Ben said, turning away slowly from the Rat to look at Buccola again. Nodded towards the locked door.

"And who told you about this, Detective?"

"President Truman. We play golf together on Saturdays. Who told me isn't fucking important. What is important, is that you tell me exactly what I want to know or you're going to have a lot of mick cops in here drinking your shit Italian coffee and busting up your business."

"Irish cops. Now, that's a very frightening threat, or maybe not, considering most of the paddy fucks are on my pad, taking my money. But to be reasonable, I'll entertain you a little more. Listen to me, I don't know who would tell you such lies, Detective. But I know no bald men. There is only Joseph, here," Buccola slapped Lombardo on the back. "His hair, it is receding, No? He almost has no hair. You're almost bald, aren't you, Joseph?"

Ben licked his dry lips again. Swallowed, "If it was this little fuckhead sat on your lap that I wanted, Boston PD would be tearing this filthy little rathole of a café to pieces already."

"Nice bedside manner you got there, Detective. Your father and mother didn't teach you no manners when you were a child, huh?" Lombardo said.

Ben blanched deep. Eyeballed Lombardo. Placed his fists on the tabletop. Buccola dropped a hand on Lombardo's arm to calm him without taking his eyes away from Ben.

"I have many friends. I'm an important man. Many people want to be my friend. Many people come here to ask my counsel.

But I must say, I don't know anyone as ridiculous as you... How did you say? With no hair."

"No hair at all. No eyebrows. Distinctive. A man that is sick. Might have had plastic surgery in the past. I believe he knows the whereabouts of a missing child. Does that refresh your memory? Remember anything now?"

Buccola's eyes flashed. He knew. He fucking knew.

"No, again, I'm afraid. I can't say that I am reminded of anyone significant. And I don't know anything about missing bambini."

Ben wanted to scream the word LIAR into the mobster's face. Buccola finished his expresso, sighed, went on, "Now, I have a question for you, Detective. When did you last see Stefano Wallace? Today, you said. What time was it?"

"I came here to ask the questions, Buccola, not answer them."

"All right, I'll ask another easier question. How about this one? Did you know Alberto was Joseph's nephew? His youngest sister's youngest son, isn't that correct, Joseph?"

"Yeah, that's about right." Lombardo's eyes, something thrashing in the darkness of them. Glimmering like switchblades in moonlight.

"I don't have the *slightest* fucking idea what you people are talking about."

"You don't? That's strange, he was murdered today in his rooming house, shot to death, by a piece of shit looking a lot like you, we're told," Buccola said.

Frankie. Fantino. Alberto Fantino. Fuck!

Ben went to stand, Buccola and Lombardo leapt across the table and grabbed a wrist each, holding his arms fixed down firmly to the tablecloth.

Ben screamed "No!" High pitched. Loathing himself for it.

The Rat suddenly behind him, snapping something long and thin tightly over his head, around his throat. The rosary, a wire noose to hang him.

Ben bucked in the chair.

The chair legs danced and screamed echoes of Frankie's death.

The Rat's stinking, panted breath on the side of his face. Diseased. Contagious. Tuberculosis.

Strangled. Choked.

Expresso splashed across the table. Coffee spread into the white cloth like blood stains.

The heels of Ben's shoes made sharp tap, tap, tap, tap sounds on the hard floor. Tap dancing into death ridiculously.

"Your boss Stefano is dead like his fucking brother and so are you, Detective!" Lombardo hissed through gritted teeth.

"*I'm a fucking cop! A fucking cop!*" Ben choked the words out. Rasping.

"Not no more, you ain't. You're a dead cop, you fuck!" Buccola grunted, laughed. The Rat snorting humid, rotten breath into his ear like a childhood secret.

Face burning, a balloon full of boiling blood about to burst. Ben sucked air.

Gasping. Choking.

Ants scurried over and around his vision. Filthy black dots growing grotesque in size. A harsh insectile buzzing in his ears. Rocking back and forth in the chair. Knees smashing into the underside of the tabletop. Crockery shook and chimed.

Ben screamed. Wrenched his feet up, pushed hard against the table with all his remaining strength.

The chair fell back, Ben and the Rat tumbled hard to the floor together.

Gasping. Choking.

He kicked out, flailing, crawling on all fours towards the door. Gasping air.

Rat Fuck pounced on his back; arms wrapped around Ben's throat. Lombardo and Buccola barking in Italian. Ben tried to scream again. Sucked air. Span around, stumbling backwards towards the plate glass window. Pushed back. Bucking. The Rat yelled out. The window exploded. Glass rattled, smashing to the stone sidewalk. Ben fell cruelly to the ground. His head struck the pavement. Dazed. Biting into his tongue to wake himself the fuck up. Blood ran hot into his eyes. The universe went a blood red.

Rat Fuck crouched groaning in broken glass like scattered ashes, holding his head in his hands. Ben fumbled, panting, stretching, grabbed at the largest shard of glass in his reach and swung it into the Rat's back in between the shoulder blades. The shard snapped. The Rat Fuck screeched. Fell prone. Moaning. Crying. A blue Buick drove by slow. Ben glimpsed a pale child's face in the back window staring as it swept past.

Struggling to his feet, holding his throat in his blood-sticky hands, Ben stumble-ran to the Cadillac. Wiping the blood from his eyes with the sleeve of his jacket. Choking. Hacking. Coughing. He fumbled with the door handle. Locked! Fuck! Screaming cracked and croaked numbers. He struggled getting the key into the lock. The mechanism clicked. He ripped the door wide. Gasping for air. Swung himself behind the wheel. Choking. Stabbed the key into the ignition. Wheezing. Gagging. Gunned the engine. Wrenched the .38 from under his seat.

He pulled the car out hard, swerving in front of a Hudson. Horns blasted. Tires squealed. The Cadillac screamed down the street. He glanced back over his shoulder and spotted Lombardo kneeling over the Rat. Buccola out of sight.

AS SOON AS he hit the freeway Ben relaxed. He took his finger off of the .38's trigger and placed it carefully on the passenger seat. Exhaling deep. Wheezy. Swerved to the side of the freeway and sat sucking oxygen, hoarse, his head in his trembling hands.

He felt the strange weight of the envelope The Chief had given him in the inside pocket of his jacket. He slid it out and ripped it open with trembling hands. Inside thirteen words scribbled on a white card. Thirteen. A fucking cursed number. Ben counting to seven to try and counteract the poison of the number as he read.

'WORD FROM MULTIPLE INFORMANTS: *THE DAGOS ARE MOVING ON YOU TODAY. BE READY.*'

Fuck!!

Ben screamed himself mute, beating his fists into the steering wheel.

London, England
Sunday, February 21st, 1926

WILLIAM STILL TREMBLING, headache a rapture from Hell, jumped into a passing taxi and told the driver to take him to Gerrard Street, Soho and be quick about it. The driver mumbled and William tried to settle down into the cold leather seats, still not used to travelling by motorized vehicles. The vibrations, noise and petrol stink were jarring. Made him queasy. He made sure the driver had his beady little eyes on the road, then slipped the Webley revolver from his heavy tweed jacket, popped the cylinder and checked the load. He enjoyed the weight of the revolver in his hand. Reassuring. His lucky shooter. Not so lucky for the dead officer he'd taken it from over in France but lucky for him all the same. He was going to talk with the owners of a club on Gerrard Street, an Italian called Darby Sabini, who he detested. A midget dago who'd married a white Englishwoman and now pimped whores. The little man always dressed over extravagantly and surrounded himself with savages imported from Sicily. A cunt, but a dangerous one. The other owner was a woman, a jumped-up divorcee named Kate Meyrick. They'd sent word that protection payments were going to stop. An Italian and a woman. Could've been Jews. Chiseling every penny from the protection payments from the very beginning. Now they foolishly thought that because William had a little bother at the stationhouse, they could stop payments or pay someone else. William was going to tell the little dago bastard and that stuck up bitch in person, himself, that the cravat wearing son of a whore and the dyke had another think coming.

As they passed Hyde Park, he coughed up phlegm, wound down the window and spat it into the street. She was standing there. Her back to him again as though gazing out into the browns and faded greens of the winter park.

"Stop!" William shouted.

"Beg your pardon, Sir. I thought you were off to Soho."

"Stop this fucking thing now!"

William jumped out of the taxi, wiping dribble from his chin.

"Sir! You need to pay the fare!" the driver called out, leaning over the front seats.

"Just bloody wait here a moment, won't you? I think I saw an old friend of mine," William said over his shoulder, making his way toward the ghostly figure, his hand grasping the revolver tightly in his pocket. He shoved his way through the foot traffic. Lost sight of her in a small, passing group and then glimpsed her again.

Golden hair hanging tangled down her back, catching the morning light dully. The filthy dress. Swaying slightly in the breeze. Mutt-like growling crawled up from William's chest and rumbled out of his throat. Uncontrollable. He'd not uttered those wretched sounds from his lips since going over the top at the Somme. He clenched his jaw to stop himself from screaming. He was on her then, squeezing his eyes shut, grabbing the little bitch's arm and spinning her around.

"Well, I say!" an old lady shrieked. Hitting him in the face with a small fabric bag with a glass bottle inside that caught painfully at his brow. Her face the tint of a Royal Mail postbox. People stopped and stared.

"I'm sorry, Mam. Thought you were someone else." He backed away from her. Bumping into someone else who shoved him hard away. "Watch where you're bloody going, wino." William fell to the damp ground, smacking his head on the cobblestones. The world span. The old lady still shrieking, "you'll be sorry."

He got back up fast, rubbing at his head. Face burning. Stumbled back to the taxi. Glancing back. The hag smiling gap-toothed, corpselike.

He swung back into the auto-vehicle and told the man to drive. The woman's shrill voice still pursuing him.

"You're gonna be in so much trouble. In this life and the next one," she hollered.

The growls escaping from his throat growing louder. Going over the top of the trenches in France. The shrieking of the officer's whistle. The bombardments falling silent. He pressed his palms to his ears and shouted at the driver again. "Drive! Just fucking drive, man!"

THE 43 CLUB had undergone numerous name changes, been closed down any number of times and Kate, the paddy 'Night Club Queen', had been jailed a sight lot more. There was very little about the woman William liked. Wouldn't even have thrown her a fuck if she'd begged him for it. She'd appeared from nowhere. A rumor brought to life in Soho's dancehalls. Started out as a partner running tea dances for social elites, spreading herself thin across London's toff society. Opened a club, had it closed down. Aiding and abetting the sale of intoxicating liquor. Illicit alcohol. Opened another club had it closed down. Opened. Closed. Opened and closed. Playing games with The Met. Hide and seek. The woman wouldn't quit, even had her kids serving drinks and checking coats in the clubs. Had uppity coloreds playing jazz and banging underage white girls. She had expensive tastes in all regards. William was expensive. He knew she never liked him and had brought that little dago bastard, Sabini, in to try and cheapen him. Complicate matters. He had the place raided in '22 and again in '24 when they'd last been late for payments. A friendly reminder that they only existed because he allowed them to exist. He was sure they were fucking each other. He wouldn't put it past the woman to fuck a snake if she thought it would get her a step ahead. William Hughes wasn't going to be outsmarted and bullied by a fucking bastard wop and a woman. Not a lot of things in life were a certainty, but William Hughes was a certainty that they both needed another reminder of.

THE TAXI COUGHED to a stop outside the unassuming, low key exterior of the club. William tossed a handful of coins on the backseat and told the driver to fuck off.

He stood outside, waving the taxi's choking petrol fumes away and glanced around. The old hag still polluting his mind. Shook up. He'd been drinking too much, is all. Or drinking too little. The situation as of late had pushed him to an edge. Seeing things. Nothing more, nothing less. Just stress. His father had been as crazy as a shithouse rat. Had hung himself with a belt from a beam in the attic. Perhaps lunacy was in the Hughes bloodline. At that moment in time, he didn't give a shit.

He twisted the end of his moustache thoughtfully, frowning, and checked out the area. Gerrard Street early morning bustling. People toing and froing from work. Ghosts. William's fingers massaging the handle of the revolver in his pocket. Staring at the peeling green paint of the club's walls and the window's drawn natty, black curtains.

Sabini was a killer surrounded by killers. Fucking little monkeys that still lived in caves in their own countries. Self-doubt crawled into his mind. Wondered if he would see the outside again, the grey sky. But he chuckled, telling himself they didn't have the gonads to take him out. He had to go into the place, yes, it was the principle of the whole blasted thing he thought, as he pushed upon the heavy wooden doors and stepped into the darkness. A bastard wop and an upstart bitch in heat weren't going to better him. Didn't even need the money really. Hadn't needed it for a very long time. He'd just become addicted to the feeling he got in his nuts when people handed over the cash with that pathetic, helpless look slapped all over their faces. The same way he felt when he took a whore off the street to the courtyard in Brick Lane. He always took what he wanted. Hell to pay for those who tried to blue ball him. Yes, just on edge was all. Seeing things. Stress, it made people sick. He wasn't going to let them pull his pants down and bend him over. He was William Hughes, he'd survived the workhouses, starvation, disease, the trenches and machineguns in that fucking war. No, he wasn't going to be outdone, outwitted by those two upstart cunts.

The interior stank like an upper-class whorehouse and was pitch black except a purple light that trickled through the dark curtains like a blackeye on the face of a flower girl. He slipped the revolver from his jacket pocket and held it out at the hip as he made his way through the darkness of the entrance towards the main hall, where a woman's laughter leaked from. His eyes adjusting to the dim. Left arm outstretched into the darkness. Thought he felt a woman's breath on his face for a moment. Swallowed the whining that tried to pounce from his jaws. Passed the cloak room with empty hangers dangling from empty racks. Gallows. A seeping white light spreading like moonlight across mahogany fixtures and oriental wallpaper.

Sabini and Kate both turned to look at him from the center table they were seated at as he stepped into the main hall. Frozen still like people having their photograph taken or criminals caught in the middle of a crime. He slid his back against the wall and gave the room a close once over, the revolver still clasped at his hip.

"Oh really, Billy? Must you always make such entrances?" Kate laughed, silk glove to her lips. "Come and have a nice cup of tea. You can stir it with your little gun."

"You would probably prefer me to come in here with just my cock in my hand, wouldn't you?"

"No, not particularly, Billy darling. It's not vaudeville we do here, you know."

The bitch winked at Sabini. Sabini smirked.

"Shut your tart mouth. And I told you, my name ain't Billy."

"Come and sit down, William. We have a little business to discuss, yes?" Sabini patted the empty chair at the white clothed table. "And put the shooter away for goodness' sake. We aren't all primitives."

"Aren't we?" William said, but slid the Webley back into his jacket pocket, his hand not leaving the smooth pearl handle. He strolled over to the table. The sounds of his black oxfords on the dancefloor echoing like drumbeats.

"Why do you two have the foolish notion that you ain't gonna pay me? I want my money and I want it now."

"Don't loom over us like that, silly Billy. Do sit down." Kate sipped at her tea, pinky finger erect in the air.

Sabini pulled a face and shrugged. Twisting the end of his finely trimmed mustache the same way William was oft to do.

"Forever discussing money. Rather uncouth, old chap. Manners are quintessentially British, yes?" Sabini poured himself another tea from an intricate china teapot, spooned in sugar.

"I'll not be told how to behave by a cave dwelling bastard dago," William said, pulling the chair a few feet from the table and sitting down.

Sabini's eyes glimmered dark, he flashed a shit-eating grin.

"Darby dear, this repartee does rather stink. Let's just get on with business briskly, shall we? I have an appointment with a Lord at eleven. However, before we proceed, I must excuse myself to use the powder room."

Sabini swallowed, nodded, reached across the table and patted Kate's gloved hand delicately.

"Yes, my dear," he said, standing up. William stood up too. Not to be outdone by this fucking little monkey costumed in finery and jewelry. Kate stood and bowed. Held eye contact with Sabini too long. Avoided William's gaze as he sat back down. It was then that he knew he wasn't going to leave the 43 Club alive.

He watched Kate move across the dance floor, her heels tapping out morse code of a heartbeat, dress moving whisp-like, disappearing through a red door behind Sabini. William's hand against the revolver soaking wet. He pushed his chair further from the table, scanning the empty dance hall, the vacant stage.

"You're out, William. I would say I'm sorry, but I'm not. It's been a long time coming. Too long, in fact," Sabini said wiping his hands on a napkin. Screwing it up into a ball and dropping it onto the floor.

"What the fuck are you talking about?"

"We don't need you anymore and frankly we're quite relieved. I've killed many men. Slit a man's throat with a straight razor when I was but a boy. Eleven years old. He was the local butcher and he had been molesting my sister. I take no satisfaction from the killing of another human being. I'm certainly no saint, but you, William, you're truly repulsive. A rapist. A killer driven to kill for his own demented desires. You're a sick twisted man and you are of no use to us anymore."

William chewed at his bottom lip, pinched at the creases in his trousers, "I'll have this club raided and smashed to pieces before dinner time tonight."

"No, William. You won't. You won't do anything of the sort, Old Chap. You see someone more powerful than you has reached out to Kate and me. Offered us a deal, and it's a far better deal, I'm afraid to say."

"Horse shit."

"Is it? You don't have a single friend in the whole wide world, William. You're alone. Suspended from the MET, you have no power here. Not anymore. This new partnership we have with your Superintendent suits us so much better," he smiled faux-glum, sighed.

"Harewood? That's absolute horse shit. You're fucking bluffing, Sabini."

"There was one condition to the deal, however," Sabini croaked, pulling his own revolver from his jacket and pointing it rigidly across the table.

Footsteps from the far end of the dance floor. Two sets of heavy footfalls. William peeped two thick silhouettes creeping behind him in a mirrored wall. A bead of sweat slid from his temple to the corner of his lips, and he licked it away. Clucking his tongue.

"Do you like fucking, Darby?" William grinned, picking up the teapot and pouring himself steaming tea with his free hand.

"I beg your pardon." Sabini said, the revolver wavering slightly in his fist.

"I said, do you like fucking? Because that shooter I came in with is now underneath the table pointing at your tiny dago bollocks."

Sabini swallowed audibly. Waved a hand slowly out in the air. Stay back. The footsteps behind William stopped.

"There are men out back, out front. More on the way. You aren't leaving here, William."

William flicked his eyes to the right, over Sabini's shoulder. "No, maybe not, but I can kill the little bitch standing over there at least."

Sabini snapped his head behind him to look for Kate and as he did William threw the table up and down on him. Sabini tumbled to the floor, the table hitting him in the guts making him gasp out, cursing in Italian. Crockery shattered and utensils rattled. Gun shots blasted like artillery shells, William ducked and dived towards the red door Kate had disappeared through. The mirrored wall exploded. The piano thumped and splintered. He fired his Webley blindly falling towards the doorway. Kicked the door, splitting it from its lock. Ducking into a bright, peach-colored washroom. The lights burned his eyes, like seeing daylight for the first time.

Kate stood against the marble sink, toying with a long pearl necklace around her throat, and chewing at her finger. Modest and shy. All ladylike.

"It wasn't me, Billy! It wasn't me," she cried.

He clocked her hard across the chin with the revolver muzzle and she fell into his arms, a damsel in distress. Choking her in the crook of his left arm, he dragged her back out of the WC and onto the dance floor.

"May I have this last dance, Darling," he hissed into her ear as she gasped, struggling to stay on her feet. Her high heels clattered to the worn marble tiles.

Sabini crouched behind a table, the top of his head, dark eyes and the barrel of his revolver glittering like stars. The two other dago thugs stood closely together, one fat and one thin, brandishing bayonets.

"Looks as though you feeble-minded cunts brought knives to a gun fight, didn't you?" William laughed, hysterical. Squeezed down on the revolver's trigger. The fat thug's features erupted red, and he fell plummeting backwards onto the floor. The steel blade rattling to the floor. William swung his Webley towards the thinner thug, who dived under the nearest table.

"Don't do anything foolish now, Hughes!" Sabini called out.

Using Kate as a shield, William dragged her past the bar, down a short corridor. He bust open a side door and slid out into a side alley that stank of piss and damp. Another Italian leaning against a wall smoking a rolled-up cigarette went bug eyed and froze. William shot him in the chest. The gun echoed through the Soho streets like an exploding bomb. Kate wailed. Started screaming out. He shoved the revolver back into his pocket. Slammed the cunts skull hard against the wall. She collapsed comatose into a pile of broken wooden crates and William ran. Out of the alley. Into civilization. He ran and didn't stop. His legs burning. Tears flew from his eyes and laughter ragged from his mouth. Not a lot of things in life were a certainty, but William Hughes was always a God damned certainty you could bet on.

South Boston, USA
Tuesday, February 19ᵗʰ, 1946

A FEW BORED beat cops loitered around Dorchester Street. A half-assed roadblock. Fat man Leary sweeping shattered glass and soapy blood into the gutter.

Ben skidded, swerving his Cadillac up onto the sidewalk. Jumped out. The Irish pouring from the club at the sounds of screeching rubber, their hands shoved in their jackets. Spotting Ben, their shoulders slumped, and they fell into a cursing cluster, standing around, numb, dumbstruck. Ben pushed through the group, "Stevie?! Stevie?!"

Leary didn't even look up. A sponge lay in a puddle of pooled blood. Leary swept muttering to himself. Ben snatched the broom out of his hand, tossed it away. It clattered into the street making an empty, lonesome noise that Ben felt in his bones.

"Where's Stevie?" he croaked, grasping at his aching throat.

Leary's eyes were very small, and a raw kind of cold when he finally glanced into Ben's face. Seeing something there he didn't like, he looked away again, towards the broom laying in the street. Muttered, "he's gone. The meat wagon carted him off not two hours before."

"Gone where?"

"Gone. It doesn't matter where, now. The morgue. He's fucking gone. Let me tell you something, those cocksuckers shot him down like a dog in the street. Like a fucking dog, Ben. It's not fucking right. Not fucking right at all."

"He's gone?"

"Yeah, I just said he's fucking gone. He was dead before he even hit the ground, English. Where the fuck have you been anyhow? You should've been here. Should've been here."

Ben opened his mouth to answer but gagged on any words that might've come.

"I want those fucking greasers dead! Every single fucking one of the dirty cocksuckers! Dead. You hear me, English. Fucking dead! Dead! Those wop cunts, Buccola and Lombardo. All of them," Leary growled out the words through clenched teeth. Coughed, spluttering.

Ben fell-sat down hard on the curb; his shoulders slumped.

Staring at the filthy, cracked ground and not caring about the dirt. Shaking his head, *no, no, no.* Blood-clotted hair hanging greasy and limp into his face.

Fingers pinching, pinching, pinching at the creases of his slacks.

He sensed Leary shuffling his large frame to pick up the broom again.

Head spinning.

Dizzy.

Vertigo. As though he'd ingested a bad batch of opium. As though he was a child again gripping at the pure white porcelain edge of the bathtub as his father's razor strop slashed into his back and legs. Counting one to seven in his head. Seven slashes. Lucky seven. His mother trying to soothe him. Naked flesh under white sheets. Li Yu. Mrs. Goodman.

He vomited into the gutter. Watched the foamy bile mix bubbling with the blood and dirty water there. A blowfly bucked and twisted in the bodily fluids. Drowning in its greed. The stink of iron, copper, eye watering. Stevie's blood still so damn red, reflecting the sunset of a dying day. Too bright.

Ben heaved. Vomited again. Guts empty and raw.

Stood shakily, slowly, wiping at his mouth with a new handkerchief. The Irish eye fucked a passing automobile, nodded to Leary, then fell back inside the club, murmuring bitterly.

"I want to know what the fuck happened to you, anyhow?" Leary said standing on the almost vacant street, leaning his weight onto the broom, eyeing Ben's throat and gashed bloody forehead.

"The Italians happened. They moved on me, as well. Moved on me. Moved on me. The Italians they moved on me. Me too," Ben bit into his tongue again. Focused on the pain, cutting off all the stuttering shit before it got truly started.

"They moved on you? A fucking *cop*? That's suicide and they damn well know it. Why'd they go and do something as foolish as that?"

"I don't know," Ben lied, "I don't know."

"They know your history with Stevie. Know you're our in to The Department," Leary massaged the nubs of his missing fingers, grimacing as though in pain.

"That's all inconsequential now. It no longer matters," Ben spat blood.

"How's that? What the fuck are you talking about?"

"I want you to get word to Paul, right away."

"Paul The Negro?"

Ben glanced around to make sure none of the cops had slithered into earshot. "Yes, if we're going to kill those fucking Italians, we need slightly more than revolvers and pistols. Set up a meet with Paul. We'll hit them all the day after we bury Stevie. The sooner we finish it, the better. Get Stevie buried quick. Grease the right palms. Deborah wouldn't want him in some locker on ice down at the morgue being cut up by some sick fuck. As soon as possible. Bury the Italian fucks the day after.

The day after. They won't be expecting such a quick retaliation. They'll think there's safety in numbers. We'll kill them all together. Like dropping boiled water on a fucking ants nest."

"That's music to my fucking ears, English."

"And after it's done, we're going to Salt Lake City for a couple of days. So, tell the others to pack their toothbrushes. Toothbrushes. Pack their toothbrushes. Fuck! This weekend."

Leary squinted, "Salt Lake City? There are better places to lam it to, English."

Ben swallowed blood. Gagged. Enunciated each word, taking it slow. "Someone very important has made me an offer. It'll be good for all of us. A good earner for everyone. Legit. I'll explain it all later," he said, fingering the wedding ring in his pocket with bloody fingertips. "In the meantime, I've something very important that I need to do now."

"You're leaving *now*? What could be more important than *this*?" Leary motioned to the small diamonds of glass and puddles of blood staining the sidewalk.

"I've already lost Stevie today. I'm not going to lose anyone else. I refuse to," Ben said, holding back tears. He'd never let Leary see him cry. The fat fuck would see it as a sign of weakness. They all would. As his father had. His mother, too, finally. Her voice echoing up from the damp, depths of his memory. "Big boys don't cry, Benny. They don't cry. I need you to be a man. Be a man for your mother, Benny." He wasn't a boy anymore. He *was* a *man*. A broken, ruined, fucking nothing of a *man*.

"In that case, I guess you should be on your way then. I'll talk to the lads. Smooth things over temporary like. Put a rein on them all." Leary nodded at him, shuffled into the club. The door closed slow, pushing a backdraft of the bar into Ben's face, bringing back Stevie's grinning pug face back from the dead for as long as it took the warm picture to fade. The grey sky tore open, and a heavy dark rain washed the blood into the sewers, as Ben stumbled back to his Cadillac letting the tears that had been bucking to be released flow freely, disguised by the rainfall.

Concentrating his mind like the muzzle of a gun.

focusing on China Town.

Thinking of Li Yu.

HE KNEW SOMETHING was wrong as soon as he entered Li's teahouse. The old man, cigar store Indian, hadn't been outside. He was *inside* seated at the table with the old women sipping tea, yapping deep in conversation. Strange as hell.

They all started squawking and waving their hands around in the air when they glanced up to see Ben standing there in the entranceway. Dripping wet. Soaked through from the downpour. His eyes bloody slits from tears. The women's eyes bulged like dumbstruck fish. The old man startled. The guy in the waiter's coat still smoking on the stairs was the only thing that remained consistent. He stood up slow and held a hand out to Ben in a halting gesture, the other he stuck inside his white waiter's jacket to the heavy shape concealed underneath his armpit.

"No. No, Yu no here. You leave now!" he snapped, like an annoying little mutt.

"What the fuck do you mean? I need to see her, right now! It's imperative that I see her!" Ben said making his way further into the tearoom, dodging tables and chairs.

"Yu gone. She no here."

"Where is she?"

"She gone. We tell you, we tell other police, Li Yu gone. You leave now."

"What the fuck are you talking about? What other police?" Ben said, going to push past to the stairs, the waiter stepped in front of him blocking his path.

"You leave! You leave, no more police fucks!"

Ben eyeballed the smooth, ugly face and sneered. "As you can see from the present state of myself at this moment in time, I'm having a rather unpleasant and stressful day. You're currently contributing to that stress and unpleasantness. Now, I'm just going to ask this one more time, *where is Li?* I really need to see her. It's imperative."

"You leave!"

Ben clenched his jaw. Bit down hard on his bottom lip. Ripped the badge from his pocket and held it aloft, above his head, flashing it around the dining room, "I am Boston Police Detective Benjamin Hughes, and this is a raid!" he screamed. Throat burning. He coughed and spat phlegm onto the floor.

The old ladies squawking tripled in decibels. Gibbering towards the waiter. Waving him away. Ben feeling another migraine like a winter wind in his skull. He pushed the badge hard into the waiter's eye socket. The man stared defiantly with his one good eye.

"You see the fucking badge now, don't you? Now move out of my way, you fucking filthy little savage."

The waiter moved. Ben grabbed him by the lapels, shoved him hard towards the other Chinese, jumped up the stairs in two bounds.

Li Yu's door.

The secret knock.

No answer. Nothing.

He banged on the door.

Nothing.

Called her name through the wooden frame.

Nothing.

Blood crusty hair hanging in his face, he stepped back and kicked the door off its hinges. Pine snapped and split. The door hung crooked. He pushed it out of his way.

Moonlight spilling through the window settling like a fine dust across the floorboards. The room bare.

Nothing.

Stripped of color. Stripped of life. The disemboweled corpse of what Li Yu's bedroom had been before.

Ben pulled open empty drawers and empty cupboards.

Nothing.

The rainy-day fund gone. Three coat hangers hung dead from the curtain rail. His smoking set placed in the center of the bare floor.

No Li Yu.

No opium.

Nothing.

Ben dropped to his knees. Screamed until his voice gave out and his throat burned. Coughed, gagged, heaved, breathless, he stood, staggered, sat down heavily on the naked mattress. More tears ran down his pale face making tracks and lines through the dried blood. He pulled the revolver from his shoulder holster and popped the chamber, spinning it. "Upon the stair, I met a man who wasn't there… upon the stair, I met a man who wasn't there… wasn't there… upon, upon, upon the stair…"

He stood up shakily, woozy, dry heaved and walked out of the room he and Li had shared hours of love together in. The bitterest tears stinging his eyes, could barely see a thing. Images and echoes crashed together in his mind.

Stevie sprawled dead in the street, blood and cockroaches spreading across the sidewalk like a rippling sheet of oncoming night.

The faces of Lombardo and Buccola, masks of razorblade hate.

The thump, thump, thump of his knees hitting the underside of the table in the café.

Li Yu shuddering to climax underneath him. Whispering his name. Her eyes passing over his face fleetingly and then gone. Gone.

Mrs. Goodman's hands on his hips pulling him desperately deeper inside her.

His mother's lips upon his face.

The razor strop cutting into his back.

His father's yells echoing throughout the house.

His mother's face so close to his. Her breath on his face.

The Beetle Man looming over his soiled bed.

A naked, screaming child consumed by ants and cockroaches.

He stumbled back down the stairs and into the dining room. Thunder crashed on the street outside. Rain assaulted the windows. The old Chinese man stood arguing with the three old women in a language that sounded like river water crashing against rocks. The waiter smoking another cigarette by the front doors. His eyes vicious little black slits in Ben's direction.

"You go, now. We don't want no trouble. We tell other policeman Jones. You go to fuck," he shrieked, waving his hands around.

Jones' name was a jab to Ben's guts, but he smiled at the waiter and pointed out of the window towards the street. The waiter turned to peer out through the grimy glass and Ben stabbed the revolver's muzzle into the back of his head, behind the left ear and squeezed down on the trigger. The side of the Hong Kong Pistol Champion's face exploded, chips of skull and teeth burying themselves into the nearest wall with a red wine splash.

Ben reached down into the crumpled corpse's jacket and wrenched a Japanese pistol from the body. Turning the barrels of both weapons on the group of elderly Chinese, a grin so tight on his face it felt as though his flesh would rip itself apart. He spoke through gritted teeth.

"Must everything I care about be stolen from me today? Is that it? Like fucking Job am I? A wager between the fucking Devil and God? My soul a gamble?" The last words came out in hysterical screams. He stood panting, scratching at his chest with the muzzle of the .38. He took a deep breath and tried to calm himself. "I usually don't shoot people in the head, but like I said earlier, I'm having quite the bad fucking day and it seems my self-imposed rules have gone out of the fucking window. Out of the window. Window. Out of the window. Now, now, now, now. Now. No, I want you to tell me why that fat fuck Jones has been sniffing around here and I want you to tell me where Li is. I want to know where she is. I need to know where she is. She. Where? Tell me. Tell me, now. I want to know where Li is. Tell me now."

The old man grabbed at one of the women by the arm, shaking her, shouting in Cantonese as she bellowed back at him.

Ben exhausted, consumed by fever and shakes, sighed heavily, shot one of the women through the face. Her body flew over a table backwards, crashing into a set of china teacups and tumbling to the floor. Her dress flew up showing flabby, veiny thighs. Porcelain smashed. Ben clucked his tongue and used the revolver's barrel to sweep the blood-stiff hair out of his face.

The most overweight of the elderly women whimpered, tried to edge her way slowly towards the kitchen. Ben let her have it in the lower back as she turned to run. She collapsed, thrashed around, moaning on the floor like an insect on its back. A cockroach sprayed with bug killer. He aimed carefully, pulled the trigger again, taking the top of her skull away.

He remembered the way his mother would cut the tops off boiled eggs so he could dip thin slices of toast into the yolk. Dipping into the yolk. Telling him to say the special words.

He swallowed bile.

His mother's skull visible as she chattered away to him from morphine dreams. Her hospital bed reeking of piss and shit. She hadn't been clean enough, she whispered. She was a dirty girl. She'd been a dirty, filthy girl. She wanted him to forgive her. Ben squeezed his eyes shut. Shook his head violently side to side.

The atmosphere in the teahouse alive with smoke and gunpowder.

The old couple's wailing and crying giving Ben a migraine.

A basement door flung open.

Naked, filthy, skin and bone bodies scrambled out stupefied, dreamingly moaning.

A trio of addicts from the den.

Ants crawling from a nest.

Ugly little crowd.

Repulsive.

Ben turned the muzzles of his weapons on the things and fired into the fleshy mass until both weapons clicked on empty and his index fingers stung.

He dropped the Japanese pistol clattering to the floor and clicked open the cylinder of the .38, letting the spent rounds scatter tinkering onto a nearby tabletop.

He turned to the old man and woman who had gone from crying hysterically to holding each other tightly in silence. Watching him. Their eyes so white and their mouths resigned, trembling, little slits.

He reloaded each round slowly with palsied fingertips.

"Tell me everything about Jones. Tell me everything about Li Yu. I want you to tell me where Li is. Tell me. Where she is. I want you to. I want you to tell me where Li is. I want you to fucking, fuck, fucking tell me everything," Ben stuttered, moving closer to the shrinking, cowering couple, the revolver shakily aimed at the space above their heads.

LATER THAT NIGHT, Ben let himself into his darkened apartment and quickly closed the front door, securing the masking tape back over the edges.

Secured the vacuum.

Locked it.

Checked it.

Rechecked it.

Counting to seven and then checking it again. And again. Touching the lock and counting. Touching the catch and counting. Running his fingers over and around the door's vacuum checking for drafts, gaps. Counted to seven. Sighed.

He slipped off his shoes and kicked them into their designated place with his feet. Took a tissue from a box of Kleenex by the front door and used it to wipe some of the caked blood from his hands. When he finished, he rolled it into a ball, dropped it onto the floor and toed it aside with piles of other discarded tissues. Slipped off the maroon spattered jacket, reeking of gasoline, blood and bile and folded it into a hemp dry-cleaning sack hanging from a brass hook on the wall.

Unclasped his shoulder holster and hung it on another hook parallel to the sack.

His shirt and slacks were removed next, folded carefully into the sack. Jockey shorts, vest and socks followed. He wiped his hands again with another tissue. Dropped it.

Picked up the can of bug spray from a five-foot pile of newspapers and sprayed around the edges of the door and entranceway. Coughing, eyes stinging from the fumes.

He then walked briskly to the bathroom across the hall, ducking his head away from the threads of red and blue string that crisscrossed through the air, marking which areas were sanitized and which spaces weren't.

He scrubbed his hands with soap and water in the basin.

Smelled at his hands.

Cursed.

Washed them again.

Sniffed at his fingers.

Cursed.

Washed them again.

Broken skin raw and stinging.

Dried them on a towel and dropped it into another dry-cleaning sack piled in the corner.

Brushed his teeth until his gums bled and the bristles on the toothbrush were stained a dark pink.

Took a bottle of whiskey from the cupboard underneath the sink.

Broke the seal.

Sanitized the neck under the flowing water from the tap.

Unscrewed the top and gulped a few mouthfuls.

Gargled and spat the contents down into the watery dank plughole.

Standing in front of the mirror glaring at the naked, pale, gangly form reflected back at him. He stared so long his body seemed to warp into something else. A creature that crawled or climbed. Something that lived in darkness. A pale white scurrying thing. He took a long hit on the bottle again and swallowed. His throat and guts bitter-raw.

Carrying the bottle with him, he stepped into the bath. Running the water into the tub as he stood shivering in the confines of it, waiting for the cold water to reach his preferred depth before sitting down. Clean. Pure. Washing away all the filth and all the bad. All clean. All clean and all better. Filth made sickness. Wash away all the bad now. Wash away all the sickness and all the bad. Splashing the water over his shuddering body, gulping heavily from the bottle and wiping away the tears that streamed from his inflamed, swollen eyes.

Murmuring her name over and over in groups of seven through chattering teeth.

Li Yu.

Li Yu. Li Yu.

Li Yu. Li Yu. Li Yu.

Li Yu.

STEPHEN J. GOLDS

London, England
Wednesday, February 24th, 1926

WILLIAM STOOD SMOKING on the hotel balcony watching tugboats make their way down the Thames, the people clambering like sheep across Waterloo Bridge. The water of the river a dark green going on black. A deep depression weighing him down like a corpse on his back. His whole body ached. His skull felt as though it was full of broken, sharp things. The wind was viciously chilled, and the day a machine grey. St. Paul's Cathedral towered over everything on the smoky landscape. Peering out over the city at the bone white structure of the house of God dropped a jagged rock in his guts. As though it mocked him. Ordering him to pray, to ask for forgiveness. He'd like to see the building burned, if only to take away the feeling he got whenever he looked at the fucking thing.

His own Superintendent had tried to have him murdered. The whole cabal of them, all the way up to the Commissioner of the Metropolitan Police. The fucking sodomites, backstabbing Judases had taken over all his money earning operations with as little as a few words and a day of telephone calls and telegrams. William had few choices left now. He'd played the cards he'd had and lost. Pushed them all too far. Lost to a bunch of toff society queers, a dago and a woman. Now it was jail or death or run. Running seemed the only logical option. He coughed up mucus and spat it over the balcony. He'd got word to his wife. Told her he had to lay low for a little while. Had told her where the bank documents were in his study. To

163

go to the safety deposit boxes he had stashed all over London. She was to bring as much cash, stocks, bonds and jewelry as she could to the Southampton Docks the next afternoon. They would set sail for the United States of America. Leave this wretched city once and for all. It wasn't much of a plan, but it was all he had left. As for Harewood and all his politician friends, there was a journalist that William was well acquainted with that drank in The Ten Bells Pub every night. He'd written a detailed account of all of the Superintendent's corruption and frailties, the house of prostitution on Berkeley Square. The Commissioner. The politicians. Their sick, twisted, degenerate sex parties. The murder of a nancy boy. It was all in an envelope on the writing desk in his suite. William would pass through Spitalfields on his way out of the city tonight, leaving the signed account with the landlord, telling him to pass it to the journalist as soon as he entered the pub. William wouldn't leave the gambling table completely empty handed. He'd leave London burning and Harewood tied to the stake at the fucking center of it.

He flicked his cigarette over the edge. Glanced down over at the streets below and went back inside. The curtains caught the wind, brushing against his face like fingertips and he startled and cursed. Walked, slouched shouldered, over to the oak writing desk, picked up the bottle of Scotch and drained it. Dropping the empty bottle onto the ivory-colored carpet dully. Went over the telephone beside the king-size bed and told room service to bring him another. Sat down on the bed staring at the painting hung above the dresser again. A painting of a poppy field in summer. He looked at his hands. His palms. The lines that crisscrossed his flesh. As though he could see every action he had taken in his life that had led him to this very room. A dried smudge of maroon brown between his thumb and forefinger.

He spat on it and wiped his hand clean on his trousers. Glanced up at the painting again. The poppies seemed to move in a breeze. A puddle of blood seeping across floorboards. Red wine spilt across white sheets. A song like a nursery rhyme.

FINISHING THE SONG, she sighed. He turned his head to the dresser she was seated at. She smiled at him in the reflection of the mirror. Lips so red against the milky white of her visage in the candlelight. Pulling her long, wavy blonde hair up into a pearl clip. Three dark brown moles forming a constellation on her right shoulder blade. He got up from the bed and went to her. Kissing the nape of her neck. Tasting lavender. The sounds of Paris at night drifting through the open window. So far away from the Somme. A phonograph started playing somewhere. French vocalists singing beautiful words he didn't understand but didn't need to. He told her he loved her. The girl who told him her name was Margaux. Told her love was everywhere in their small tenement room. *L'amour.* He walked around touching the sparse furniture, the walls and shouting the French word for love over and over. She giggled with her hands to her mouth. A picture of eternal beauty and eternal youth. Margaux. Every night together like this for weeks. He wanted to tell her that she was his first. She couldn't understand his English. He held his forefinger up into the air of the room, whispered one in French and then pointed the finger at her. She giggled again. Still nothing more than a very young woman. Her creamy face in the candlelight angelic. Wanted to tell her so badly he wanted to stay in Paris. Stay in this place for always. With her. Margaux.

He went to her again. Pulling the pearl clip softly away from her head, tossing it onto a bureau and letting the waves of gold fall down her naked back. Like something from a renaissance painting. Her hair in his fingertips like the threads of something very fragile and he felt himself become hard. He took her by the hand, leading her to the bed. Pushing her softly down on the white covers.

"I love you so much," he whispered, reaching up her thighs, pulling gently at her knickers.

A HARSH KNOCKING at the door jarred him from the memories. The room appearing a little darker.

"Who is it?" his voice broke. He growled. Clearing his throat.

"Room service, Sir. You requested a bottle of Scotch, Sir," came the answer.

"Just leave it outside."

"Very well, Sir. Will you be needing anything else, Sir?"

"Do you have a time-machine like in that novel?"

"Urm, I'm afraid not, Sir."

"Well, fuck off then, you dozy cunt."

"Yes, Sir. Very well."

He jumped up, staggered, placed his ear against the smooth, cool wood of the door and listened to the clatter of a tray and glasses being placed on the floor outside, footsteps fading down the hall. He unlocked the door, peering up and down the empty, elegant hallway and snatched the bottle, leaving the tray and glasses where they were.

He'd been in the suite going on two days. Felt longer. The walls seemed to be breathing. Constricting, choking him. The furniture creeping towards the center of the room when he's head was turned. The flowery, ornate wallpaper made his head spin. Vertigo. He needed air again. Trapped in Limbo. Purgatory. Even in dreams *she* came for him. The song sung from the throat

166

of the dead. The stench seeping from rotten orifices. No peace for the wicked. No rest for the dead.

Since coming to the Savoy Hotel, he'd drunk himself into blackouts but still she came. He'd known she'd always been there somehow. Never really left. Hovering always at the periphery of his vision, a sunspot, or mark upon the eye. In crowds, always her back turned. In the songs of children. In his wife's eyes on their wedding night and in the voice of the priest echoing through the church aisles. In his son's smiles and tears. She was in the silence of the early mornings and in the loneliness of the nights. In the desperate, beautiful face of every single whore he saw on the streets of London.

He unscrewed the cap from the scotch and drank greedily from it. Sat down on the bed. The poppies swayed and poured. He jumped back up. Ripped the fucking painting from the wall and slid it under the bed.

Standing a moment, staring down at the floor, he changed his mind, retrieved the painting, took it out onto the balcony and slung it out over the railing to the street below. stumbled back inside and sat down on the carpet, his back to the wall, drinking until he couldn't lift the bottle to his lips anymore.

THEY CALLED PARIS the 'City of Light'. A metropolis of artists, writers and painters. He knew why artists loved the city. It was the way the rays of the sun hit the boulevards and monuments. A wash of gold and yellow. A city born for spring, for summer. The scents of flowers weaving through a soft breeze. The light came down on Margaux's tenement building warming the bricks and stone. People on bicycles rode past him in pairs talking amicably. He really loved Paris. He really loved *her*. The bitterest of tears fell from his snarling face onto the bouquet of roses he held crushed in his fists. Waiting.

After watching the third man come and go from the vestibule of her tenement building that morning he dropped the bouquet atop a pile of trash, let himself in and wiped his eyes on his sleeve. Jogged up the stairs to her apartment. Knocking at her door. Gasping at the stale, dusty air. Not trying to wipe away the tears any longer but allowing them to trickle down his face freely.

She opened the door, smiling, saying something in that elegant, musical language of hers. Then she froze, momentarily stunned by his sudden presence. Not who she was expecting at all. He always called by in the evenings. She murmured his name the same way that had always caused the breath to catch in his chest like a kite moving higher into a pastel blue sky on a string in the hand of a small boy.

He'd prayed outside, slouching against the chipped brick wall. Prayed that he was wrong. Prayed it was just his foolish mistake. A misplaced lover's jealousy to be laughed off later after they had made love. The men were family members. A brother, an uncle, perhaps. But standing there in the doorway, looking over the room, the disheveled sheets, the coins tossed scattered on the mattress, the bottle of wine, glasses half empty on the bedside table. The lipstick and rouge smudged across her face, standing there in her fucking stained nightgown coming off at a bruised shoulder. The fucking stink dripping off the walls and the furniture. He realized he had fallen in love with nothing but a cheap, fucking whore. He *had* been giving her money, but it was for food and clothes. Things she needed. A *gift*, not payment.

Margaux said his name again, but this time it sounded empty. Meant nothing to him anymore, like the prayers, the city light and the music on the phonograph seeping through the hallways.

She reached out a palsied hand to him, bottom lip trembling. He shoved her hard back into the room, following her inside and kicking the door closed. She sat on the end of the bed, drinking the wine from the bottle, resting it on her thighs. He glared down at her. His mouth opening and closing like a dying fish. Unable to find the words for the unbelievable pain in his guts. She shrugged, started singing her song. Her blue eyes on his shoes as he made his way to her, telling her how much he loved her. He loved her so fucking much. Did she know that? Understand that?

When she giggled it was like a blow to the face, the chest. He stood there, swaying, shaking uncontrollably as she giggled and smirked at him like a disobedient child with her hands to her smeared-red mouth.

His teeth clenched tight.

The hands around the little fucking whore's throat clenched so much tighter.

THE BOTTLE TUMBLED to the floor. The scotch seeping from the bottle into the carpet, into his trousers mixing with the piss and the shit already soiling his bottoms.

William vomited until his eyes and throat burned like a soldier in a cloud of mustard gas.

Coughing out her name.

Margaux.

Margaux.

Margaux.

Margaux.

South Boston, USA
Thursday, February 21st, 1946

STEVIE'S WAKE AT The Seven Shamrocks had finally wound down. The last of the old timers to leave was Mikey Spillagan. He'd come all the way from New York City, had spent most of his time at the wake telling '*remember when*' stories about him and Stevie's formative years, Kerryman jokes, and trying to convince Ben to come out to Hell's Kitchen to work for him. Said he needed good men like Ben to fight off the encroaching Sicilians. Said he'd heard a lot of good things. Ben lied to the guy, said he'd give it some thought, and Mikey finally shuffled out into the street to go back to where he'd come from, leaving the Dorchester Street gang sitting silently around a table with trays of stale ham and cheese sandwiches that had been slapped together by Stevie's widow Deborah and daughter Meghan.

Ben's guts growled; he hadn't eaten in a long while. Didn't feel like it. Couldn't. He stared at a piece of boiled egg that had fallen onto the ring scarred tabletop, sipping poteen from his flask and scratching at the back of his head. Throat still sore. Voice still broken in parts.

Deborah came from behind him and kissed him lightly on the stubbled cheek. Took his hand in hers. Squeezed. He didn't avoid it. Her eyes were the bluest Ben had ever seen. Watery. Lined in red. Always so damn kind. She didn't say anything. She didn't need to. She kissed his hand and placed it back in his lap.

Meghan came over and started to clear the table. Attempting a smile at Ben but failing badly. She tucked a long, wavey strand

of red hair behind her ear, nodded at the men and carried the
tray of half-eaten sandwiches away. Ben covered the piece of
crumbly egg yolk with a napkin trying his best not to look at the
absolute disorder scattered in front of him. He pushed his chair
even further away from the table. Taking longer drinks from the
flask and waiting for the women to leave. None of the Irish
spoke. A silence with a sharp, violent edge pervading. The most
dangerous kind of quiet. The Mulligans were drinking hard.
IOU dozed. Leary puffed at a cigar, blowing smoke rings
towards the yellowed ceiling. The man who everyone called a
negro was actually Portuguese; Negro Paul spoke first, breaking
the hush with the tact of a sledgehammer.

"How about that fire in China Town last night, huh? They
reckon it was one of those junkie dens went up in smoke. *Puff!*
I hear they identified some of the dead. Wei Tu Hot, Ouh Chi,
Ho Li Fuk and Sum Ting Wong. An Irishman was among the
dead, too. O. Howie Burns."

Ben stared at the creases in his slacks and sniffed at his
fingers. Still smelling the gasoline. "Can you just get to the
fucking point of why you're actually here, Paul," he shot the
words out, slurred. Not looking up.

"Jesus, it was just a joke, English. Trying to lighten the mood
is all, it's like a funeral in here. No need to get all cunty about it."
Negro Paul brought a beer bottle to his lips and flashed his
eyebrows around the table.

"They'll be another funeral soon enough, if you don't start
showing some respect, Negro." Leary blew smoke across the
table at him.

Paul shrugged, hooked a thumb over his shoulder. "Alright,
alright. There are two crates out in the back. The very best for
all of you guys."

"Did you get us what we asked for?" Christopher Mulligan said, examining the label of the whiskey bottle he was drinking from. Blowing grey smoke rings.

"I did what I could. It was difficult," Negro Paul shrugged.

"How many?" Ben asked.

"I got two."

"We asked for *five*," Ben said.

"So, you asked for five and I could only get *two*. It wasn't a small thing you asked for. It being short notice, like I said."

"We asked for five," Ben repeated.

"St. Valentine's Day was last week. This is Boston, not Capone's Chicago. Getting my hands on two Thompson machine guns within a day and a morning was pretty fucking good work, if you ask me."

"We ain't asking you," Connor Mulligan sneered.

"Okay. Alright. Two Thompsons'll have to do. What else do you have for us?" Leary shrugged.

"I got you a couple of shotties and a machine gun pistol as well."

"That sounds good enough," Connor nodded.

"Continuing with the topic of Valentine's Day in Chicago, how about the other things we asked for?" Ben said.

"I thought it strange you asking for those. Being who *you* are?"

"Did you obtain them or not?" Ben looked up, locking eyes with Paul for the first time that day.

Negro Paul got up, went out the back for a moment and came back hefting two large olive canvas duffel bags. Dropped them on an empty table and started pulling midnight blue fabric from out of one. He tossed the bundle at Connor. An uneasy laugher rippled out into the club as Connor stood up and pulled on the jacket of a Boston beat cop.

"I'm Portuguese."

"You got the complexion of a spook, maybe your mother
fucked one and your father ain't really your father. For shame.
But I *do* have to say you've done grand work here, Negro. How
much are we to owe you then?" Leary said.

"Today being the day that it is, I'll let you have the guns and
the uniforms at seventy-five percent of what I originally asked
for. *But,* on one small condition. I want in on the Salt Lake City
job that you told me about, Leary."

Ben eyeballed Leary. Leary blushed and popped sweat.

"You let the cat out of the bag on the Salt Lake party, did you, Leary?" Ben leaned forward, knocked on the table as he spoke.

The Mulligans rolled their eyes.

Leary held his hands out, half surrender, half shrug.

"Why do you want in on the party, Paul?" Ben said.

"Are you kidding me, English? Two thousand bucks to sit around the lobby of a lace curtain hotel for two days eating room service and flirting with the maids? Do you even need to ask? Besides, I can take all you guys in my Hudson. It's big enough for sure. Never been to Salt Lake City, anyway, always wanted to go. Drive'll be fun. Like a road trip."

"It looks like that's settled then," Ben said, finishing his flask and getting up to go and sit at the bar. The wake had him beat. Having to talk to so many people, pretending he was all right, normal, exhausted him physically and mentally. Drained.

Voices, memories and the words spoken by Li Yu's mother as the teahouse burned flying around his skull with switchblade wings the entire day.

The chances of finding the boy were becoming slimmer by the day and he'd lost track of where he was supposed to be and what he was supposed to be doing.

He slid the newspaper page from out of his pocket and opened it up on the bar, trying to smooth out the creases with the base of his fist. Formulating some kind of a plan. First, fix all of the North End Italians for Stevie once and for all, go babysit the groups of spoilt, overindulged cunts in the Salt Lake City hotel, stamp on a cockroach that had been crawling around his feet for too long, and then finally come back and investigate the case properly, pull in all the favors that were owed.

He knocked on wood.

STEPHEN J. GOLDS

He'd find the boy. On his soul. If he had anything of one left to barter with.

And then there was Li Yu. She would've heard about the fire and the dead by now. He massaged his eyes, twisting his head away from the thoughts that ripped through his head like electric shock treatment. Lobotomy sometimes seemed the only answer to his fucking problems. Counting echoes in his head.

One.

What's the matter with Uncle George?

He thinks too much,

yesterday, upon the stair, I met a man who wasn't there!

worries too much about things that

aren't real, and it makes him very

sick.

Two.

So he stays in the hospital where the doctors can look after him.

Where he can be properly cared for. That's why you mustn't

worry

too much about that silly

upon the stair, I met a man

Three.

Beetle Man

who wasn't there!

and other such nonsense. There are more important things to

be worried

Four.

about in the world.

Such as what,

Mother?

Five.

Say it, Benny, say the words.

Tell me

175

Six.
you love me.
Seven.
I love you, mother.
yesterday, upon the stair, I met a man who wasn't there!
Sickness and disease.
very dirty... Filthy.
A filthy, filthy
Beetle Man
Tell me you love me, Ben.
Seven.
Say the words to me
I love you,
Li Yu.
And I love you. Even I know all the
terrible things
you've done;
seven.
who wasn't there!
I still love you
yesterday,
upon
the stair,
who wasn't
there!
Ben drank until he blacked out.

The North End, Boston, U.S.A
Friday, February 22nd, 1946

BEN BREATHED SHALLOW in the front passenger seat of the blue Ford truck Negro Paul had acquired. Closest thing he could steal appearing similar to a BPD paddy wagon. Hungover with the shakes. Trying to hold his breath. Leary stank fucking filthy. Unwashed. Ben yawned, tasted something foul on his breath and gagged. The Thompson machine gun cradled in his lap smelled strongly of gun oil and mean intentions. He checked his wristwatch. Ten minutes past ten. A misty Friday morning. Hanover Street empty and damp. Grey. Something haunted. An edge of Hell. Foot traffic almost nonexistent. The café's front window boarded up with sheets of plywood. He used the sleeve of the dark blue uniform jacket to wipe away the condensation on the windshield and wound down his window. Cleared his throat. Spat. Breathing the chilled morning air. The jacket fit loose and brought back memories of his time walking a beat. Then Li Yu there at the forefront of his mind again. He wrestled with the images of her. Too bright. Too colorful. He poked at his temples and frowned into another migraine or the same chronic headache he'd had for days. Li Yu — a razor blade dragged slowly across his flesh. Recollections that throbbed like a bullet wound in the back. His guts like cruel chips of ice. Stabbing.

Counting to seven in his head. Repeating the poem his mother taught him. His only Hail Mary. *Mother.*

He gazed up at the building opposite the café. IOU on the roof with a pair of army surplus field binoculars. He'd give them a wave when he confirmed Buccola, and Lombardo were present. So far a big, fat nothing. Ben rubbed his bruised throat, thinking Rat Fuck's presence in the café would be a very nice bonus. A ruby red cherry on top. Today was the day he wanted to end it all. Dot all the i's and cross all the t's. A flying insect landed on the windscreen and Ben cursed, twitched, twisted his head to squint at Leary. Scratching at his cheek.

"Leary, you still know how to ply your specialty?"

"How do you mean?"

"From your days in Belfast."

"Oh, that? For sure. It's like riding a bicycle. Let me tell you, you never really forget. Especially when you got half your jerking-off hand missing to remind you how to do the job right." Leary chuckled bitterly, waving his deformed hand through the air above the dashboard in a jerk-off motion and then dropping it back down on the steering wheel.

"There's something I want you to do for me tonight."

"If you're wanting me to blow up the guineas with a car bomb, I'd say it's pretty fucking late notice, wouldn't you?" Leary said, lifting the Thompson aloft from his lap, sucking air through grit teeth.

"It's not the Italians."

Leary gave Ben a long hard look.

Ben noticed a puss filled spot on Leary's chin and looked out the windshield. The flying insect had seemingly disappeared.

A group of kids appeared from a side street, ran around with sticks in their hands playing cops and robbers, squealing machine gun *ratatatat* noises excitedly at each other.

"Hope those kids fuck off before we get the showtime wave," Leary murmured to Ben or himself, pawing at a lucky rabbit's foot hanging from the rear-view. Ben let the comment pass unanswered.

The Mulligans' voices bouncing back and forth came muffled from the rear. Leary leaned over the steering wheel and squinted. The man really reeked crusty, stale, rotten and Ben rolled down his window further and tried to breathe the outside air deeper. Heard one of the kids yell, "You're dead!" Another kid, shouted, "no, I'm not, you stupid liar. I'm a good guy."

Ben grinned. Fucking children. One day they'd realize there were no good guys. Just bad people who gradually became worse.

"Couple of the guinea cocksuckers coming down the street now. That them, you think?" Leary said shifting in his seat. The leather squealed under the pressure.

"I can't make out their faces," Ben said, eyeballing the figures on the sidewalk.

The two Italian men flicked cigarette butts into the carless street and entered the café. Ben and Leary stared up at IOU. No wave. Nothing. No Buccola. No Lombardo.

"What's the betting that little eegit is half asleep up there?"

"It's still early. Give it time," Ben said, pushing his body as far as it would go against the passenger door, away from Leary and the stink. Checking his wristwatch again.

"Anything yet? We're freezing our pricks off back here," one of the Mulligans hissed from the back.

"Nothing. Now keep it the fuck down back there," Leary said, grinning at Ben and banging on the back with a fat fist. Ben swallowed another gag. Squeezed the oily Thompson in his hands. He'd last fired one at basic training, before the first *Dear John* letter from his wife and before being kicked out of the army.

"Those two make five of the wop cocksuckers in there. They've got some fucking balls meeting up all together like this so soon after…" Leary trailed off, squeezed the steering wheel hard. Growled.

"It would appear as though they're having some kind of an important meeting," Ben said, checking his wristwatch for the umpteenth time. Ten-sixteen. "No doubt planning how they're going to take the rest of us out. I'd say it's extremely fortunate for us. Exactly what I was hoping they would do. Mindless fuck heads."

"Dumb wop fucks. We're gonna bury them all. Fuck the Roman Empire," Leary thrust his hips. Ben wound down the window even further.

Two more well-dressed men turned the street corner and strode confidently into the café. Ben's heart skipped beats. The stagnant air suddenly electric.

IOU gave the wave. Leary banged on the back of the truck three times hard. The vehicle rocked on its axles as the Mulligans got out, slammed the back doors and walked briskly up the sidewalk towards the café. Looking exactly like two of Boston's finest.

One of the kids dropped his stick and threw up his hands. Clutched at his chest. Fell into the street for ten seconds. Waited. Grabbed his stick again and ran towards the other children, shouting, gunning them down. Ben wondered if the kid's branch was a Tommy gun. He unfolded the newspaper looked at the Goodman child's face, counted to seven three times under his breath and then folded it away again.

Loud shouting drifted down the street from the café. Crockery smashed. Bellowing. Voices raised in anger and surprise.

Ben and Leary waiting the pre-agreed ninety seconds. Eyeballing the slow-moving hands of their wristwatches.

"All right. Let's go, Leary," Ben said, tying a bandana around his mouth and nose.

"What the fuck is that for?" Leary stared.

"Protection," Ben stared back.

"Like a disguise? I thought that's what this fucking cop get-up was for."

Ben stared back.

"Maybe it's none of my business but you're letting your, how do I say, fucking eccentric ways get the best of you lately. You need to watch that shit. You'll end up in a mental asylum shitting your pants and finger painting with it."

"You're right, Fat Man. It's none of your fucking business."

"Fuck it, this is for Stevie. For Stevie," Leary nodded, shifting his gross body out of the swaying truck. They jogged up the street towards the café. Leary gasping, panting. Out of breath. Ben counting to seven slow. They burst through the doors, shouting their throats raw.

The interior was dim and lit with lamps. The silver expresso machine still hissing clouds of steam, stopped Ben dead in his tracks. Heart spasmodic. Cold sweat popping. He grasped at his throat. Guts painful. He bit his lip and tried not to shit himself.

The Mulligans waved their shotguns around nomadic, barking orders. Leary flipped a table with coffees and small baked pastries smashing to the floor.

"Get your fucking hands up, you wop cocksuckers! This is a fucking raid!" screamed Christopher.

"He said *get your fucking hands up!*" Connor drove the butt of his shotgun into backs and necks. Italians whelped, cried out and shook. Others played it tough. Christopher made an example and cracked a young guy's hard head clean open. He collapsed over the coffee bar ridiculously, like a drunk after last orders. Christopher cackled and pointed. Look it!

The other North Enders got the message and lined up against the bar quick. Hands up and backs turned. Cursing. Six Italians. Ben scanned the sides of sweat moistened olive faces and the backs of greasy heads.

No Buccola. No Lombardo. Fuck!

"Where the fuck are Buccola and Lombardo?" he hissed out of the side of his mouth, through the fabric of the bandana. His breath stinking of something metallic.

"The top two pieces of shit ain't fucking here?" Leary yelled.

"Wait a minute! There was a seventh? Where's the fucking seventh?" Ben called out.

The Rat peered over his shoulder. Recognizing the voice. Locked eyes with Ben. Features screwed up. Wailing something foreign and garbled. Italians span round. Faces like death masks.

"They know we ain't cops," Christopher shouted.

"Fuck it! Let 'em all have it! Now!" Connor bellowed.

Ben and the Irish pulled down on the triggers. A rapture. Bullets tore into the huddled line of screaming Italians. Bodies twisted. Hands waved seizure like. Legs kicked out. A death dance to the soundtrack of gunfire. The Thompsons and shotguns roaring and ripping into the shrieking flesh – something primal. Chips of wood and plaster flew. Lost in the fog of gun smoke, fire and blood, the Southie gang fired on empty. Guns *click, click, clicked.* Loud. Ben held his breath underneath the fabric covering his mouth and nose. Ears ringing. He couldn't hear a fucking thing. Connor emptied the cash register. Christopher reloaded his shotgun, kicking bodies, answering gargled, begging prayers with point blank resolution. Leary pawed over corpses, looting pockets, billfolds, chains and wristwatches. Ben stepped over slick puddles of red going on black. Broken glass and porcelain ground under foot. Kicked open the back-office door. A cheap desk. Steel filing cabinets. A lamp. An Esquire cheesecake calendar tacked to the cracked wall. Nothing. Vacant.

He stepped inside, Li Yu's bedroom rupturing his mind. Frozen in the memory. The cigar store Indian on his knees, bloody with the muzzle of the .38 stabbed into the cracked flesh of his forehead as Li's mother yammered in broken English. Jones. Li Yu. Confessions. The crucifix his mother wore around her neck pulsing from the recesses of his childhood. The black dressing gown she wore with a hood. Silk. He remembered how it felt underneath his fingertips. Made his stomach feel as though there were an octopus writhing inside it. Just a boy. The boy in the newspaper photograph. A flash of darkness.

Something crashed from behind the door, collided with his chest sending him sprawling. A glimpse of a ghostly white face. All gaping eyes and mouth. The face of a deformed baby. No eyebrows. No hair. Whimpering and clattering towards the front door of the café. High pitched wailing. A baby crying for its mother.

Mother.

Say the words. Tell me you love me

Ben yelled, "NO! DON'T!"

A machine pistol barked into the void of static silence.

Ben pulled himself to his feet, tumbling back through the doorway.

The hairless man facedown and bloody, sprawled on the floor.

"Fuck! That was lucky. One of us, should've probably checked the back office, ain't that fucking right?" Christopher said, waving the machine pistol towards the wide-open back-office door.

"Fuck! Fuck! Fuck!" Ben hissed, glaring down at the dead mass in a navy suit.

"What's the matter with you, English? You know that guinea or what?" Christopher asked.

"The boy! I need to find the boy. He was going to tell me where the fucking boy is."

"What the fuck are you talking about, English? We gotta go. Now!" Leary said, dropping his fat hand on Ben's shoulder. Ben shook it off. Used the toe of his mirror-shined Oxford to roll the body over. Its eyes flickered open, focusing on the space above Ben's left shoulder.

"Look at that, the piece of shit is still alive, but not for long," Leary swung the muzzle of the Thompson towards the dying man's face and Ben slapped it away. Grimaced. The smooth faced creature choking claret in between Latin prayers.

"Not until he's told me what I want to know," Ben kicked the ugly thing hard in the side of the ribs. It groaned and spat blood up across its face.

"Where is the boy? Where's James Goodman? The boy? Tell me now! Where's the boy? I need the boy!" Ben shouted.

The thing swiveled its dark eyes over both Ben and Leary, continuing the muttered, gasping prayers. The words *I'll pray when I'm dying,* echoing in Ben's mind. The words his father had always shouted at Ben's mother when she asked him to accompany them to mass on Sunday mornings. The anniversary of the man's death impending. Ben kicked the revolting thing in the ribs again. A sound of dried wood snapping, reminding Ben of Li Yu's door hanging from the frame – his ragged, broken heart hanging from a noose in his chest.

"We gotta fucking *go*, lads! *Now!*" Christopher shouted.

The Mulligans pulled the visors of their cop caps down low. Leaving slow, casually together. Not glancing up at the small crowd of gawkers and onlookers beginning to cluster on the street outside.

Pushed for time, Ben found a bloody gaping hole in the thing's guts. Shoved the muzzle of his Thompson in deep. The thing screamed soprano. Ben's ears rang. He grit his teeth so hard he thought they'd shatter like the porcelain and glass scattered across the floor amongst the dead.

"Where's the fucking boy? Where's James Goodman? You cockroach fuck!"

"...*eary*. ...*eary*." It whispered with blood-crusting lips.

Ben and Leary glanced at each other. Ben stared. Leary shrugged.

"I don't know this fucking guy. Why the fuck's he saying my own selves' name for? Never seen him in my life before."

Ben shoved the muzzle in deeper. "Where's the fucking boy, you wretched cunt?!"

The thing screeched, squealed, gasped, slumped down slack-jawed and died.

Leary pulled at Ben again, "He's gone. I don't know what the fuck this is about, but we've gotta get gone too, Englishman! Right now!"

Ben shoved Leary away. Bent down, tearing through the dead thing's slacks.

Coins clattered across the floor.

"There has to be something. Something. Something. Something... Something... Fucking something! Something!" He snatched at the contents of the deformed fuck's jacket, shoving everything he grabbed into his own.

Leary grabbed Ben's arm hard, squeezed, "I'm leaving now *with* or *without* you, Englishman."

The smell of shit and blood unbearable, seeping through the cotton fabric of his mask. Glaring down at the bald thing's face. It's legs akimbo. Arms outstretched. There was something terribly unnatural to the body. Heinous. Sinful. A giant white cockroach or ant.

Ben gagged and vomited into his bandana. Ripped it from his face. Tossed it at the corpse. Wiped his face on his jacket sleeve.

"Fuck!"

He followed Leary towards the door. Heart-wracked up. Panting. Dizzy. Ben thought he was having some kind of a heart-attack. They strolled out together. Faux-casual. Ignoring the shouted questions of the people that stood as slack jawed as the dead men within the confines of the café, from a safe distance in the street.

Ben scoped around for the kids. They were gone. He let out a sigh he hadn't realized he'd been holding. The Mulligans were almost at the Ford. IOU waiting with the truck started. Revving the engine. The exhaust backfired, sounding like a pistol shot. Everyone froze mid-step. Someone giggled nervously. Christopher swung in the front, tossing the cap on the dash. Leary, Connor and Ben hopped in the back slamming the door behind them.

IOU got the truck started and pulled hard into the street. Ben and Leary tumbled to their knees and cursed. Onlookers squealed. Ben heaved, coughing into his fist. The taste of vomit still thick in his mouth and on his tongue. He wiped his hands on his leg. Vertigo building to a crescendo then tapering off and diminishing.

Leary still cursing softly underneath his breath. Connor grinning, eyes glazed. Ben fell onto a pine bench, tearing at the bulging contents of his jacket pocket. The boy's silently screaming face exploded through his skull like a shotgun blast at point blank range.

He took out the blood-soaked billfold, rummaged through it with fingers that shook uncontrollably. Cash thick. One-hundred-dollar bills. Soggy. Nothing else. No cards. No identification. Nothing of any consequence. He tossed the cash to the floor of the truck. Leary and Connor locked eye contact with each other and pulled faces. Ben reached back into his pocket. His fingers brushed against the corner of something. Square. Card. A matchbook. He withdrew it, holding the scarlet matchbook up to a crack of light seeping through the backdoors. 'THE FAMOUS PARKER HOUSE BAR'. A bar in one of the oldest, classiest hotels in Boston. The Parker House Hotel on School Street. John Wilkes Booth had stayed there eight days before putting a bullet in old Abe's head. Popular with the Kennedy clan and other Boston lace curtain elites.

He flipped the matchbook open. A couple of the matches were gone. The matchbook nearly new. THURSDAY, 7. $, scribbled on the inside cover in what looked like kid's purple crayon. A rendezvous. He'd bet the rich woman Frankie had talked about would be there to pay the bald man off. A lucky break, at last. He squinted at his wristwatch. Ten twenty-two. More than enough time to kill.

"You not wanting that then?" Connor said, toeing the cash strewn on the floor.

"I think I may have what I wanted," Ben nodded grimly. Turning the matchbook over and over in his clammy fingers.

Leary and Connor nodded, fell to their knees and started to stuff their pockets with the blood splashed cash.

"And, Leary?" Ben said.

"Yeah what, English?"

"It's an emerald-green Ford Coupe that I want you to use your special skills on."

"That piece of shit? Are you fucking kidding me?"

"When have you ever known me to have a sense of humor, Leary?"

"He's got a point there, Fat Man," Connor said.

"I want it done, tonight," Ben said.

Leary stared, bug-eyed. Wiped sweat from his eyes and pulled at his beard.

"But, English…" he stuttered.

Ben cut him off, "just get it done. I'll explain later."

He shook off the patrolman's jacket, pulled on his sport coat delicately from a paper bag on the bench. Banged a fist hard on the side of the vehicle, shouted "I'm getting out here."

IOU pulled the truck over and Ben nodded at Leary as he pushed open the back doors.

"I want there to be fireworks while we're on our way to Salt Lake City tomorrow morning, Leary. Get it done. Done. Get it done and dusted. Done."

Leary tightened his lips but nodded. Went to say something but Ben slammed the backdoors on anything the ex-IRA man was going to say.

Stood at the corner of the junction watching the truck disappear into a side street. Ben checked his wristwatch. Flagged down a taxicab to take him back to the Old South Church in Southie where he'd parked his Caddie earlier that morning. He had one last place to be before The Parker House Bar.

Li Yu.

He was going to see Li Yu.

THE BAR IN the Parker House Hotel was after dinner bustling. Conversations coming in waves. The atmosphere thick with smoke. The chimes of glass on glass. Bursts of laughter. Soft lighting, dark woods, ox-blood leather. Boston's party crowd and elites rubbing shoulders. Suffocating. An insect nest of crawling bodies and mouths and eyes and teeth.

Ben slipped into a seat at the end of the bar. Turned his collar up and told the barkeep eyeballing the still raw scratches across his face to bring him an unopened bottle of bourbon and a clean glass.

"Looks like you went and pissed off yourself a tiger, Mister," the barman said with a thick Southern drawl, placing the bottle and glass down on top of crisp, white napkins.

"Something like that, yes." Ben touched the long gashes tenderly. Chewing at his ruptured bottom lip, Li Yu's screams echoing from somewhere across the crowds of people making him spin around in his seat to glance around the room.

"Oh, yeah?" The barman raised his eyes to the ceiling for some reason, whistled and placed both hands on the bar. He looked like an undertaker with plucked eyebrows. He wore a navy-blue bowtie that was crooked and compelled Ben to finger the collar of his own open shirt uncomfortably. The stink of stale cologne caught at the back of his throat. He leaned back and away on the stool.

"Yes, my wife, she's rather hotblooded." He slid out his badge and laid it on the bar. The gold reflected in the barman's cringing face and black eyes. "Now, brass tacks. Have you perchance ever seen a completely hairless man come in here, no eyebrows, bald, meeting a woman of rich appearance?"

The barman's eyes bulged for a split second. He peeped over at the door. "I ain't seen that fella around here for a month or so, I'm guessing. Kinda looks like one of them China dolls. Gives me the heebie jeebies, sure as night is dark. What's he done?"

Ben ignored the question. Asked his own. "How about the woman?"

"The woman, I can't say I rightly recollect."

Ben brought out his billfold and pushed a five spot across the dark, highly shined wood. "How about now? How's your recollection now?"

The barman licked his lips, reptilian. "Yeah, all right. Sure, I've seen the woman a couple of times with the China doll man."

"She here now?" Ben glanced over his shoulder, taking in the bar. The groups stood chatting, touching each other, laughing. He'd never understood how people could ever be so happy. Confident. Comfortable. He'd never had anything remotely like that. Had been alone his entire life. Even when he wasn't alone, he was isolated and alone. A roach captured under an overturned glass.

The barman glanced around the crowded room. "Nope, that she ain't."

"What does she look like?"

"Well, Sir, on the topic of tigers. She certainly looks like one. Don't know what the heck she sees in bowling ball head."

"I want to know about her appearance."

"Well, lemme see now. She's a beauty, all right. Tall, slim, blonde, all legs and tits. Real chesty. I'm more a derriere man, myself, though." He winked. Ben sneered.

"I don't give a fuck about what you are or aren't. Keep to the woman. How old is she approximately?"

"Well, now. There ain't no call for rudeness."

"Well, there isn't any call for me jumping over this bar and busting your fucking skull open either, but I'm presently certainly considering it."

"All right, all right. She's in her forties, I'm guessing. Early forties. Now if there isn't anything else, I've got other patrons to serve."

As he reached out for the five spot, Ben grabbed his wrist, twisted it. "You are sure she isn't here now?"

The barman snapped his head around again, face screwed up. "Yeah, I'm sure. She ain't here. Now lemme go. Ain't no wonder your woman scratched your face up." He ripped his arm free and walked down the other end of the bar rubbing at it. *Your woman scratched your face up.*

Ben drank hard and fast. Trying to smother the jagged glass images of Li Yu hours before from his mind. Her throat underneath his hands. That look of absolute fear in her dark eyes. *Tell me you love me, Ben. Say the words to me.*

Nine fifty. The bottle of whiskey reaching half empty. Attempting to focus on the faces in the room contorting every time he glanced over his shoulder. A kaleidoscope of tight grins, crawling hands, canine teeth and stretched eyes. The bar span. Topsy-turvy. He pulled out the crumpled newspaper page with the boy's photograph from his chest pocket, spread it out in front of him. Sipping at his glass, wincing at the picture like it was a gangrenous wound. Head in his hands. The fucking woman wasn't coming. A no-show. He almost fell off the seat. Vomited on the empty stool beside him. His fist to his mouth. Bile seeped down his chin and dripped onto his shirt front. Frankie's screaming broken face. Li Yu writhing underneath his fists. Ben pulled his .38 and slammed it down on the bar when the barman started over, a concerned, disgusted look all over his insectile face. Disarray and disorder. No symmetry to anything. People's whispers grew earsplitting. A beating heart of hate. *Crazy. Sick. Father. Mother. Weak. Ill. Dishonorable discharge. Sick. Filthy. Sick. Crazy. Buggy.*

Sweat or tears fell splashing onto the newspaper. Ink smeared like lipstick, like blood.

"I think you've had more than enough, my friend," the barman, standing in front of him, hands on hips. Eyebrows crooked like a cockroach's legs. "You're making quite a scene. Go home and sleep it off."

"Who the fuck are you? The Beetle Man?" Ben glared at the figure in front of him. Mouth drawn wide, forehead swollen, horned, grotesque in shadow. He snatched up his .38, waving it at the Beetle Man. The whispers of the crowd, papercuts all over his itchy, scratched flesh.

He squeezed the trigger, squinting down the muzzle at the Beetle Man. Stopped. Realizing he was pointing the revolver at his own reflection in the mirror at the back of the bar. He vomited again. The bile burning, seeping through his fingertips. He stumbled from his stool, pushing overgrown ants and cockroaches out of his way. A hive. A nest.

He fell into an elevator. Gagging. Told the operator to take him down to the first floor. Bronze. The chiming bells. The world a jumbled jigsaw puzzle. Marble floors. Piano music. Li Yu's throat underneath his hands. Flowers in Grecian urns. Spinning. That look of absolute fear in her eyes. Concierge in red coats. Faces for masks. Masks for faces. Bellboys in little hats pushing cages of weeping children. Footsteps tapping lunatic morse code. *Tell me you love me, Ben. Say the words to me.* The Beetle Man. Joseph P. Kennedy walking arm in arm with a blonde woman through the lobby, and out together through golden doors. Ben staggered after them. Hitting the street. Falling to his knees on the ice-cold concrete. Gone. His hands filthy. Filthy. Filthy. Filthy! His mother said she had been a filthy girl. Li Yu—a filthy girl. He stumbled to his feet, steadying himself, gripping at a lamppost. Filthy. Infected. Diseased. Soulless. The hotel a block away. He needed to wash. He brought his diseased, infected wrist to his face, frowning at his wristwatch.

Hours gone by.

Hours missed.

Missing.

The boy smiling from a missing poster.

Something black and shiny crawled from the shadows into the freezing night. Scurrying up Ben's foot, his leg, his chest and burrowed itself into his ear to lay pulsing inky eggs in the soft tissue of his brain.

Ben slid down the lamppost onto his ass.

Ben vomited.

Ben screamed.

London, U.K
Wednesday, February 24th, 1926

WILLIAM PULLED THE peak of the flat cap lower over his eyes.
Ran a finger over the smooth flesh of his freshly shaved upper
lip, feeling naked without the mustache. His other hand buried
deep in his overcoat pocket. Brandishing the pearl handle of the
revolver. Confident even his own mother wouldn't recognize
her son if she passed him by.

He made his way quickly down Commercial Street towards
the Ten Bells Pub. The pale spire of Christ Church penetrating
the night sky. A subtle knife in the dark. Hungover. His head
rattling like a train over rusty railway lines. He told himself the
shakes convulsing his body were only caused by the chilled wind.
Just the cold. He just needed to drop off the letter with the pub
landlord and be gone. A quick nip of the hair of the dog that bit
him. Ripped a chunk of flesh from him. Calm his nerves.
Smooth himself out. Ease off the tremors. Take a taxi. The
overnight train from Kings Cross to Southampton. He could
make it. He grinned. He was going to make it out of the shithole
East End, out of London, out of England. When everything
blew up in the faces of Harewood and all his fairy politician
mates, William would be in the First-Class cabin of a White Star
Line ship sailing across the Atlantic Ocean to America. He
patted at his chest at the thick envelope of secrets concealed in
his inner pocket and grinned again. Walking so fast he started to
hyperventilate, out of breath. Should quit smoking, he thought.
Spotted a couple of constables come out of The Ten Bells pub

at the bottom of the street and start strolling down the road towards him. Voices loud, lost in conversation about yesterday's football match. He ducked into an alley. Taking a piss with his back to them as they passed by. Hand pressed against the icy bricks of a wall. The urine smoky. The alleyway awash in rubbish and dozing tramps.

Buttoning his trousers, he heard a soft giggling. Snapped his head towards the sounds, squinting down the alley at a figure swaying there, caped in gloom. Her back was to him. Hand on a pushed-out hip. He closed his eyes, rubbed at them, screwing his sight up against the shadows and bitter cold. A red dress. Dark hair. Not a ghost at all. Flesh and blood. A tramp stirred from piles of soiled newspapers croaking curses at him and William stamped the filth unconscious. Moving down the alley towards the woman. She turned to face him, mouthing words that were meaningless in the dank, inky blue night. Her lips making intricate shapes. Giggling. Two words or a single two syllabled word. He shrugged theatrically. She beckoned to him. Drawing him in. A swarthy looking whore in a red dress. A rose in her hair. Blossomed like a wound against the sable color of the long wavy hair falling down to her shoulders. The February breeze frigid on his face. A beautiful girl smiling at him with lips painted blood red. He kicked old beer crates out of the way, telling himself he had time. He had time for one last hurray. Then he was next to her. His hand on the small of her back. The fabric of her dress as smooth as skin underneath his fingertips. The scent of her perfume bringing tears to his eyes. She threw her head back and laughed into the space above the bricks and mortar. Eyes sparkling like flares over No Man's Land.

He pushed her hard against the side of a building, "I love you so much and you always hurt me so, Margaux," he hissed, reaching up her thighs, pulling roughly at her knickers. She pulled herself free from his grasp, spat in his face and took off quickly. Running like a ghost story into the night. He wiped saliva from his face. The echo of footsteps around him. Vengeful spirits seeping out from the darkness to take his hand. The blade across his throat flashed faster than an unwanted memory. Cold knives puncturing his back. Penetrated. Raped. He could smell lavender and red wine. Paris on the night air. He fell to his knees. His son's face there in front of him. Weeping. Then the woman who had taken everything that had remained of him after the war. He spat out her name hot with blood.

"Margaux!"

Sabini stood towering over him. "This shall be as satisfying as finally popping a puss filled spot I think, William."

The muzzle of a revolver pushed cruelly against the top of his skull.

Is this really how it all ended?

He stared down at the cracked, soaked cobblestones, stuttered out the beginnings of a half-remembered prayer and then his entire life snapped to black.

Charlestown, Boston, USA
Saturday, February 23rd, 1946

FUCKING YAP, YAP, yap, yap. His bitch of a wife never stopped her incessant nagging. Jones couldn't even remember why he'd married the cunt. He hurried down the stairs, pulled on his jacket from the coat rack and shouted back up towards the bedroom, "I'm going into work, don't bother waiting for me."

"What time will you be home? I'm cooking your favorite tonight," the bitch hollered down.

"Jesus Christ, leave it in the oven and I'll eat it whenever," he yelled.

"I don't even know why I bother anymore," she shrieked.

"Quit your pissing and moaning, it ain't ladylike."

"What would you know about it?"

"Evidently not enough, I married you, didn't I?"

Jones' throat hurt from all the back and forth. He thought about going back upstairs and giving the old lady something to really screech about, but saw his son watching from the parlor. The constantly sad, confused look on the boy's little face always disappointed him. Those big blue eyes. Like a kicked dog, cowering. Why couldn't he have a normal kid like the other fellas? Fucking cursed genetics. Probably his wife's fault. Her side of the family were all suckers, retards and morons. Maybe the kid wasn't even his. The wife had always been a round-heels. He went over to the kid and picked him up and hugged him. He didn't know why. The action surprised them both.

"You look after your mama while I'm away, kiddo, okay?"

The kid nodded. Those eyes too wide and too moist. Little body stiff in Jones' arms. He dropped the kid down on the couch, ruffled his spikey hair and switched on the wireless for him. The kid sucked his thumb and stared. Jones cursed, shaking his head at the boy, picked up his car keys from the coffee table and left without saying another word. He paused a moment at the bottom of the stoop, one foot on the sidewalk to look back at the house for a final time. Wondered when his wife would find the note he'd left on the dining table. He was leaving them both. He'd had enough. Had met someone else. Someone better. A real woman. One that could fuck like an alley cat and had some real dough. One that *could* and *would* testify against that murdering fucking freak, Hughes, finally. Hopefully, they'd give him the death penalty. Jones' partner had been found dead in parked car in Southie two years ago. Two bullets in the chest. No suspects, but he had always known deep down in his heart it was that prick Hughes and those paddy fucks from The Seven Shamrocks. Hughes would get a black hood over his head and then Jones would use all the information he had against The Chief as a wedge. Hang it all over Sullivan's fat fucking head until he was cut into whatever dirty little deals he and Hughes had going on. Get promoted finally. Hell, become Captain. Chief. Commissioner. The fucking President of the United States. The future was going to be bright. So bright.

A shit-colored stray dog trotted up next to his ride and hitched its leg to take a leak on his front step. Jones gave it The Old College Try and kicked the mutt as hard as he could. Giggling as it hobbled away down the avenue yelping pathetically. Funny, reminded him of Hughes.

He unlocked his automobile, grinning and swung himself into the green Ford Coupe, glanced back at the house again and slid the key into the engine. The engine farted and spluttered. Died. The fucking thing wouldn't start. He cursed under his breath. Must be the cold. He didn't want to get out and start the fucking heap of shit manually. The son of a bitch kicked back like a mule on the crank. His eyes caught on something red, white and blue on the dashboard. He picked it up and peered at it. A small paper Union Jack flag on a cocktail stick, the kind you'd find in a lousy bar. He tossed it over his shoulder into the backseat, tried the engine again. It choked to life and the automobile exploded killing him instantly. Windows shattered, his wife smeared lipstick across her jaw and his son screamed for his daddy. The emerald-green Ford Coupe and Jones burned fiercer than Hell. The thick black smoke could be seen from all over Charlestown.

Salt Lake City
Saturday, February 23rd, 1946

THE MAN THE Mob had sent from Los Angeles to kill Joseph P. Kennedy sat by the window of his second story room on a stool watching shit kickers and shoppers wandering up and down Broadway as the day started the blood-red decline towards its end. He had a great view of the Peery Hotel opposite. Had lucked out with there being a smaller motel across the way from the more prestigious one. Prestigious because it was the only hotel with air conditioning in the whole of Salt Lake. Hell, probably the whole of Utah. His motel didn't have jack shit. Business must have been a bitch for the little dump having to keep up with those kinds of standards. He snubbed out his cigarette in an overflowing ashtray and leaned back on the stool, glancing at the old man slumped in the ensuite bathtub. Bled out and dead. A shocked look smeared all over his face. Maybe he'd been excessive with the old timer. The good old boy had spotted the Thompson machine gun leaning barrel up against the wall in the far corner when he'd come into the room to fix the radiator. He'd acted impulsively, sliding his bayonet up into the old man's ribs. He had closed his eyes for a moment and was back at Shuri Castle, Okinawa. Sliding the same bayonet up and under the ribs of another old man. A Jap civilian who didn't know when to quit. The Pacific. Everything in life was a battle. It couldn't be helped none, the old guy had to die but now the room was fucking freezing and the owner of the little motel was dead. No one to fix the radiator. Foolish old fuck. Another casualty of war, the man from Los Angeles thought, scratching at the three-day stubble on his jaw.

He lit another cigarette, turned his attention back to the street below and the Peery hotel again. He'd been watching the fucking place for twelve hours straight. Hadn't slept since the stopover in Cedar City a day and a half ago. Not that he ever slept much nowadays, anyway. Had a bad feeling in his guts about this job. The first for the wops. Didn't like the look of the Peery Hotel either. Something about the architecture was jarring. Disquieting. Haunted. The way the red bricks caught the sunlight like blood from a fresh wound. The windows reflecting empty like a corpse's eyes. The target too. Disquieting to say the fucking least. Joseph P. Kennedy. The wop, Anthony Cornero, who'd given him the job had told him they wanted to hit someone, when he asked who it was, he'd been told '*the biggest vegetable*'. A big fucking vegetable indeed. One of the biggest. He didn't ask why they wanted Kennedy dead. Knew it was something about heroin being imported from Europe or some bullshit. Corsica, maybe. Joey P. had fucked the Italians over on the deal. The man from Los Angeles had been promised a large chunk of change and more work if he proved himself and gunned Kennedy down publicly. Cornero had told him to 'make a fuckin' example of the fuckin' prick'. No problem. He'd done much worse things for free in the Pacific. Much worse. And to people who deserved it much less than a piece of shit like rich prick Kennedy.

He'd counted at least three Irish goons hanging around the hotel's lobby wearing tan trench coats and looking bored as hell. The kind of coats used for hiding the type of artillery that killed you quick and bad. The kind of faces that were dull and mean as hell. Killers. No other patrons that he'd seen had gone in the front. A few flashy Rolls Royces had pulled in the back the night before. Strange as hell. Yeah, he had a feeling in his guts this was a kamikaze mission. Kept telling himself he'd survived worse. He'd already been to Hell. Okinawa. Sugar Loaf Hill. Salt Lake City would be a piece of cake. Nothing. A stroll in the park. But the feeling in his guts was rarely wrong. He leaned back on the stool again to take a peep over at the old man slumped dead in the bathtub. Red going on thick black blood trickled from the corner of his mouth and he stared the same way all the ghosts from his dreams stared. Always the Dead. The man from Los Angeles shook his head to clear it and puffed smoke rings at the ice-frosted window.

The people in the room upstairs thumped around. Talking loud. More wops. He'd seen a couple of them on the stairs, talking hushed when he'd first checked in. They'd given him the stink eye and he'd given it back. The type of wops that stuck out in Utah. Had the look of very well-dressed hard cases. He wondered if they were there to steal his payday, because they sure as shit didn't look like they were in Salt Lake City to ski the slopes and enjoy the views. He'd spent the last of his family's dough on the gas for the three-day drive. The last of their savings. Left his wife and kid back in Bunker Hill without a single red cent. It was this job or fucking bust. The wops upstairs had another damn think coming if they thought they were going to steal his fucking meal ticket to a better life for himself and his daughter.

He snubbed out the cigarette on the windowsill, pulled the scrap of paper with the emergency contact telephone number on it from his pocket, went over to the telephone on the bedside table and told the operator the number. She asked him to hold, then said she was putting him through, telling him to wait. He sat down on the bed, spinning a Colt .45 on his finger.

"Yeah?" a deep voice boomed down the line.

"Mr. Cornero?"

"Yeah, who's this?"

"Scott Kelly?"

"Who?"

"The guy you sent to Salt Lake City. Scott Kelly."

"Oh, shit. The fuckin' marine. That's right. Sure. You done the job, already, huh?"

"No, not yet. I wanted to ask if you'd sent any other guys over here?"

"What? No, we ain't. People gave the job to me, and I gave the job to you. That's it. This ain't the army, marine. One guy's all it takes most of the time. If you ain't up to the fuckin' job, you better say now."

"The job's as good as done, but I want you to know I don't appreciate you sending in back-up. I'm not sharing the salary with anyone else. That wasn't the deal we agreed on."

"What the fuck are you talking about?"

"There are other mob guys around here, I've seen them. Italians. They're not exactly inconspicuous. I've put a lot of time and effort into this thing, Mr. Cornero." He glanced over at the bathroom door, the dead geezer going stiff there. "And I'm not sharing the proceeds. You see what I'm saying to you?"

"Marine, look here, I ain't bullshitting you. You're the only guy we got anywhere fuckin' near that fuckin' dump Salt Lake City. You drinkin' on the job or what? You fuckin' micks. No offence intended."

Kelly raised his eyebrows over at the half-empty bottle of whiskey on the bedside table. "No, no, I'm not drinking."

"I hope not. I know what you fuckin' Irishmen are like. Look, Kelly, kill that double-crossing Mick fuck Kennedy and call me after it's done. No more fuckin' telephone calls until then. We clear or ain't we?"

"All right. Okay, thank you, Mr. Cornero. We're clear. I won't disappoint you."

"I hope not, marine. And call me Tony for Christ's sake. You sound like my mother." Anthony hung up.

Scott Kelly placed the telephone down on its cradle, picked up the bottle and took a long drink and went back to the window again. The feeling in his guts twisting tighter. He lit another smoke and told himself he'd survived much worse.

BUCCOLA WAS GROWING impatient, and the small, shitty motel room was giving him cabin fever. Ice cold. The radiators hadn't worked for a day. He slapped down the newspaper he was pretending to read on the bed and jerked his chin at Lombardo sitting on a chair by the dresser. "What does he see?" Lombardo slapped his cousin Calacante with the back of his hand. "Well, what you see?"

The stick-thin man peering through curtains with a brass telescope, took it away from his eye and spoke over his shoulder in a thick Sicilian accent, "No change. The men you want are in the entryway of the hotel. Always. Sometimes they change. Two go, three stay. But they are there. Always."

"What they doing?" Lombardo asked.

"They sit, they talk. Drink. Smoke tobacco. Sometimes they get up and walk around. They appear, what is the word? Bored."

"What about other guests? You see any?" Buccola said.

"No one. I see no one else. Just the men you hate. The Irishmen," Calacante brought the spyglass to his eye again and spoke while peering out of the curtain.

"Well, where are the other hotel guests?" Buccola said.

"I don't know. They turned a man and woman away a couple hours ago," Calacante took the spyglass away from his face, breathed heavy on it, wiping the lens with a handkerchief.

"How's that?" Lombardo said.

"I don't know. The couple, they went in and the men with the orange hair told them to go and they went. Perhaps, I saw some motor vehicles go round the back. Many black cars. They had the man who drives with the special hat. Last night this was," he said, replacing the spyglass to his eye again.

"What the fuck is going on?" Lombardo said.

"I think they're making the moves here, yes? Something is going on and it must be *molto importante* they come all the way to this fucking cowboy city," Buccola said.

"Maybe they got a floating casino going. Something like that," Lombardo shrugged.

Buccola glanced at his gold wristwatch, lay back down on the bed, his hands behind his head, speaking to the ceiling. "I never thought I would feel this way, but I would like to go back to Boston very soon. Already I miss the place like a beautiful woman. We wait until the sun sets behind those mountains and then we go down there. They think they can destroy my business? Kill my men, our blood, and continue their lives? They're foolishly mistaken. Lombardo and me, we go in quick. It will be like it was when we were younger, hungrier men." He nodded to Calacante. "You be waiting outside in the automobile with the engine running. Then we return home. We will have the whole of Boston. The spoils of war. Heroes." Buccola grinned and picked at his teeth. Lombardo checked his nails and Calacante stared through the spyglass.

South Boston, U.S.A
Friday, February 22nd, 1946

BEN SLID THE key into the door of his Cadillac, heart still jerky from the hit on the Italians in the café. The sting of gun smoke still burning his eyes. Boston alive with the howls of sirens. He paused, gazing up at the bell tower of the Old South Church. The symmetry of the architecture was calming. Soothing. He remembered bringing his mother there a few times, before she went into the hospital for the final time. He strolled slowly over to the front and seeing that the heavy doors were pushed ajar, slid inside the place. That aroma of old wood, prayer and sin. A bitter twist of nostalgia trickled down his spine with beads of sweat.

Watching his mother hobbling down the aisles, running her grey fingers along the redwood, worn pews. So much white light from chandeliers and filtering through the stained-glass windows basking her in a saintly halo.

He guessed she had found some kind of a peace there. She'd spent so much of her final years jabbering away to priests and plaster models of Jesus Christ. Scrambling around for some kind of redemption. Her blue eyes on Ben's face always. Something there in the irises. Dark and shiny, glistening like black glass. He sat at the back of the church. The pew nearest the door. His hands trembling viciously. Breath coming out in gasps. Ragged. Strained. The sounds of the outside world crashing into the silence. He gripped onto the pew in front, trying to steady himself. Took out the silver flask from his pocket, drained the remnants of poteen, shook it, ran his fingertips over the inscription '*Love Always, Mother*' and tossed it down in the empty space beside him. Suddenly revolted by it. Sucking the dusty, ancient air through gritted teeth. Irises. Black and shiny. Glistening like black glass. The color of the abdomen of a cockroach on its back, its legs twitching madly in the air.

"You promised, Mother! And now what? What have I become?" he shouted it out towards the ends of the church. To the figure draped over the cross, hanging over the altar, the candles flickering with each spat word.

"Are you all right, my son?"

Ben jerked his head behind him to see a priest standing there. Draped in black. Concerned. Understanding. Lies. Lies all over his face, in every wrinkle of his aged skin. The bible held to his chest like a dead child. He moved closer to Ben, reaching out a filthy hand. "Would you like to pray with me?"

Ben stood up, handing the priest the flask, "Go to Hell, Father. I'll pray when I'm dying."

The priest shrunk, gawped, backed up, stumbling into the pew across the aisle. Ben walked out, not looking back, the keys to the car held in his fist like a jagged piece of glass.

HE PULLED HIS Cadillac up at the curb and down the street. Slumping over the steering wheel, watching the address that Li Yu's mother had scribbled down on a paper towel with a revolver pressed into the flesh of her neck. An apartment over a bakery in Charlestown. Eyes itchy. Heavy. He hadn't slept in days. Things seemed to be moving around him too fast or too slow.

He twisted his neck until he heard the bones click and slid out of the automobile. He counted his steps in groups of seven.

He reached the bakery in four sets. Four was an unlucky number. He turned around and walked back seven spaces, turned and walked back. Cancelling out the bad. Creating order. He sighed. Coughed. Walked around the back of the building. Bread baking warmly on the cold air. A rusty fire escape led to the apartment on top. He counted the steps up to her door. Twelve. Went back over two steps to make it fourteen. Two sets of seven. Felt relief. The door was green. There was a spyhole. He pushed his thumb over it. Knocked twice. Heard movement inside. A lazy kind of shuffling that sent shivers down his spine. A child again awoken in the night. He wiped his palm over his face and pressed it over his mouth. Glancing around nervous. Footsteps. Her voice, "Lewie? Finally!" Ben's eyes sharpened to slits. Lewis Jones. Of all the things the filthy, backstabbing, treacherous whore had had in between her lips, that piece of shit's name was the worst. Fucking bitch. He gripped at his Adam's apple, making his voice sound gruffer than it was, croaked out a "yeah." The lock clicked; the green door opened an inch. Ben slammed all his weight into it and bust the thing wide open. Li Yu yelped, falling hard to the floor. Wearing a lime green dress with patterns of purple grapes on it. She cried *no, no, no, no* when she saw him step into the apartment kicking the door shut behind him. Opened her mouth to scream. He slapped her hard across the face, her head rocked back, features slacked as though momentarily blacking out. He choked her in the crook of his arm, dragging her over to a disheveled bed, throwing her down onto the soiled sheets. A bottle of wine, glasses half empty, an opium box and a pipe on a bedside table. Her lipstick and rouge smudged across her face. Stains on the pillows. A stink coming off the walls and the furniture. He stood there panting, staring down at her, his fists opening and closing, a broken heart's beat. She scrambled back on the mattress, her knees pulled up under her chin, staring back at him, hands wrapped tightly around herself. The sunlight came golden through a crack in the curtains, illuminating her face and regressing her back to childhood. Ben's eyes blurred.

Finally, he cleared his throat, sniffed, tears stinging his vision, "I just want to know why, Yu?"

"You killed momma! I saw the newspapers! The fire! The bodies! You killed her and burned our home!" She screamed. Hysterical. Mucus ran from her nose. Ben looked away at a fine crack in the light blue wall.

"I didn't kill your mother, or the old man. They're in the precinct's drunk tank. They'll be released tonight."

"You fucking liar!"

"That's pretty hypocritical coming from a fucking lying whore like you, isn't it, Li Yu?"

She just glared through him.

He stepped closer to her, and she flinched away.

"I just want to know why? That's all. Why?"

Her lips quivered but she said nothing.

"Tell me why, Li Yu? I killed for you! Stevie died because of you! I loved you! I love you."

She backed up on the mattress further, her eyes burning with hate, and shrugged.

Ben's face broke out in spasms. Twitches. She shrugged. She shrugged. She fucking shrugged. Shrugged. As though he were insignificant. As if he were something that crawled. Less than a bug. He leapt on her, wrapping his hands around her throat, cutting off her shrieks and squeezing down hard. Feeling her windpipe giving.

She raked her fingernails across his cheeks. Her small fists hitting his mouth and ears.

"I tell you Stevie fucking *died* for *you*. That I'm going to *hell* because I love *you*. And you *shrug*? You fucking *shrug* at me?" The words hit her face hard with spittle and blood.

She gasped deep, bucking her hips against him, clawing at his features as he pushed a knee hard into her chest. Holding her down with his weight. Her eyes so wide. So white.

"Scared! I was frightened of *you*!" she gasped it out.

Ben pulled his hands away from her. Holding them out in front of him as though he was seeing them for the very first time.

Li Yu gasping, weeping and coughing.

He glimpsed his father's ghost glaring at him from across the room, but it was just another mirrored reflection of himself and everything that he hated.

He stumbled from the bed knocking the wine bottle smashing to the floor. He snatched the opium box and the pipe. Fleeing her apartment. His face awash with tears and blood and the sounds of her relieved crying.

Salt Lake City, U.S.A
Sunday, February 24th, 1946

SHAKING. TREMBLING.

The sound of fabric against fabric. Skin against skin. Another creaking of floorboards. The dragging of feet sliding softly, delicately over the carpet of his bedroom floor. He felt it then. The heavy, magnetic atmosphere of being watched. Observed. He couldn't move. Frozen in place. The dragging of feet moving closer to his bedside. Closer. The wet sound of something breathing.

Ben snapped awake, revolver clasped in one hand, the opium pipe in the other.

"Jesus Christ, Englishman. Don't point that fucking thing at me. This place reeks, man." Leary waved his stump-fingered hand through the thick blue smoke cloaking the hotel room. "It's our shift. For the watch. Time to get up and look like you give a shite."

Ben stared at the Fat Man for a moment, attempting to remember where he was and then nodded. The Peery Hotel, Salt Lake City. The party. The twenty-year anniversary of his father's death. The start of his disease. Sitting up like moving through wet tar. Leary pushed out a sticky hand to help him and Ben ignored it. Stood up slowly from the bed. Swaying. Pushed the revolver back into his shoulder holster and picked up the Thompson from on top of some cushions on a couch, giving it a wipe over with his handkerchief, concealing it under his long trench coat. Running his palsied fingers through long, greasy hair. Pushing his crumpled fedora on his head and following a few paces behind the waddling Leary out of the room and down the brightly lit, carpeted hallway. Leary stank worse as the days went on. Ben sniffed at himself and cringed, realizing the filthy smell was coming from his own body. He hadn't washed or shaved in days. Had hardly eaten. His slacks slipping from his hips. Lost weight like loose change. His fingernails grown into sickening yellowish claws. He'd grown a moustache. A beard. A shadow of a Boston Police Detective.

Bach's *Air on a G String* filling the whole hotel from the party upstairs. Booming out. Leary grinned over his shoulder at Ben, "What about this fucking music? I gotta say I prefer Mozart. Some fucking party, let me tell you."

Ben grunted, pulled the peak of his fedora down low, trying to block out the lights that burned through his eye sockets into the back of his skull. Vomit boiling in his guts.

"IOU says he was upstairs messing around with one of the maids and saw that FBI prick from the moving pictures and the radio wandering around on the second floor drunk," Leary said, stopping to look at a painting of cherubs on the wall. "You believe that shit?"

"IOU says a lot of things, Leary. A lot of things. IOU says a lot of things," Ben croaked. Head splitting. He'd been repeating himself more frequently over the last twenty-four hours and he'd given up trying to stop it. The Irish didn't even look at him strange anymore. It was as though his whole life had led up to this point of unravelling. The kid and Li Yu, the only things that could have saved him were both gone. He patted his breast, the folded newspaper in his pocket that seemed aflame. Burning to be taken out. Examined. Solved. Saved. He stopped, leaned his back against the wall, took out the picture of the boy and screwed the newspaper page into a ball and dropped it onto the floor, chewing at his bottom lip.

"Yeah, true, but get this, he says the guy was all dressed up like a dame with rouge, make-up and shit like that on his face," Leary said.

"It takes a fool to believe a fool. He's a fool. Fool," Ben cleared his throat and spat brown mucus onto the maroon carpet. Scratched at the bearded growth on his chin. Fingered the scabbed-over itchy remnants of the final time he'd seen Li Yu.

"That ain't even the worst of it. He says that FBI guy was walking around with another guy on a leash that was acting like some kind of a dog or something." Leary chuckled uneasily, continuing down the hallway.

"IOU is a strange man with a short attention span obviously. Tell him to lay off the mini-bars and the maids. We're here to do a job and lay low. Lay low. I said, lay low."

"Says the man that's been off his gourd on poppy since we arrived," Leary muttered.

Ben pulled the peak of his fedora lower. Sucking at the blood from his broken open bottom lip. Ignoring the comment.

THE PAIR CAME out of the corridor into the simple yet beautiful lobby of the hotel. Cream colored marble pillars and marble flooring. Dark wood fixtures. A grand chandelier hanging from the ceiling aglow, and a grand piano pushed to the side near a small glass gift shop counter. A rack of postcards with pictures of snowcapped mountains. Ben looked over the empty check-in desk. The rich leather chairs the Irish had pulled into the center of the room on top of a huge, intricate Persian rug. The whole place looked like an abandoned, derelict building. An elegant crime scene.

"Well, looky here! Finally! It's Fat Man Leary in The Peery! About fucking time. I'm bored as all hell," Christopher called out from the couch he was sprawled across. IOU, Negro and Connor playing a game of cards in front of the fireplace on a table and chairs they'd dragged in from somewhere. Empty bottles strewn about the place. A maid came out from one door, nodded to the group shyly, hustled across the lobby, passed Ben and disappeared down the hallway that led to his room and further on another wing of the vacant hotel.

"Is that the one you were banging in the broom cupboard upstairs when you saw the dog man, IOU?" Leary asked, leaning against the piano and getting a cigar started.

"Nah, not her. My one was prettier. Mexican. Can't get enough of those little senoritas."

"It was probably the dog man he was banging," Negro sniggered and shuffled cards. IOU held out the back of his hand and mimed a slap. The Irish laughed.

Ben went to the soberly designed entrance doors, taking a glance outside. The day terminal, the sky streaked with pink and a dark orange. The foot traffic on the street outside a trickle. The mountains looming over the city like ancient gods. A motel opposite with a few lights on in the windows already. Ben thought he saw a curtain twitch, blinking into a dying orange sun. The breeze that rolled through the doors around him a spiteful kind of cold. He pulled the collar of his overcoat up and turned back inside. Running his fingers over the tender scratches on his face. Li Yu. Feeling empty in the chest. Bottomless.

Tell me you love me, Ben. Say the words to me.

Her throat underneath his hands. That look of absolute fear in her eyes.

Scared! I was frightened of you!

Ben bit into his bottom lip hard again and squeezed the Thompson machine gun in his fist harder. Guts full of acid, ghosts and shit. He shuffled over to the check-in booth and leaned his weight against the desk, staring down at reflections crawling towards him on the marbled flooring.

"This place gives me the willies. Don't seem right, empty the way it is. That music playing all the time. It's like a ghost house or something," IOU said, uncorking another bottle of wine from a collection beside him and gulping at it.

"I second that. Something feels strange. Not right," Leary said.

"I think it's fucking hinky that there's a party going on and I ain't seen hide nor hair of any guests. The music's giving me a headache," Negro said.

"The maid told me she saw a whole bunch of them arriving in flash cars. Said she saw some famous movie stars," IOU said to the ceiling.

"Who'd she see?" Leary asked.

"I don't know. She didn't say no names. She just said famous movies stars. Besides, I was preoccupied trying to get her apron untied," IOU sniggered and wiggled his eyebrows.

"Go on and tell them what you heard, Connor. It'll put a chill down their backs." Christopher nodded at his brother, sitting up on the couch.

"I don't know what I heard; the music's so fucking loud. Got a pounding headache myself too. Was probably nothing." Connor shrugged, slapping an ace of spades down on the tabletop. Lighting another cigarette.

"What did you hear?" Ben said, wiping the seat of a leather chair with his handkerchief and sitting down underneath a painting of a poppy field. Blood red. Laying the Thompson on the floor beside him on a cushion so it wouldn't be contaminated.

"Well, I was taking a look around on the second floor. Wasn't looking to steal anything of course. Just looking out of interest, you know. And one of those songs, the music being played so fucking loud on the top floor came to a stop for a few seconds and I thought I heard a kid or something."

Ben jolted like a man in the electric chair. "You heard a child? Here? In the hotel?"

"Yeah, maybe. A kid. Crying. I mean, really fucking crying. Screaming. In pain. Then the music came back on and I couldn't hear nothing no more. Scared the shit out of me, to be frank. Got myself the hell off of that floor. Got my ass back down here. Not been back up there since. Won't again, that's for sure. Something don't feel right about this place, like the atmosphere is off or something. I don't like it. Hotel's ain't supposed to be this empty. Fucking classical music playing nonstop."

Ben gagged and then vomited on the marble floor. Bile splashed across the cuffs of his slacks. The Irishmen stared at him for a moment and then looked away. He shook a handkerchief from his pocket, wiping vomit from his scraggly beard and mouth as he spoke.

"Say it again, Christopher, what you said when you saw me and Leary. Say it again. Say it again. Say. It. Again."

"What? Nothing." Christopher's eyes popped wide.

"What did you say?" Ben coughed. Pulling at the creases in his slacks as though they were hurting his flesh.

"Nothing. Just said I was bored. That's it. Didn't mean nothing offensive by it."

"No. No. No. Before. Before that. What did you say? What did you say? You say?" Ben took off his hat and screwed it up in his hands like a wet towel. His mouth constricted to a slit.

"You mean, *Fat Man Leary in the Peery*?" Christopher shrugged, looking at Leary. The Fat Man shook his head at Christopher.

"Fuck!" Ben scratched at his neck. His face. Scabs tore loose and blood trickled down his face.

"What are you talking about, English?" Leary slid his machine gun onto the top of the piano and pressed a couple of keys. Playing *Shave and a Haircut*.

"The hairless man was trying to say '*Peery*' not '*Leary*'..." Ben stood up shakily, stumbling towards the stairs.

"What the fuck are you talking about, Englishman?" Leary called after him.

"The hairless man in the café. Frankie told me about him. He was trying to say '*Peery*' not '*Leary*'... The kid is here. He's here. In the Peery. The Peery. He's here."

"Wait a minute!" Leary called out again.

Ben couldn't hear him. In a trance as he made his way up the stairs. His hand sliding over the oak banister. Touch wood. Touch wood. Touch wood. Touch wood. Touch wood. Touch wood. Touch wood.

"Ah, let him go," Connor said, waving a dismissive hand. "He hasn't been right in the head since Stevie died."

"The Englishman? When was he ever right?" Leary walked across to the fireplace, threw his cigar into the flames, kicked off his shoes and collapsed into a couch, the frame gasped. Leary closed his eyes.

BEN DEAF TO the words they said. He was a child again climbing the stairs of a house in Chelsea, London that had poisoned his body and stunted his growth. Lost. In a trance. A man on the moon. Making his way slowly up the steps. Felt like he was traveling down. Inverted. Twisted. The lights burning down on him setting his flesh ablaze. The music, *The Flower Duet, Duo des Fleurs* choking his heart. Vibrating through his bones. Bringing tears to his eyes.

He fell to his knees on the second-floor landing, staring at his blurry reflection in a smoky floor to ceiling mirror.

Yesterday, upon the stair, I met a man who wasn't there!

Then stumbling up the staircase to the third floor and the banquet room. Every step upon the stair a point-blank bullet of memory and violent imagery ripping and tearing its way through his brain.

Upon the stair, I met a man
Beetle Man
who wasn't there!
Mother
Say it, Benny, say the words
A razor strop ripping into the flesh
Pillow soaked with tears
you love me
I love you, mother
Just a scared, lost kid
yesterday, upon the stair, I met a man who wasn't there!
Sickness and disease
very dirty... Filthy
A filthy, filthy girl
The Beetle Man
Tell me you love me, Ben
Say the words to me
I love you
Mother
Li Yu
And I love you. Even I know all the

terrible things
you've done
who wasn't there!
I still love you
yesterday
upon
the stair
who wasn't there!
Cold
Freezing
Goosebumps speckling his pale skin
Toys on a shelf with eyes that glistened in the moonlight
Twisted on string like dead men
hanging from the ceiling
Fabric on fabric
Skin on skin
Intoxicating
Scent of a woman
Her eyes
sucked him
in
Drowning him. Icy blue. Desperate
Inside of her
Whispering the words
Please, please, please
over and over
Crazy
Mother
Weak
Sick
Filthy
Crazy

Buggy
Mother
Mother
Mother
Mother standing in a silk black robe at the end of his bed
Mother with a black hood pulled over her head
Tell me you love me, Ben
Say the words to me

Ben stood swaying in front of the large banquet room doors. Cold. Freezing. Goosebumps speckling his pale skin. Dark yellow piss trickling down his legs and puddling around his dark brown oxfords onto the carpet of his childhood home. The hotel floor. Hand shaking sickly as he reached out to the golden doorknob. Reflected like an insect in its smooth surface. The soprano's screeching within the music assaulting his face and ears like blows of an angry parent's fists. Couldn't breathe. Suffocating. Hyperventilating, drowning as he twisted the handle and pushed the doors open wide onto a landscape of darkness, spotlights, and absolute pandemonium. Hell.

Insects crawling over cowering children. Ants. Cockroaches. Beetle Men.

Ben's eyes ripped open. Very wide. Very white. Slapping a hand to his mouth.

He screamed and screamed into his palm. A pain like a knife blade slicing through his stomach. His bowels collapsed. Shit pouring through the fabric of his slacks.

A child's screams.

Ben. The boy in the photograph.

The ants and pale cockroaches scurrying over the boy's small body nipping and biting. Smothering. Infesting.

The boy from the newspaper photograph shrieking in pain.

The music screeched, skipped, stopped.

Bugs twisted their grotesque faces to gaze at Ben.

The boy moaned, ants crawling from his dead eyes and gaping mouth.

Then a sickly, naked white figure standing in front of Ben. Its bulbous stomach bulging. A human's flaccid penis hanging vile from its body.

"Hughes, what the *fuck* are *you* doing *here*?! Get out and close that fucking door! Now!"

Ben stared at the thing's face. Eyes too black and too empty. Horns sticking from its head a cockroach's antennae. He stared at the masks burning in his direction. Rubber Halloween masks. A masquerade of depravity and sickness. Masks pulled too tight over faces grotesque and ancient.

"Close the fucking door, Hughes. You were never here. You saw nothing. A single word of this and we'll fucking destroy you, you hear me? Destroy you! We'll see you in prison for the rest of your fucking life."

Ben stared at the boy in the photograph. The boy's eyes. Cast in ink shadow. Black gaping holes. Screaming from an abyss of darkness and things that scurried naked. Eyes that were empty graves. Just a scared, lost kid. So many children missing.

"Get the hell out of here, Hughes. Now!" the thing growled.

The Boy screamed, reaching out a small, begging hand.

The doors closed slowly on Ben.

Bile exploding from his mouth, down the smooth surface of the shut doors.

Ben screamed until his voice broke.

Gun shots exploding.

The child's screams.

The boy in the photograph.

Gun shots exploding.

Ben fell backwards down the stairs. Vomited again. His hands to his knees. Staring at himself in the large mirror. The Beetle Man staring back him. It had been *him* all along. He was the Beetle Man. He had always been the Beetle Man.

Gun shots exploding.

IOU screaming in agony. Leary calling out for him and then silent. Connor cursing. Machine gun fire. Shattering glass.

Ben pulled the .38 from his shoulder holster. Glaring back at the banquet room's door, hesitating and then tumbling down the rest of the stairs towards the chaos and explosions below.

BUCCOLA, LOMBARDO AND Calacante peered down, grinning at the arsenal spread across the mattress. The red, orange light from the sun setting over the mountains washing over the room and the weapons. Buccola had spared no expense and, like everything else in his life, opted for Italian made. A Beretta Model .38 submachine gun and a Glisenti 1910 pistol for each of the two of them. Fully loaded. Calacante spinning the car keys on his finger.

They pulled on their coats and hats. Slapping each other on the back and wishing *'buona fortuna'* as they left the room and quietly made their way down the stairs and out of the motel.

SCOTT KELLY SPAT the whiskey he was drinking down the windowpane. Dropped the bottle clunking to the floor. Muttering curses under his breath. Fuck! Standing up quickly. His palms pressed against the cold glass of the window, watching two of the wops he'd seen on the stairs jogging across the street towards the Peery Hotel. Right hands buried deeply in their overcoats. The Italian fucks were trying to steal his fucking pay day. He cursed under his breath repeatedly, quickly pulling on his overcoat, grabbing the Thompson from the corner, shoving the Colt 1911 into the base of his spine.

As he went out the door, he glanced back into the room, at the dead man in the bathtub, wondering if he was going to end up the same. Cocking the Thompson he smiled confidently, knowing it was Salt Lake City, not the hills of Okinawa and these were a handful of two-bit hoods and a failed politician he was dealing with, not the Japanese Imperial Army.

The metallic roars of multiple machine guns ripped through the Peery hotel and out into the dying day as Kelly made his way across Broadway. The smile disappearing from his face as though it had never been there in the first place. Confidence AWOL. Heart jackhammering. Life nothing but a never-ending circle of bullshit and blood.

IOU SLUMPED AGAINST the wall at the bottom of the stairs gawping sadly at Ben as though a man shocked awake from a deep sleep in a puddle of blood and scattered postcards. Bullet riddled. Gun smoke drifting. Wood and marble exploded. Ben dived for cover. Piano keys chimed. Christopher still seated on the couch. The top half of his skull gone. The lower jaw pink and raw. Exposed. Ben scurried on all fours, over the bodies of Negro Paul and Connor, hair hanging in his face, diving behind the check-in desk. The gun fire coughed to a stop, fell silent. A tossed empty magazine clattered to the marble floor. The cold, metallic clicking of a machine gun being reloaded.

"Behind the pillar on the far right, English!" Leary called out from behind the grand piano. The machine gun exploded into life. The piano played the music of a madman as bullets tore it to pieces. Leary screamed earsplitting, gurgled, then was hushed like the piano, and the gunfire too fell silent again.

Ben wiped the damp hair out of his eyes, cocked the .38, and swung it over the counter of the desk, squeezing a couple of shots off at the pillar. Marble shattered into dust and the man hugging the structure, brandishing a Thompson machine gun, leapt down the corridor Ben and Leary had come out from earlier.

Ben let off another shot towards the hallway, glancing around the lobby, trying to comprehend the situation. Two dead men laying closely next to each other in front of the entrance. Bullet wounds like angry ants swarming all over their backs. Italians. Looking a lot like Lombardo and Buccola. A blood-splattered maid slumped against a crumbling far wall. Leary dead underneath the piano, his insides spread all over the floor. Ben grimaced at the sights and smells. Swallowed.

A woman's hysterical screaming came from the hallway the shooter had disappeared down. More gunshots in quick succession. The screams muted abrupt.

The classical music boomed constantly from the third floor had stopped. Ben couldn't tell when. The hotel eerily silent.

Ben kept the muzzle of the .38 on the hallway entry. His eyes scanning for his Thompson. Still in the place he'd left it. Next to the destroyed couch. On the cushion. Clean.

"Hey, Englishman!" Connor hissed, sprawled on the floor next to Negro Paul.

"I thought you were dead," Ben hissed back, his eyes darting from Connor to the Thompson to the hallway entrance.

"Nah, I've been fucking pretending. Had to. Gonna make a run for the doors real soon."

"Who's the shooter?" Ben asked.

"A fucking white man! Buccola and Lombardo came in blasting. They fucking killed IOU and Negro. The Fucks! Then *that* fucking mad dog came in and started killing everyone. He killed my fucking brother," Connor gasped, spluttered. Jutted his chin towards the corridor. "We gotta get the fuck outta here. I think he's gone now."

Ben's eyes jumped towards the machine gun again. If he could reach that. Get up the stairs, he could still save the kid. Kill all those sick fucks. Cockroaches. Ants. Save himself. Save the kid. Save his soul.

Connor started to push himself to his feet. Nodding at Ben, gesturing for him to follow. Ben shook his head *no, no, no.* Broke away from the check-in desk, stumble-ran towards the Thompson. Time perverted. Slowed. Seconds retarded. Ben counted steps. Four. Four steps. Sirens howling. His fingers clasping the muzzle. The soles of Connor's shoes clapping down on marble. Four. The scream of machine gun fire. The sound of metal on stone as the killer dropped the machine gun. Connor begging, "please, please, PLEASE,' a final POP from a small caliber weapon, something wet splashing the interior and then nothing more.

Ben almost at the stairs. His hand upon the oak banister. Touch wood. Touch wood. Touch wood. Touch wood. The stairs shattering, splintering around him. Touch wood. *Yesterday, upon the stair, I met a man who wasn't there! He wasn't there again today. Oh how I wish he'd go away!*

Impact. A burning hot pain like hell.

The bullet exploding through Ben's lower back, shattering ribs, puncturing his stomach, and throwing him hard against the wall, bursting out through his abdomen like an insect leaving the chrysalis. His skull connecting dully with brick. Ben fell to his knees. Gazing up the staircase. Sirens like church bells. The screech of tires from outside. Shattered glass. More gunfire. The chaos of the hotel lobby spilling out into the streets of Salt Lake City. The boy in the photograph screaming. Or was the shrieking coming from his own jaws? Ben didn't know. Then shadows falling like a winter rain. The woman's face there in front of him. Weeping. Begging for forgiveness. The woman he loved who had taken everything from him that might have mattered.

He spat her name out into the aching quiet.

No prayers. He had no soul to pray for.

Darkness.

His entire life went a slick black like the body of a cockroach climbing up a light blue, cracked wall.

Epilogue

HIS EYES FOLLOWED IT. The cockroach. Yellow light from a lamp across the room reflecting off its smooth, disease riddled back. It ran parallel to a fine crack in the wall. Symmetry. Order. He wanted to scream but couldn't. The stench of shit and ammonia crawled down his nostrils and nested in his body. Gags convulsed from his dry throat. Could hear the nurses chattering away insanely in the hall. Blue curtains shook trembling with a dusty draft. An old man in the bed across the way snoring. Ben's eyes burned with tears, blurring his vision until the cockroach was nothing more than a dark smudge floating erratically in his sight. The pain in his back and guts pure hell. More morphine. He wanted more morphine. MORE FUCKING MORPHINE!!!!

He squeezed his eyes shut.

Opened them to darkness.

Squeezed them shut.

Opened them again to daytime.

He watched a cockroach scurry across his baby blue sheets. Up the wall. Dancing over the fractured paint. A giant, pale, naked cockroach wearing a masquerade mask was looming over the bottom of the hospital bunk. Reading the clipboard. Tossed it on top of Ben's numb legs. The mask fell away. His father. The top half of his forehead jagged, splintered, missing. Eyes white, rotten boiled eggs. Blood crusted lips twitching. The Chief telling Ben to keep his fucking mouth shut. Telling him he would get better. The bullet passed right through him. Up and around in no time. He'd go to Los Angeles. They needed good men out there. Just keep his fucking mouth shut. He had a lot of important friends now. Very important. The Chief grinned with teeth pinkened with blood.

Ben closed his eyes.

Opened them again.

Night.

Ben closed his eyes.

Opened them again.

Daylight streaming through a window burning his face. Aflame. Itchy.

The cockroach gone. Just the crack on the wall like a thread of hair remaining.

His mother washing him down with a damp cloth. Her blonde hair hanging down in coils of gold. Telling him she was a filthy girl. Not his mother. Mrs. Goodman. No, it was mother. The cancer that killed her leaking from the corners of her lips, thick and black. Holding a paper cup to his lips. Drink the water. Dark yellow and warm. Drink it. Mother. Her hand crawling underneath the covers towards his prick. He wanted to scream but couldn't. He loved his mother. He was the man of the house now and big boys didn't cry.

He closed his eyes.

Opened them.

High heels stabbing at marbled flooring. Closed his eyes. The rattle of a door. The scent of her perfume. Chanel Number Five and opium.

Opened them.

Li Yu sitting in a chair next to his bed like a broken heart. All dressed in black. A lace veil across her face. Ben clenched his teeth and fists until he spasmed. She lifted the veil. The face of the dead child. Eyes a cloudy grey. Skin swollen. Bruised. Bloated.

"Ben, I need your help."

Ben screamed.

Authors Note

I'll Pray When I'm Dying is my ballad for the bad guy. In all types of media, literature, film, and so forth, the bad guy is still a character that is, in the majority of examples, used to give the protagonist/good guy something to overcome, to beat. Cannon fodder. Two dimensional characters that are bad or evil for no other reason than they just are. I wanted to make the bad guy from one of my earlier novels into the protagonist of I'll Pray When I'm Dying so we could see a side of the story that we so rarely get to see. Why is the bad guy bad? Surely they need help more than the actual good guys, no? Here my protagonists, bad guys lead the story. They're deeply disturbed people. More importantly they're deeply wounded souls suffering from serious mental anguish that pushes them to do the awful things they do. Someone once said, 'there are no bad people, just bad actions.' That's why I wanted to write this novel.

In this novel I have also tried to hint at a few serious themes. One of the themes I wanted to explore was that of Obsessive-Compulsive Disorder, which is a mental illness that has yet to be portrayed accurately within the media. We often see the same tired old tropes of characters washing their hands repeatedly. Cleanliness. When these are in fact just one small facet of OCD. I wanted to try and bring the reader's attention to the other debilitating aspects of the mental illness. The constant, disturbing, jarring mental images that get stuck within one's mind. The checking, rechecking that can take up a huge amount of the sufferer's time. The frustration. The fixation on ritual, symmetry, order, symbolism. Counting to particular numbers that have meaning to feel some kind of relief only for the negativity to repeat again in cycles. The repetition of certain words and phrases to get them sounding right or ordered correctly when under stress and pressure. OCD is a multifaceted mental disability and I have attempted to shine a light on something that is still massively misunderstood. Perhaps not the most entertaining thing to write about but fuck it, someone had to try, and I am happy I did.

You may not like my characters, but I hope you'll find yourself rooting for them regardless because as Ben Hughes says in the novel 'it's important to have empathy.'

Stephen J. Golds
May 2021

Acknowledgments & Thanks

First and foremost, I would like to say thank you to a few people who championed and aided my work from the very beginning. Moy McCrory my university professor who told me to keep writing. Brian 'Zygote in My Coffee' Fuggett for being the first editor that I submitted my poetry to. Laura Hird for being there from day one. Rob 'Blackstoke' Parker for always being there to help a struggling author out. Sean Coleman who took a chance on a stray that occasionally pisses on the rug. Martine, Barbara, Scott, James, Nate, Kirstyn, Travis, Gabriel, John BN, Alec PM and Kev for your efforts, support and aid in proofreading and editing.

I would like to say an incredibly special thank you to those whose constant love, support and help were indispensable to me throughout my writing.

My daughters M and N for letting papa write when you wanted to play.

M for being M. Just keep watching!

Mother and Father, Family.

Friends.

Okinawa! I love you!

The authors, editors, bloggers, reviewers and beta readers who have helped me throughout. You know who you are. Much love. Thank you.

And **thanks to YOU** the reader!

Stephen J. Golds

About the Author

Stephen J. Golds was born in London, U.K, but has lived in Japan for most of his adult life. He enjoys spending time with his daughters, reading books, traveling, boxing, and listening to old Soul LPs. His novels are Say Goodbye When I'm Gone, Always the Dead, Poems for Ghosts in Empty Tenement Windows, Cut-throat & Tongue-tied Bullet Riddled & Gun Shy, and the story and poetry collection Love Like Bleeding Out with an Empty Gun in Your Hand. He is co-Editor of Punk Noir Magazine.

Made in the USA
Coppell, TX
18 September 2021